First Kiss

THE BRIDESMAID CHRONICLES

KYLIE ADAMS

A SIGNET BOOK

SIGNET
Published by New American Library, a division of
Penguin Group (USA) Inc., 375 Hudson Street,
New York, New York 10014, USA
Penguin Group (Canada), 10 Alcorn Avenue, Toronto,
Ontario M4V 3B2, Canada (a division of Pearson Penguin Canada Inc.)
Penguin Books Ltd., 80 Strand, London WC2R 0RL, England
Penguin Ireland, 25 St. Stephen's Green, Dublin 2,
Ireland (a division of Penguin Books Ltd.)
Penguin Group (Australia), 250 Camberwell Road, Camberwell, Victoria 3124,
Australia (a division of Pearson Australia Group Pty. Ltd.)
Penguin Books India Pvt. Ltd., 11 Community Centre, Panchsheel Park,
New Delhi - 110 017, India
Penguin Group (NZ), cnr Airborne and Rosedale Roads, Albany,
Auckland 1310, New Zealand (a division of Pearson New Zealand Ltd.)
Penguin Books (South Africa) (Pty.) Ltd., 24 Sturdee Avenue,
Rosebank, Johannesburg 2196, South Africa

Penguin Books Ltd., Registered Offices:
80 Strand, London WC2R 0RL, England

First published by Signet, an imprint of New American Library,
a division of Penguin Group (USA) Inc.

First Printing, July 2005
10 9 8 7 6 5 4 3 2 1

Copyright © Jon Salem, 2005
Excerpt from *First Dance* copyright © Karen Moser, 2005

Printed in the United States of America

PUBLISHER'S NOTE
This is a work of fiction. Names, characters, places, and incidents either are the product of the author's imagination or are used fictitiously, and any resemblance to actual persons, living or dead, business establishments, events, or locales is entirely coincidental.

The publisher does not have any control over and does not assume any responsibility for author or third-party Web sites or their content.

ACKNOWLEDGMENTS

Kara Cesare—My editor. She's an absolute doll, even in the face of my worst Barbra Streisand moments (I tend to be opinionated/difficult about plot points, character motivations, cover art, back cover copy, font type, marketing plans, basically everything but the routine maintenance of the printing press).

Karen Kendall—Author of Books 1 & 3 in this series. Her e-mails are an absolute hoot, and somehow she managed to bang out a manuscript while moving and fighting a hurricane. She's practically Xena, Warrior Princess.

Julie Kenner—Author of Book 4 in this series. She's prolific beyond belief (by comparison, Danielle Steel works at a snail's pace). Plus, she's raising kids. An amazing multitasker.

Shelley Powers—My hilarious friend. We share a certain solidarity—that would be a common obsession with Tom Welling of the WB's *Smallville*. Episodes that feature him without a shirt routinely get a second, third, sometimes fourth viewing. And we can spend entire lunches waxing lyrical on how this event (Tom Welling taking off his shirt) is simply just good for America.

Men who have pierced ears are better prepared for marriage. They've experienced pain and bought jewelry.

—Rita Rudner

From: kiki@misstexas95.com
To: suzix2@hotmail.com
    80sdancer@aol.com
Subject: Venting

Suzi-Suzi and Danni!

It's after midnight and too late to call, so here I sit banging away on my laptop. May I please share two things that are currently driving me insane?

1) Polygamy! Why is this a crime? The multiple wives/husbands are at least sharing responsibilities. Meanwhile, there are no laws to protect bridesmaids. I'm already booked for four weddings this summer, and now my brother is getting married. That's five new dresses to buy that I will only wear once! Five trips to spots on the map that require me to get on a plane and fly coach! Five bridal shower gifts! Five wedding gifts! And you know my luck. If there was one straight, single, smoking-hot groomsman to look forward to, then it might be worth it. But that's never the case. I get stuck trudging down the aisle with the teenage boys fighting acne, boring salesmen who are already married, and gay cousins. Never the straight hot guy. Ugh! It's so unfair. I should write my congressman. Hmm. Who is my congressman? Wait! I'll e-mail Hillary. She's a senator. That's

higher up the political food chain. I'm sure that she'll want to help. I mean, Chelsea's probably just starting to go through this sort of thing. I imagine that she'd be a very popular bridesmaid. Don't you think?

2) Botox! I can't afford it this month. Why? Because of all these wedding expenses! And there's also the fact that I'm not working right now. That doesn't help. Anyway, I don't know what's worse for my frown lines—not getting Botox, or stressing out about not getting Botox. All I can do is double up on my new Principal Secret products. Victoria's new Reclaim line has an ingredient called Argireline that's supposed to smooth out lines. I've been applying it every two or three hours. You know, I think it's starting to work.

PS This is way off point, but I would totally get behind the controversial cloning issue if a brilliant scientist agreed to duplicate Jude Law.

Air Kisses,
K

Chapter One

At the crack of eleven, Kiki Douglas slowly began to stir. To the crunchy guitars of Hoobastank blaring from the alarm clock radio. To the steady hum of traffic thirteen floors below. To the incessant yapping of the Scottish terrier next door.

For a moment, she simply lay there as the cold, hard realities began to sink in. The weight of the obvious seemed to push her deeper and deeper into the Tempur-Pedic mattress. Sleeping on one of those was a dream. And Kiki had bought it for a steal, thanks to Suzi-Suzi's married boyfriend, who worked for the company. Poor Suzi-Suzi. She was struggling to find work as a model *and* involved with another woman's jerky husband. But Kiki had her own problems to face down this morning.

Like no job. Damn those writers on *All My Children* for pushing her character off a cruise ship!

And no money. Damn American Express for expecting that she pay all those Bergdorf Goodman charges at once!

And—worst of all—no one to blame it on. If she had a husband/boyfriend/whatever, then she would at least be able to make *him* responsible for all of this.

WOOF! WOOF! WOOF!

Kiki erupted from the bed and pounded on the wall. "Shut up, Alfie! Your mommy won't be home for seven hours!" Now fully awake, she shuffled into her tiny kitchen to snatch a bottle of Voss water from the could-go-at-any-moment fridge. And the landlord called this cramped one-bedroom *newly renovated*. Only in Manhattan.

She eyed her Macintosh iBook atop the sleek desk situated in front of the window. The arrangement was very Carrie Bradshaw from *Sex and the City*. In fact, when Kiki tapped out her philosophies on the message board of her Web site, sometimes she could feel the muse of Sarah Jessica Parker as her fingertips went *peck-peck-peck* over the keyboard.

Ten years. An entire decade. Practically a lifetime ago. That's how long it had been since Kiki represented her home state of Texas in the Miss America Pageant. Thinking back on that crushing moment, when she realized that Miss California had won the title, when the cruel truth of being forever banished to the forgotten Siberia of *first runner-up* crystallized in her brain . . . well, even now it still conjured up that familiar feeling called gut-twisting nausea.

And how many times had she played the events over and over in her mind? The evening gown competition. The swimsuit contest. The talent showcase. The all-important onstage interview. God, it was like her own version of the Zapruder film.

The swimsuit memory triggered Kiki's most intense regrets. How in the world had Miss California scored higher? The woman had ugly knees. And when the surfer girl did her turn-step-turn-spin in front of the judges, she tottered slightly and almost lost her balance. Robbery! That bitch had beaten her in the talent showcase, too. What did those judges know about opera? The idiots probably gave her high marks by default just for singing in Italian. Meanwhile, Kiki's dramatic monologue from the movie *St. Elmo's Fire* had earned a lukewarm reception at best. *So* over their heads. What did Charo know about acting anyway? Please. A few skits on Bob Hope specials hardly made a dinosaur like that the second coming of Meryl Streep.

Kiki pushed the replay of her personal Waterloo out of her mind and logged on to www.misstexas95.com to check her message board. It was amazing that she still had fans from that era. But the truth was, more girls seemed to seek her out from her pageant days than from her soap exposure. No wonder. The moment she felt settled into a role on a daytime drama, the writers dreamed up a plot twist to kill her off. On *One Life to Live*, she'd been the victim of a mob hit; on *Guiding Light*, she'd been poisoned by a psychopathic husband. God, what she wouldn't give to slip into a coma on one of those shows. That could mean months of dramatic screen time without having to worry about memorizing lines. Heaven.

As expected, Kiki found a new posting from Ariel C. A high school senior now, Ariel had represented Texas in last year's America's Junior Miss competition and routinely sought Kiki's counsel on everything from makeup tips to dealing with parents. But today's missive was her most serious to date.

From Ariel C: Kiki, my boyfriend (we've been together for six months) is really pressuring me to have sex. I'm one of the few virgins still left in my class, and he says there are plenty of girls who want to hook up with him. He also wants me to quit the Abstinence Club because his friends make fun of him about it. Part of me wants to hold on to my convictions, but another part of me doesn't want to risk losing this guy. I really love him. What would you do?

Kiki was determined to craft a response that would steer Ariel in the right direction, and for a moment, she was so engrossed in the assemblage of her own thoughts that Alfie's barking receded into white noise.

From Kiki D: Ariel, take it from a girl who remembers—sex with high school boys is no trip to the moon. They care less about bringing you to orgasm than your future husband will a few years after marriage. This guy sounds like a creep who's more concerned about what his retarded buddies think than he is about your feelings. I say stick to your principles. He's not worth the compromise. Don't get me wrong, though. I'm not a staunch moralist who advocates saving yourself for marriage. I mean, that could be disastrous. What if future hubby is an absolute bore in the bedroom? Better to learn such things before involving innocent bridesmaids. I've been one of those more times than I want to count, and whenever I hear about a divorce (so many occur within just a few years, and it's usually about sex or money), I feel like demanding a refund on the tacky dress and any gifts that I bought. Anyway, I digress. Back to the main point—losing your virginity. Are you traveling abroad this summer? If not, you should plan a trip. There's nothing like a hot foreign affair to awaken a girl's sexuality. I vote to save yourself for an Italian named Antonio or a Frenchman named Jean-Paul. It could be so delicious!

Kiki signed off, her spirits soaring. A few minutes upon rising and already she'd set a young woman on the proper path. What a glorious feeling of productivity. Suddenly, it dawned on her that she should write a book. Some sort of quasi-autobiographical/self-help/practical solutions tome.

First Runner-Up . . . But Still a Winner.

The inspirational title hit her like an internal thunderbolt, causing the fine, tiny hairs on her arms to tingle. What a brainstorm. She scribbled the thought on a Post-it, then wrote CALL ASSHOLE AGENT, and underscored the reminder three times, each successive line scratched with increasing hostility.

Keith Bush. The bastard never returned her calls and so far had done nothing to turn around the slump in her acting career. But he did have the William Morris Agency clout behind him.

One more chance, Kiki thought. Better to give him the opportunity to redeem himself than shop around for new representation from a point of weakness. Word could get around that she was desperate. Which she was. But the trick in the industry was to never let anyone see you borrow money from your parents. Or was it to never let them see you sweat? Hmm. Maybe it was both. No matter, she made a second note to call her father. Rent was due soon, and American Express was stalking her. Come to think of it, they always called about this time of day. Yikes. Time to go.

Kiki rushed to get ready and get out. A quick Reclaim routine. The lines *were* fading . . . or was she simply fooling herself? Truth be told, there was nothing like the magic of Botox. Amazing. Certainly the best medical advancement since . . . penicillin! A brilliant observation. Must save that for the book. She gave her teeth a good brushing with Sonicare, swiped on some mascara and lip gloss, dressed quickly in a tight Junk Food–label Cookie Monster baby tee and matching hot pants, tossed on a Juicy Couture charm bracelet for a bit of trendy flash, and dashed out the door just as the phone started to jangle. Thank God those pesky bill collectors didn't have her mobile number. The torment would be endless.

She stepped out into the middle of the street and raised her right arm to hail down a cab. It would gobble up her last bit of cash. Whatever. How could she walk in this suffocating heat? Nobody wanted to show up at an important luncheon shiny with perspiration. Okay, in all honesty, it was just a quick bite with the girls—Suzi-Suzi and Danni. But still. They deserved the same consideration Kiki might reserve for, say, the League of Women Voters. Hmm. This reminded her. Better register to vote before the next presidential election. Anyway, trying to tough it on foot was out of the question. And so was the subway. Way too early to deal with a pervert rubbing up against her or a mother with a stinky baby. Yuck.

A taxi jerked to a stop. Finally! A survey had been done revealing that unattractive people have to wait even longer. How awful. Kiki lamented the horrible injustice as she tumbled inside. That had been a good five minutes in the blistering heat. She could empathize with what it must feel like to just stand there like a statue in the park. Where were the social crusaders when you needed them? They should make this cab situation a priority. Hmm. More fodder for the book. Maybe a whole chapter. A mini-polemic on aesthetic worthiness in America. That could get her on *Meet the Press*. It was all about expanding your audience. Face it, the whole beauty queen/soap star bit all but guaranteed her a slot on *Regis and Kelly*. She had that demographic in the bag. But the Tim Russert crowd—they had no idea who she was or that she had great ideas for, say, all the hullabaloo about the obesity crisis in America. Example: Manufacture refrigerators with photos of Brad Pitt and Salma Hayek built in to the doors. *That* will curb late night snacks and make people want to exercise!

Suddenly, Kiki took one look at the cabdriver's posted identification and realized that his name had, like, fifteen consonants. Impossible. Out of sheer frustration, she screamed out the address for Pastis and told him to drive on the sidewalk if he had to. "Otherwise, you might not get the full fare. I'm short on cash."

He took off like Dale Earnhardt Jr.

Kiki slumped back in the battered seat and fanned herself in an attempt to help the car's clunky air conditioner do its work. No mercy. The long wait on the angry, steaming concrete. The stifling cabin. Her legs were actually sticking to the leatherette. God, it felt like a tour of duty. This definitely made her an honorary Swift Boat Veteran.

At last! They pulled up to Pastis on Ninth Avenue. Kiki handed over the fare (plus a little tip!) and swung out. She was only twenty minutes late. For her, that was basically early. Definitely on time. Suzi-Suzi and Danni would be so proud, as she was working on punctuality as a personal improvement issue, and this represented significant growth.

The French bistro bustled with buoyant chatter and the requisite power lunch activity. Surreptitiously, Kiki checked her reflection in one of the antique mirrors as she click-clacked along the mosaic floor tiles to find her adorable friends at a corner table.

"Oh, my God!" Suzi-Suzi squealed, beaming as if Kiki had just put on a magic show. "You are *so* early!"

Danni checked her watch—the Chanel J12 number. Kiki *loved* that timepiece, and if any woman in the restaurant other than Danni were wearing it, then she would have to hate her on principle. But sweet Danni got a pass. "We've only been here for about twenty minutes."

Kiki plunked down with a dramatic sigh and immediately flagged a waiter for a Diet Coke with lime. "You don't know what I went through to get here." She glanced around quickly for famous faces. Celebrities frequented the eatery all the time. Ooh. Wasn't that the hot guy from *Survivor*? Yummy. Civilization definitely agreed with him. "I have two dollars to my name," she announced without preamble. "And a credit card that the manager will probably cut up in front of my face."

Danni opened up her clutch to flash a thick wad of cash. "No worries, sweetheart. I did a new routine to 'Pour Some Sugar on Me' by Def Leppard last night. After I nailed my new move on the pole, it rained money."

Danni Summer worked as an exotic dancer at Camisole, the hottest gentleman's nightspot in Manhattan. The hysterical part was this: She never took off her clothes. For Danni, a nice Christian girl from Mississippi, it got no skimpier than a modest bra and panties set. She merely loved choreographing and performing dance routines to songs by her favorite bands from the eighties—Def Leppard, Poison, Bon Jovi—the list went on. Where else could a girl do that but a strip club? And who else could get away it but Danni Summer? She was drop-dead beautiful. A near dead ringer for Nicole Kidman with her auburn hair, lissome body, and porcelain skin. Management at Camisole kept her on because she packed the club even without flashing the goods.

Suzi-Suzi glanced at Danni with imploring eyes.

"Everything's on me today," Danni offered. As if

anyone had to hold their breath. She was one of the most generous people Kiki had ever known.

"I didn't get that feminine pain relief commercial I was called back for," Suzi-Suzi grumbled. "It's all because of that irritable bowel syndrome campaign. I just know it. People already think of me as the girl with cramps. They want a fresh face."

Suzi-Suzi had to be the *un*luckiest model in the entire world. Or maybe she just got hooked up with the worst agency. PLK Management had done nothing for her. They goofed and allowed her to sign a few modeling releases with broad language. With considerable legal latitude at work protecting "editorial usage" of photographs, she had no recourse when the trouble started. Like the public service announcements for STDs. Or the photo illustrating the advice column in *Cosmopolitan* dealing with a wife whose creepy husband wanted to "swing" with a neighbor couple. Now Suzi-Suzi was part of an aggressive ad blitz promoting a new treatment for IBS. People stopped her on the street all the time to talk about diarrhea. She wasn't supermodel gorgeous. Her beauty was much more accessible than that, nonthreatening to women, yet still captivating to men. Most people said she had a girl-next-door quality like Jennifer Garner. Only Suzi-Suzi didn't have the action heroine body. She hated working out.

The waiter swooped by with Kiki's Diet Coke but forgot the lime.

"I'll die without the lime," she told him.

He smiled tightly in apology and off he went.

"Did you get my e-mail?" Kiki demanded.

The girls nodded.

"It was hilarious," Suzi-Suzi put in. "I want to know who this girl is that your brother's marrying all of a sudden. But I guess the more pressing question is . . . when's the baby due?"

A chorus of girlish giggles.

"She's from *New Jersey*," Kiki said, putting enough topspin on the words to equate New York's neighbor state to the hills of Appalachia.

Danni pointed to Kiki's Diet Coke, which sat there untouched and sweating, as if angry about its no-lime status. "*New Jersey*? You're going to need a stronger drink than that."

"Ugh—that's only the beginning," Kiki said. "Her family owns a chain of motels. *Marv's Motor Inns.* Can you imagine?"

"Is that the kind of place where kids with no money go on prom night?" Suzi-Suzi asked.

"They're actually not that bad," Danni put in. "I have an aunt and uncle who love road trips. I've heard them rave about the chain."

Kiki remained skeptical. "Oh, and here's another fun fact. Guess who's best friends with the bride?"

Suzi-Suzi's eyes sparkled. "Is she famous?"

"Yes," Kiki answered. "Famously awful. It's *Vivien*. That horrible woman who represented Walter in our divorce."

A look of alarm flashed across Danni's face. "Is she a bridesmaid?"

Kiki nodded. "Why can't my brother elope? Or just get drunk in Vegas and be done with it like Britney and Nicky Hilton managed to do."

"Um, I think both of those marriages were annulled," Suzi-Suzi pointed out.

"Whatever," Kiki grumbled. "It's just so unfair. I don't expect this Julia girl to know any better. I mean, she's from New Jersey. But Roman's my brother! And did he consider *me* in any of this? How self-involved can one person be?"

The waiter returned with the lime and stood poised for their orders. It was salads all around plus an entrée to share of steak *frites* with the thinnest, most perfectly salted fries in the world.

"Why couldn't Roman have been gay?" Kiki went on. "It would've been like having a sister all these years, and I wouldn't be dealing with any of this."

"Look at the bright side," Suzi-Suzi offered. "In a few months, you'll have a niece or nephew to spoil rotten."

Kiki blanched. "No more baby jokes. *Please*. One day, yes, but not so soon after the wedding. I think a couple should be married for at least five years before having kids. I mean, you have to build in time

15

for the possibility of divorce." She shook her head and sipped on her drink before erupting with, "All these weddings! And none of them are mine!"

Suzi-Suzi piped up again. "That's okay. We shouldn't be made to feel less than just because we don't have husbands." She halted. "Well, I sort of have one, but he's not mine legally, and I never get him on holidays. And when he's around, he never wants to do manly things like fix the running toilet or move furniture. He saves that part of himself for his real wife. Chad just wants to have sex. Come to think of it, he's really just some asshole guy who calls me up when he happens to be free and horny. Remind me to break up with him. But back to my point. Most of the married women I know are not the happiest bunch. They pop Xanax and Paxil like Tic Tacs and constantly complain about their husbands not being interested in anything they have to say. If that's the case, aren't we better off single?"

"Most days," Kiki said. "But right now I wouldn't mind having a husband with a nice income to rely on." Thoughts of Kiki's short-lived first marriage smoked her brain. Walter Sharpe. What had she ever seen in that rich old bastard? Besides all the exotic trips, new clothes, and jewelry. Hmm. That list seemed fairly complete. Basically, it was a starter marriage. Every girl needed one of those. These days, a first husband was sort of like a first heartbreak—something you just *had* to muddle through.

"Don't worry. Everything will work out," Danni whispered soothingly. "You're just in a bit of a slump. I can help you out. In my bedroom closet, I've got shoe boxes stuffed with cash I've earned from dancing. Just take one. I'll never know the difference."

"Do you really think it's safe to keep all that cash around?" Suzi-Suzi asked. "Why don't you put it in the bank?"

Danni shrugged. "I keep meaning to, but the banks are closed when I get off work." She reached for Kiki's hand and squeezed it for emphasis. "I'm serious. Come over and grab a box. Take the one my Gucci boots came in. That's a big box with lots of money."

Kiki was touched. "You're so sweet. But since I'm taking the box anyway, do you mind if I borrow the boots, too?"

"Not at all," Danni said. "And they will look so cute on you."

Kiki experienced a surge of relief. Financial crisis averted—for the moment. Suddenly, it dawned on her that there would be no funding emergency at all if Walter had not been so well represented by Vivien. Evil divorce lawyer. Sworn enemy. Now a fellow bridesmaid. "Whenever I think about that prenup, I just feel like screaming. So what if I didn't read it before I signed. I barely have time to read *Us* magazine, and the courts expect me to study a thick legal document? Besides, what sane person would agree to anything other than lifetime alimony? I should've been declared incompetent just for signing it in the first place. God, it's ridiculous. I gave that man ten months of my life, and all I got in return was three years of support and a gag order to never speak about him in public."

"It's all because of that Vivien," Suzi-Suzi spat. "How are you going to stand being in the same bridal party with her?"

"Keep in mind that what happened had no personal intent," Danni reasoned. "Think about it. Walter hired her to do a job. She would've fought just as hard no matter who was on the other side."

"You know, I've read that women are the real sharks in divorce law these days," Suzi-Suzi said. "Men are hiring them left and right because they work like hell upholding prenups and even get fathers full custody of their children. What, I ask you, has happened to sisterhood?"

Kiki sighed wearily. "I don't know. But I bet you anything these women were *not* popular in high school. I mean, take Vivien. She's *very* tall. You know how boys are about that. I can't see her having many dates back then."

Suzi-Suzi and Danni nodded in agreement.

"I probably represented every mean girl who called her *beanstalk* and then turned around to win homecoming queen. That's why she worked so hard.

It's called anger transference. Dr. Phil did a whole show about it once."

"It's so classic," Suzi-Suzi remarked. "She makes *you* pay for her childhood wounds."

"I know," Kiki said. "It's so wrong. And they say beautiful people go through life with such ease. If you ask me, it's the pretty girls who suffer the most."

From: kiki@misstexas95.com
To: breckin@withthisring.com
Subject: SOS

Breckin!

It's been a million years. At least. But here I am, reaching out via e-mail to beg for help. Please say yes. Do you remember Roman, my adorable brother? Certainly you do. As I recall, you had a mad crush on him all through high school. Well, he's getting married. To a GIRL. How many times did I tell you he wasn't gay? At least five hundred or more. That was just your wishful thinking at work. Homosexuals can be so optimistic! Isn't that how those Tom Cruise rumors got started? Hysterical. Okay, where was I? Oh, the girl. Ugh. Get this—she's from New Jersey, and her family runs a chain of roadside motels. You know, the kind of places where people in scary movies are always killed. Anyway, I'm coming back to Fredericksburg for Roman's big day. Can you believe it? After all these years. But you *HAVE* to agree to help plan this wedding. Okay? This is me begging . . .

Air Kisses,
Kiki
P.S. You do know that I dropped Sonntage for the snazzier stage name of Douglas, right?

Chapter Two

The day was in complete turnaround. First, a fun and supportive lunch with the girls (very therapeutic). And now, a little shopping spree with the girls (equally therapeutic). All these women marching in and out of psychiatrists' offices to blather on about old childhood wounds or to tick off the top five reasons they feel unfulfilled were just wasting their time. Hmm. Another good insight for the book. "Doctor Visa Is In." A great chapter title!

"What do you think of these?" Kiki asked, donning a pair of funky mirrored sunglasses and vamping appropriately. They were in the Stella McCartney boutique on Fourteenth Street, one of Kiki's favorite places on earth.

"They're *so* you," Danni said. "You should get them."

Kiki consulted the mirror. The sunglasses *were* definitely her. Hmm. But did they make her look like

Teri Hatcher? People always told her that. Of course, it was a flattering comparison. They both had gorgeously styled brunette hair, inviting smiles, Yoga-perfect bodies, and the uncanny ability to wear skimpy outfits *without* coming off slutty. But deep down, Kiki would've liked—at least every once in a while—to hear someone say, "Teri Hatcher looks like *you*." Kiki removed the shades to check the price. Two hundred dollars. Very reasonable. Especially when you considered the fact that they came emblazoned with the Stella McCartney name. Face it, that woman was only going to put her moniker on a fashionable, well-designed product of impeccable quality. After all, she's Stella. In fact, to not snatch up the glasses immediately would be practically insulting. And Kiki would never dream of offending Stella McCartney.

"Can you see me in this?" Suzi-Suzi inquired, holding up a sexy, lacy top with a loose, plunging neckline.

Kiki visualized. "With some shrewdly positioned invisible tape and those breasts, you might even make the gayest of men stop and reconsider their orientation."

Suzi-Suzi smiled as she consulted a mirror. "Chad seems a little distant lately. Maybe I need to sex it up a bit. You know, really differentiate myself from his wife."

"You're not covered on his insurance," Danni put in. "Isn't that enough?"

"And ten minutes ago you wanted to break up with him," Kiki added.

"I still do," Suzi-Suzi insisted. "But first I want him to really get into me again. You know?"

Kiki meandered a bit, checking out a few handbags, a sales rack, some shoes. From behind a privacy wall, she heard the chatter of shopgirl to VIP customer and stopped cold.

"Mrs. Brock, that is *too* hot. It's impossible to believe that you were pregnant six weeks ago," a raspy, Demi-like voice praised.

Kiki gasped. *Mrs. Brock. Pregnant six weeks ago.* That could only mean Kirsten Brock.

"You're officially a MILF," the salesgirl went on.

"What's a MILF?" Kirsten asked innocently.

Kiki frantically motioned for Suzi-Suzi and Danni to come over.

"It's a guy expression for hot moms," the salesgirl answered. "Kind of vulgar."

"Oh, I get it," Kirsten said. "Did you hear that, Tom? I'm a MILF now."

Kiki stifled a shriek. *Tom.* That could only mean Tom Brock!

"What is—"

Kiki clamped a hand over Suzi-Suzi's mouth before she could get the question out. "Tom and Kirsten Brock are behind that wall," she hissed.

"Oh, my God! Are you serious?" Danni asked in a voice way too loud.

23

Kiki hushed her. "Of course, I'm serious. Would I joke about Tom and Kirsten Brock?"

Tom Brock was possibly the sexiest, most romantic man alive. Imagine Brad Pitt singing and sounding just like Frank Sinatra. Now multiply by one hundred. Yes. That hot.

Kiki experienced a warm flush. "Is my face red?" she whispered.

Suzi-Suzi began to fan her with the sexy top.

Tom Brock was New York's top cabaret act. To see him perform live was standing room only. He did a sweep of shows each fall and spring, and tickets sold out faster than J.Lo can scribble her name onto a marriage license. Kiki had seen him once during a special limited engagement at Feinstein's at the Regency. Oh, God. When she heard him sing "Put Your Head on My Shoulder," Kiki cried so much that her eye makeup got ruined. Now that was real emotion.

Suzi-Suzi and Danni were whispering and craning their necks, brainstorming ways to get a closer look at Manhattan's supercouple.

Tom was a total dream. No debate there. But Kirsten Brock, his wife of just a few years, was an icon of class, style, and sophistication. So perfect. She was the sacred object of envy/worship for single and married women alike. What clothes she wore. The exact shade of blond her colorist used. Where she

ate. Everything she said. It was all slavishly moni-
tored. And subsequently imitated.

"I forgot to tell you," Suzi-Suzi whispered. "Last
week I saw Kirsten racing down Fifth Avenue on a
mint green Vespa."

Silently, the girls processed this important information. Then, in almost perfect harmony (practically
Destiny's Child, but, in all honesty, Danni chimed
in a smidge late), they murmured, "We should all
get one."

"I'll make inquiries at a dealership," Suzi-Suzi
offered.

Kiki realized that riding a scooter in New York
traffic probably meant risking their lives at every mo-
torized moment, but if Kirsten Brock thought it safe
enough, then it must be okay. After all, she was a
mother now to a beautiful baby they called Music.
Kiki had seen a picture in the *New York Post* of Kirsten pushing Music in a Lulu Guinness stroller. So
inspiring. A true testament to family values. It made
Kiki want to rush out and demand that Tom Brock
get her pregnant.

"Go back there and try that on," Kiki told Suzi-
Suzi, pointing to the barely there top. "See if you can
get a good look at them. Maybe strike up a conversation."

Suzi-Suzi looked uncertain. "What would I say?
As much as I love Kirsten, she would take one look

at me and know that I want to sleep with her husband."

Danni just stood there with a bemused little smile. "Could definitely put a strain on a new friendship."

Kiki huffed and snatched the blouse from Suzi-Suzi's hands. "Then *I'll* try it on." She made a beeline for the private fitting area.

Suzi-Suzi and Danni squealed like two little mice.

Kiki boldly stepped into the VIP sanctuary to find Tom Brock playing the role of bored-silly husband as he sat patiently in a chair holding his wife's purse (a gorgeous quilted Chanel bag in pink with white logo).

Tom gave her a slight grin and a rolling of the eyes.

Kiki smiled back. It was a real moment with Tom Brock! Would it be rude to ask him to sing for her? Just one song. Maybe "Fly Me to the Moon." That was a jaunty number. He could just snap his fingers and give it a go.

Clink.

What was that? Damn! Kiki realized that the heart charm had just fallen off her Juicy Couture bracelet and landed somewhere near Tom Brock's Prada-clad feet. He had great taste in shoes. The sign of a very sophisticated man.

Kiki crouched a bit to scour the area.

"Did you lose something?" Tom asked.

Kiki rejoiced in his unsolicited heroism. Memo to

the women of America: Chivalry is not dead! "Oh, it's just a stupid charm from my bracelet. It's got to be around here somewhere." Kiki bent down to retrieve it, momentarily lost her balance, and found herself between Tom's denim legs. Actually, not a bad place to be (but only under the proper circumstances).

All of a sudden, Kiki sensed the firing of flashes and the *snap-snap-snap* of a shutter release. She glanced up to see a photographer. The icky, unwashed variety. The kind of bottom-feeder who hides in a Dumpster to get shots of Paris Hilton stumbling out of a nightclub. But just as quickly as he appeared, he scampered away like a rodent.

Kiki looked away, terribly embarrassed, trying to put all the pieces together about what had just happened. The charm! There it was, right under Tom's chair. She snatched it up and presented it to him as evidence. "This is just a fun costume piece. I really have better taste in jewelry."

"I'm sure that you do," he said graciously as he helped Kiki stand up. How gallant!

"God, I'm so clumsy. Do you think I looked retarded in that picture? I could use some good PR right now. I'm an actress. Mostly soaps. But right now I'm in between projects."

Tom Brock laughed. "If I'm being honest, I don't think it was the best angle for either one of us."

Up close, Kiki realized that his teeth could stand

to be bleached. This upset her terribly. It put a major ding in the picture of perfection she had built up. Regardless, the man still oozed charm.

"I love your last CD—listen to it all the time. But I have to say, as gorgeous as your voice is, it's becoming a bit of a bore. I want a new set of tracks."

Tom seemed amused by her candor. "Actually, I'm just starting on a new record. Should be out early next year."

"May I be so bold as to suggest a song?" She didn't wait for his answer. "What about 'Almost Paradise'?" You know, from the movie *Footloose*. It's a great love ballad!"

His look was quizzical, as if half wondering if her idea might be a joke.

Kiki merely peered back at him earnestly.

"Um . . . that's an interesting idea . . . but I tend to stick with standards," Tom said.

"That *is* a standard, silly," Kiki informed him. "Do you have any idea how many schools have used 'Almost Paradise' as their prom theme? *Thousands.*"

Kirsten emerged from the changing room. "Tom, I'm almost done here. I promise. You must be about to die."

"I'm fine, baby. Take your time," Tom said.

Kirsten glanced at Kiki, then back to Tom.

"I'm sorry. What's your name?" Tom asked Kiki.

"Kiki. Kiki Douglas." She extended her hand to

Kirsten, who returned a sincere smile and a firm shake.

"Kirsten Brock. Nice to meet you."

"Kiki and I were just mugged by one of those tabloid photographers," Tom explained.

Kirsten gave him a strange look.

"I'll tell you later," he said, laughing and waving off the joke at the same time.

Kirsten glanced at Kiki's selection and raised her perfectly waxed eyebrows. "That's nice. Don't you just love all of her stuff?"

"I do!" Kiki said. A bit too enthusiastically. But this was Kirsten Brock talking to her about fashion. The excitement level was off the charts. Possible comparison: a political junkie getting the chance to talk shop with Bill Clinton.

"Don't even think about trusting a dry cleaner with that," Kirsten said. "I hand wash all my couture. It's a chore, yes, but it's the only way."

"Oh, I agree," Kiki lied. "Totally." The truth was, she had never hand washed so much as a delicate wineglass. If it shattered in the dishwasher, then it just wasn't meant to be. And then Kiki stood there, overjoyed. To be on the receiving end of confidential information from Kirsten Brock! It was a major social coup. Lesser events have ended up as items in "Page Six," the gossip column in the *New York Post* that everybody reads. "A friend of mine saw you riding a Vespa on Fifth," Kiki said, racking her brain for anything to extend the conversation. "I'm thinking about getting one."

"Oh, you should," Kirsten encouraged her. "It's great freedom, and they're easy to ride."

Suddenly, Kiki was distracted again by the discovery of Tom Brock's less-than-sparkling-white teeth— even more so by Kirsten's complicit role in the matter. Why was she dragging her feet on the issue? If Tom were Kiki's husband, then she would've just pushed him through the doors of BriteSmile and been done with it. At the very least, Kirsten should refuse the man blow jobs until he used those over-the-counter Crest Whitestrips.

The shopgirl appeared and gave Kiki a cool appraisal that translated *You don't belong here.*

That's when Kirsten piped up with a friendly, "You look so familiar, Kiki. Where have I seen you before?"

Kiki shot the bitchy shopgirl a look of triumph. "Well, I've done some—"

"Wait a minute!" Kirsten interjected, reaching out to claim Kiki's wrist in her excitement. "You're Jeannette from *All My Children*!"

"Actually, I *was* Jeannette," Kiki corrected. "I got pushed off a cruise ship, remember?"

Kirsten shrugged. "I haven't watched a single episode since the baby was born."

"I've seen pictures," Kiki said. "She's beautiful."

"Thank you." Kirsten glanced at her watch (a sleek little Dolce & Gabbana number). "It makes me crazy to be away from her for even this long." She turned imploringly to Tom. "Do you mind if we skip the bakery? I'm anxious to get back. Music didn't poop before we left, and I'm worried."

Kiki blanched. Talking about bowel movements in a Stella McCartney boutique . . . well, that should get you arrested for public indecency. Okay, one free pass for New Mother Syndrome.

Tom's sigh was equal parts exasperation and uxoriousness. He patted his stomach, generally firm but not necessarily in fighting shape. "I guess it won't kill me to go without a few cupcakes."

Kirsten laughed at him. "A few? You always eat at least half a dozen." She gave Kiki a little smile, as if in confidence. "He's completely obsessed with the cupcakes at Magnolia Bakery. It's on Bleecker. Have you had them?"

"*Yes*," Kiki answered dramatically. "That frosting is addictive. There should be a surgeon general's warning on those things."

The shopgirl lingered, waiting for direction from Kirsten, glowering at Kiki.

"Could you have everything I tried on sent to my apartment?" Kirsten asked.

"Of course," the shopgirl said, practically tripping over her own words as she no doubt factored out the killer commission that came with such requests.

"Great. Thank you. If I don't get home to my baby right away, I think I might explode." Kirsten offered Kiki a demure wave. "Nice to meet you." With a conspiratorial wink, she pointed to the blouse in Kiki's hands and whispered, "Buy it. You'll look amazing in that."

Kiki watched the supercouple go, then peeked at the price tag. She swallowed hard. Eight hundred dollars. Completely out of the question. Especially considering her current financial circumstances. But Kirsten had told her under no uncertain terms to purchase the top. And who was Kiki to second-guess the fashion judgment of Kirsten Brock?

She rushed back to the sales floor to rejoin Suzi-Suzi and Danni.

"Oh, my God!" Suzi-Suzi gushed. "We wanted to listen, but I made Danni rate the way I looked carrying every Stella handbag. Did you talk to them? What did they say? What did you say? Tell us *everything*!" The questions came with the rat-a-tat-tat rapidity of assault weapon fire.

"And please tell me you didn't tell Tom that ridiculous idea about recording 'Almost Paradise' for his next CD," Danni put in.

Kiki reeled back with imperial indignation. "I most certainly did. And he's considering it."

Danni smiled, shaking her head.

Suzi-Suzi's face was a masterpiece of desperation. "I'm *dying*! What were they like? What was he like?

What was she like? Did she act like a bitch? I read somewhere that she once snapped at a waitress for bringing her coffee that wasn't decaf."

Kiki went over the encounter in luxurious detail, feeling like a college professor who might be lecturing to a gifted class. After all, Suzi-Suzi and Danni were well-versed on the subjects of fashion and celebrity. They got the nuance and subtext. Kiki didn't have to dumb it down.

"I can't freaking believe it," Suzi-Suzi said after minutes of paying silent, rapturous attention. "How could his teeth be that way? They live just a few blocks away from a BriteSmile!"

Kiki nodded somberly. "I know. Isn't it awful?" She glanced down at the skimpy top, then back to Suzi-Suzi. "Kirsten told me that I should buy this. She said it would look great on me."

Suzi-Suzi beamed. "And I picked it out, which means Kirsten and I practically have the exact same taste."

"So you don't mind if I get it?" Kiki asked.

Suzi-Suzi shook her head. "Any finders-keepers claims are trumped by a direct recommendation from Kirsten Brock. It's yours." One beat. "Besides, I can't afford it anyway. It's eight hundred dollars, and I have to get my hair colored this week. And you know how much Trish charges."

"But she's *so* worth it," Kiki said.

"Completely," Suzi-Suzi agreed.

Kiki turned to Danni. "Are you sure there's lots of money in that Gucci boot box? I mean, if it's filled with ones, I'm going to be in serious trouble."

Danni smiled shrewdly. "What do you think I am? A stripper in a small town? I do *not* dance for single dollar bills."

Kiki marched back to the bitchy salesgirl and nervously chewed on her lower lip until the credit card was approved. Amazing! Maybe MBNA raised her limit on account of her on-time payment history. Well, many times Kiki had been late, but she always called to offer detailed reasons why. Certainly creditors appreciated that.

Walking out of the Stella McCartney boutique with her Stella McCartney bag and the secret knowledge of her new almost-friendship with Kirsten Brock, Kiki felt the day could not get any better. Of course, a job would improve things. Not to mention a man in her life. Preferably an independently wealthy and straight one.

Suzi-Suzi wanted to step into Jeffrey, another expensive boutique, but this time Kiki begged off. She would at least have to count the money in Danni's boot box before entertaining the idea of more shopping.

"Well, *I'm* going in," Suzi-Suzi said defiantly. "I need an outfit to drive Chad insane with desire before I dump him. I know I said I was broke, but now that I think about it, this is an emergency situation."

Kiki and Danni left her to the seduction/destruction plan, jumped into a cab, and headed for Danni's digs on the Upper West Side.

"So," Kiki began once inside the taxi, "do you really think that she'll break up with him?"

"Absolutely not," Danni said.

And then they both laughed.

"Leave it to Suzi-Suzi to go about things the bizarre way," Danni went on. "You're in what—four weddings this summer?"

"*Five*," Kiki corrected. "Counting my brother's shotgun thing."

"So most girls are doing it the old-fashioned way. You know, getting engaged and driving all their friends insane with a big wedding. But our Suzi-Suzi is doing a practice marriage with somebody else's husband."

Kiki shook her head with a giggle. "Maybe she's onto something."

The taxi kaboomed along, a few hours ahead of the worst traffic.

"So this guy keeps coming into the club," Danni announced. "Have I told you about him?"

"The creepy one who wants you to star in his independent film?"

Danni pulled a face. "Oh, God—not him. By the

way, I found out he was legit. But his movies are low-budget horror. I'd be running around in the woods getting chased by a psycho with a chain saw. No thanks."

Kiki rolled her eyes. "Sounds like my first marriage. Except for the woods and the chain saw, of course."

Danni gave her a quizzical look.

"Walter was psycho," Kiki explained. "And the prenup was definitely low budget."

"*Anyway.*" Danni pressed on. "Usually, I don't look twice at any guy that comes into the club. But there's something about this particular one. He's really sweet, and he shows the girls a lot of respect. Every dancer has tried to get him into the Champagne Room—"

"What's that?" Kiki asked.

"That's where they do private dances. Management says every customer who goes into the Champagne Room should walk out with a maxed-out credit card. But I don't go there. Champagne Room guys tend to get touchy-feely. Besides, I need a full stage to do my choreography."

"So what about this guy?"

Danni's eyes sparkled. "He works on Wall Street. Hedge funds, I think. His name's Thad Davis, and he loves, loves, loves eighties music. He says I remind him of Tawny Kitaen. Remember her? The girl from the Whitesnake videos?"

"I heard she went crazy and beat up her husband," Kiki said. "It was all on the *E! True Hollywood Story*. But I'm sure he means that you remind him of pre-arrest Tawny, the girl who was rolling around on top of David Coverdale's car."

"Exactly," Danni chirped proudly. "So this Thad guy keeps asking me out. And it's not like, 'I'll sit here until you get off work, and we'll go back to my place.' He wants to pick me up and take me out for dinner and a show."

"A real date," Kiki said. "This guy really does love the eighties. I mean, he's so retro."

"I know!" Danni sighed. "But I have this personal policy about never dating guys I meet at the club."

"Okay, I'm great at rationalizing loopholes for constricting policies. You should see me do my taxes." Kiki gazed out the window. "Ooh—hot guy jogging." She pointed to a half-naked Adonis sweating bullets in the midday heat.

Danni raised her brow in appreciation.

Kiki moved on. "Let's see . . . what do you think is the core reason behind your policy?"

"Maintaining a professional distance," Danni said right away. "And avoiding losers and heartbreak. Every dancer who's ever dated a regular she met at the club has ended up crying on my shoulder."

"It's simple then," Kiki remarked in a singsong voice. "Ban him from the club. Then go out with him."

Danni brightened. "In a weird kind of way, that actually makes sense!"

"I mean, if he's not willing to give up going to Camisole to date you, then he's not worth fooling with anyway."

Danni smiled. "*You* are brilliant."

"Did I tell you I'm writing a book?" Kiki asked.

"No! Are you serious? What kind of book?"

"Sort of a self-help, autobiography, relationship recovery thing. Well, I don't know exactly yet. It's all over the place. I just think I can help a lot of women out there. For instance, take a girl in, say, Ohio. She wakes up with a pimple on the morning of the night she has a very big date with a guy she's mad for. Does she know that the only way to make it disappear is to put a speck of toothpaste on the eruption and keep it covered with a Band-Aid all day?"

"Probably not," Danni said.

"My point exactly!" Kiki thundered. "Why should I limit all of my knowledge to just you and Suzi-Suzi and the occasional girl I strike up a conversation with in a nightclub bathroom? I could be helping women all over the world."

"It's not just a book," Danni said. "It's a humanitarian project."

"Hello!"

The taxi rolled to a stop outside Danni's building, and the girls swung out, blew past the leering doorman, and rode the creaky elevator up to Danni's sixth floor studio.

Danni was a compulsive organizer, so it took no time to find the Gucci box piggy bank. She sat on the bed and gestured for Kiki to join her. "Let's count it. I want to make sure there's enough here to tide you over."

Kiki just stared at the box. Cash had been stuffed inside to the point of spilling out once the cover was peeled off. They both began to count, but Kiki gave up after the five grand mark. Whatever the final figure was, it would be plenty to see her through this minor funding emergency.

"You can take another box, too, if you want," Danni offered.

"This is more than generous," Kiki gushed. "And I'll pay you back every cent." One beat. "Once I'm rich again, of course. I mean, really. If I pay you back too soon, then I might just have to borrow it again. And that would just be tiresome." She scanned the floor of Danni's closet in search of the Gucci boots that had once been nestled inside the cardboard ATM machine positioned on her lap. Suddenly, she saw them—a gorgeous brown pair with gold "G" buckles hooked around the ankles. A little yelp escaped her lips.

"Help yourself," Danni said.

"You're the best friend in the world." Kiki practically negotiated a dive-and-roll for the coveted shoes.

"That's what you told Suzi-Suzi when she got you front row seats to see a taping of *The Daily Show with Jon Stewart*."

Kiki grinned. "I meant it then, and I mean it now." A soaring sense of exuberance rushed though her body. What a day! A great book idea, a meaningful encounter with Kirsten Brock, a new Stella top, enough money to momentarily keep the vultures at bay, and these fabulous boots. "You know," she announced sunnily, "everything in my life is starting to move on the right track."

From: kiki@misstexas95.com
To: breckin@withthisring.com
Subject: Just Imagine . . .

Breckin!

I've had the most delicious thought. Why limit ourselves to a ceremony in Fredericksburg? Think about this: How fabulous would a New York wedding be? You would go wild planning it, and it's so much more convenient for me. I'm sure Roman won't mind. Let's discuss.

Air Kisses,
Kiki

Chapter Three

The telephone jangled violently.

Who on earth? And why at this ungodly hour? Kiki stirred, spewing curses in a low growl as she fumbled for the receiver. But first she squinted to make out the clock. A few minutes past nine. What kind of barbarian would dare to call now? As if everyone lived by a farmer's crack-of-dawn schedule.

"This better be an emergency," Kiki croaked instead of hello.

"I'd say the end of your career in New York qualifies as one."

Kiki rose with a start, recognizing the voice instantly. It belonged to Sarah Ann Duckworth, the Birmingham, Alabama debutante turned Manhattan publicist. But forget transplanted sweet Southern girl. In this case, long-lost Soprano child rang with more truth.

"And if you expect any help with damage control," Sarah Ann went on, "then I suggest that you pay your overdue bill."

"What are you talking about?" Kiki asked, feigning ignorance about all of it when she really was only clueless about half. In all honesty, she had been thinking about Sarah Ann's recent invoice (the one with DEADBEAT! scribbled across it in red Sharpie) while the girl at Stella McCartney had been ringing up the eight-hundred-dollar blouse.

"I'm talking about a public image holocaust!" Sarah Ann shrieked. "I would rather explain why you pushed an old blind woman in front of a bus than this!"

Kiki paused to consider the situation. It could very well be that Sarah Ann Duckworth had bipolar disorder. Oprah had done a whole show about it. Hmm. If this proved to be true, then Sarah Ann could hardly be an asset to Kiki's career.

Beep.

Oh, thank God for call-waiting. The perfect escape chute for unpleasant interruptions or boring conversations. "That's my other line, Sarah Ann. I'll have to call you back."

Click.

But before Kiki could get so much as the "H" in hello out, Suzi-Suzi was screaming bloody murder, then asking, "Are you dying? You must be dying. I would be *so* dying. At least it's not a bad picture, though. I mean, you look great."

43

"What are you talking about?" Kiki demanded. And this time, she really had no idea.

"You haven't seen it?"

"Seen what?"

"Oh, God," Suzi-Suzi said, her voice down an octave. "Uh—you shouldn't be alone when you see it. I'm coming over there. But whatever you do, *don't* go out and buy the *New York Post*. Promise me you won't. *Promise!*"

"I promise," Kiki said earnestly. So the first thing she did as soon as Suzi-Suzi hung up was shove her feet into a pair of Uggs, toss on her Hello Kitty terry cloth robe, and race downstairs to the newsstand on the corner.

From several feet away Kiki saw it. Almost instantly, her stomach dropped. And then a sense of personal doom settled somewhere in her gut and threatened to stay.

HOME WRECKER!

Those two words were stacked on the front page of the *New York Post*, each offending letter billboard big. To the immediate right was a photograph of Kiki between Tom Brock's legs, looking like she had graduated Phi Beta Kappa from Lewinsky University.

Kiki just stood there in a foggy tableau, as if watching the scene outside of herself. Slowly, she reached out for the tallest stack to touch one of the tabloids, if only to prove it real. And the smudge of newsprint that stained her fingertips provided the answer: Oh, hell, yes.

She slapped down two dollars, grabbed a copy, and started back to her apartment as she read. The photo caption alone infuriated her: "Washed-up soap starlet Kiki Douglas makes a desperate play for Tom Brock, New York's very own young Sinatra." Kiki could feel a flush of red heat start up at her neck and move to her cheeks, which were burning. *Washed-up soap starlet?* First of all, she was hardly washed up. Her career was merely in . . . a period of transition. And what's this about a *desperate play?* Please. Not that she was even trying to offer one, but the fact is that she gave a very good blow job. Any man should be quite happy to get one from her. Even Tom Brock!

Ripping through the paper to get to the story, she found the rest of it a few turns over, basically a single column running down the page, accompanied by publicity shots of her (a nice one, actually; she was wearing a Pucci halter), Tom, and Kirsten. Not much there as far as information goes. It was all vague speculation about what might or might not be an affair. Pretty boring and pointless, actually. Even the most gullible moron would have thought so.

Kiki continued to read. All of a sudden, she halted. How did they discover her real age? Damn those tabloid hacks! Now she couldn't go ahead with plans for her thirtieth birthday party. Still consumed with every image and syllable, she found her way back inside her apartment as if by muscle memory alone.

The telephone blasted Kiki away from her private Mars. Like a zombie, she moved to answer. All she did was pick up. Not even an intake of breath.

And Suzi-Suzi shouted, "I *knew* you would go down and grab the first paper you saw! I called Danni. She's on three-way. I think. I'm always screwing that up. Either hanging up on someone when I want them on the line, or not hanging up when I want to gossip about them. Danni, are you there?"

"I'm here. Don't panic, Kiki," she offered soothingly. "The morning's scandal is the afternoon's fish paper."

"And what's the old saying? Oh, yeah. There's no such thing as bad publicity," Suzi-Suzi put in.

"Everybody's going to know that I'm really thirty-four," Kiki whined.

"What? That's crazy. They didn't say anything about your age," Suzi-Suzi said. One beat. "Oh, you're right. There it is. Well, don't worry. At least it's buried in the article. Hardly anybody will notice. Most people just look at the pictures. I only read the whole thing because you're my best friend."

"Nobody is going to pay attention to this," Danni went on. "There's *nothing* to this story. It must be a really slow news day."

Kiki gasped. "Are you saying that I'm not a worthwhile scandal queen?" Almost worse than the public humiliation would be the prospect of boring the public. After all, at the end of the day, Kiki considered herself an entertainer.

"No!" Danni and Suzi-Suzi exclaimed in perfect unison.

"You're a *great* scandal queen," Suzi-Suzi assured her. "Way better than, say, Amber Frey. I mean, has she ever heard of Google? That's how I found out Chad was married. I just Googled him. Come on. You don't have to be Nancy Drew."

"What we mean," Danni added, "is that there's no meat on this bone. It's an innocent situation completely blown out of proportion. If it lasts longer than this morning's news cycle, then I'll choreograph a dance to 'Two of Hearts' by Stacey Q. And you know how much I hate that song."

Suzi-Suzi started singing, " 'Two of hearts . . . two hearts that beat as one.' " Then she sighed. "I used to love that song! Whatever happened to her?"

"Girls!" Kiki scolded them. "Would you shut up about Stacey Q already? I'm the one with the problem. Focus!"

"Sorry," Suzi-Suzi murmured. "Do you want us to come over?"

Kiki thought about it. "No, I'm fine." Her stomach did a low rumble. "God, I'm starving. Do you realize that I haven't eaten a thing since lunch yesterday?

And there's not a speck of food in this apartment. I think there might be a jar of jam in the fridge, but I have no idea how old it is."

"So go to the market," Danni suggested. "That will help take your mind off things."

Kiki sighed miserably. "Ugh. That's too much trouble. I'd have to go there, pick everything out, haul everything back . . . I'm exhausted just thinking about it. I'll just pop in somewhere for an egg white omelet." She said her goodbyes, signed off, tossed on a Krista Allen SexBrand tee emblazoned with the phrase YOU WERE NEVER MY BOYFRIEND, squeezed into distressed denim cutoffs, slipped on the nearest available pair of Manolo Blahniks, and hit the door.

"There she is!"

Kiki heard this the moment her expensive shoe hit the sidewalk. She glanced up to see a gaggle of photographers positioned in front of her building. Right away she regretted not putting any makeup on. God! All she wanted was an omelet! Hmm. Note to self: Maybe you *don't* want to be as famous as Jennifer Aniston. But you *do* want her hair.

"Are you in love with Tom Brock?" The question came from a sweaty man with bad acne.

Kiki ignored him and started down the sidewalk. Honestly! The idiot needed a lesson in priorities. Shouldn't he be more concerned with ordering a trial package of Proactiv Solution?

"Why are you going after a married man with a

young family?" It was a female voice this time. Probably the butch-looking girl with sideburns growing down her face.

Kiki walked on imperviously, never once looking back, doing her best to pick up the pace without coming off as frantic.

"How much did the plastic surgeon charge for those tits?"

Kiki stopped cold, spinning angrily to see a short, balding Danny DeVito look-alike smirking at her as he snapped off several shots. She stood there in a state of horrified silence, wondering how these vultures found out about her boob job. She had them done in Brazil. And everybody had always assumed they were real. Even her last boyfriend, Mike Jovie, a real estate developer and self-proclaimed connoisseur of breasts, was completely fooled by the teardrop implants. Ugh! Her real age. Now the truth about her breasts. Why not just film her next visit to the gynecologist and be done with it?

Suddenly, Kiki felt the impact of the personal invasion. She experienced a tight fight-or-flight sensation. So as any sensible woman would do when faced with the same set of circumstances, she slipped off her Manolos and sprinted down the sidewalk, pedicure be damned. She *had* to get away from these pigs.

Thank God for all those spinning classes. And designer sample sales. All that pedaling and dashing about had really whipped her into great shape. Kiki commanded a quick lead, but the paparazzi gained on her fast. For people who looked like they lived on Krispy Kremes and Coke Classic, they sure could move.

Just ahead, Kiki saw a cab jerk to a stop. Out stepped a distinguished woman who looked at Kiki's bare feet as if she were a refugee from one of those countries that's impossible to spell.

Kiki tumbled inside and found herself momentarily paralyzed by the driver's body odor. Beyond awful. She wanted to suggest a new super-strength time-release deodorant. This worked for Adam, a writer friend whose fiancée broke up with him over his odor problem. Of course, this happened before the new deodorant hit the market, and by then she had met someone else. Now she was married and lived in a great apartment in the West Village. Poor Adam! Hmm. Mental note to include this story in the book. An important object lesson about proper grooming.

For now, Kiki just told the stinky man to drive.

He demanded to know where because his shift was about to end, and if it was too far, then she'd have to get out.

What a horrible attitude! She decided to keep the deodorant tip a secret. Kiki thought for a moment. Where to go? Suddenly, it dawned on her. In all of yesterday's hurly-burly, she really didn't get a chance to see all that Stella McCartney had to offer. A little shopping should help curb the morning's anxiety. She announced the boutique's address.

Obviously it was close enough, because the driver took off.

Kiki fired up her cellular and got Suzi-Suzi on the line pronto. Luckily, the girl was always sitting by the phone hoping that her modeling agency might call. In the middle of Kiki's story about being chased by ugly people with bad diets, Suzi-Suzi halted her to say, "That's not even the half of it."

Kiki blanched. There was *more*? "What do you mean?"

Suzi-Suzi sighed. "Radio is all over the story. DJs are ripping you to pieces, and listeners are calling in to say you're a skank. You know that show with the shock jock who's always prank-calling his mother?"

"Stevie G?" Kiki asked.

"Yeah," Suzi-Suzi said. "By the way, that's so cruel. I mean, she's got Alzheimer's! Anyway, he's been the worst. But don't worry. I called in and defended you on the air. I told him that you were just like other women in the city. You *wanted* to sleep with Tom Brock, but you haven't. He sort of twisted my words around, though, so I'm not sure if I helped or if I made things worse."

Kiki sat there totally perplexed. A simple charm falls off her bracelet, and it had come to this. Suddenly, a sobering realization hit her. The public's love affair with Tom and Kirsten was *not* to be underestimated. What if they turned her into the next Monica Lewinsky? Of course, she would be considered a thinner, beautiful version. But they still might feed her to the wolves faster than you can say "Gap dress!"

The cab stopped in front of Stella's shop.

Kiki swung out in a funk but was soon levitated by the environment of upscale retail. Way better than nature. What can a babbling brook do other than make you think that you have to go to the bathroom?

The same bitchy salesgirl was there. Only this time she stared daggers at Kiki and traded contemptuous looks with another associate on the floor.

Kiki ignored them and began to browse the racks.

Then the newer girl walked over to snappishly announce, "I'm sorry, but I'm going to have to ask you to leave. Your business is not welcome here."

Kiki was appalled. "Excuse me?"

The girl nodded to the security guard. "Let's not cause a scene."

At first Kiki couldn't believe it, but then the burly man in full cop gear took a menacing step toward her, so she stepped out onto the sidewalk and just stood there, stupefied.

Suddenly, the screeching of brakes startled her. Kiki looked up to see an SUV being driven by one of those disgusting photographers. He gave her a creepy smile and aimed his big protruding lens at her as if she were fresh kill.

Kiki dashed off, doing her best to lose him while

still staying on the fashionable end of the Meat Packing District. After all, one scandal was enough for the day. So she stayed south of Fourteenth Street, ducking in and out of the crossroads of Little West Twelfth Street, Gansevoort Street, and Greenwich Street. Having successfully eluded him, she sought refuge inside a discreet-looking building.

Once inside, she took in the mood lighting, sumptuous furnishings, and romantic ambiance, instantly realizing where she was—Affair, the swanky new hotel that everybody was talking about. Kiki rolled her eyes, the irony not lost on her. Here she was seeking sanctuary at Affair because people were chasing her for an affair she wasn't having. Could there be anything more ridiculous?

Kiki moved to nestle into a discreet spot in the cozy lobby only to find a couple locked in a passionate canoodling session. *"Please,"* Kiki snapped. "You're in a hotel. Get a room already."

But the kissing thundered on.

Kiki sank down into a love seat nearby to call Suzi-Suzi and fill her in on the latest. "I feel like a hunted animal. These photographers are like bloodhounds. And they kicked me out of Stella McCartney! Can you believe that? I'm, like, her biggest fan. It's not Stella's fault, though. If she knew, I'm sure that she would call to apologize. And fire that horrible sales-girl. She should be working at H & M and feel lucky to be there."

Kylie Adams

Suzi-Suzi was oddly silent.

Kiki grew pensive. There was more. She just didn't know about it yet. "Suzi-Suzi, what's going on?"

"It's worse. Much worse. Somehow between yesterday and today, you've become the most hated woman in Manhattan. The rumors are out of control. There's even one going around that you said Tom and Kirsten's baby looks like a monkey."

Kiki was horrified. "Oh, my God! I would never say that about Music!"

"I know. I mean, you have her picture on your refrigerator. You practically think of her as your niece. But it's all over the radio."

Kiki felt a sense of panic begin to envelop her.

Meanwhile, Suzi-Suzi babbled on. "Danni said most of the strippers at Camisole are on Kirsten's side."

Kiki found this particularly daunting. When strippers are against a girl, then she's really swimming against the current of public opinion. "What should I do?"

"About the strippers?" Suzi-Suzi asked. "I wouldn't worry about them. But if you really want to plead your case, I'm sure that Danni could arrange a little talk between shifts. Addressing them woman-to-woman would probably change some minds."

"I mean the whole mess in general!" Kiki snapped.

"Oh," Suzi-Suzi murmured. "Too bad you don't have a publicist."

Sarah Ann Duckworth! Kiki gripped her cellular tighter. "Suzi-Suzi, you have to help me."

"Name it. As long as it doesn't involve calling Stevie G again. That man is vile."

Kiki's brain computer was processing at Intel speed. "You still have an extra key to my apartment, right?"

"Of course. Remember when the pipes in my building burst, and you were out of town, and Chad and I spent the night there?"

Kiki huffed. "How could I forget? He left his business card on my nightstand with a rude little note that I needed a new mattress."

"But then he got you a good deal on that Tempur-Pedic," Suzi-Suzi said brightly.

"That's true. And it *is* a dream to sleep on."

"And he hated your old mattress so much that we did it in other parts of the apartment—the couch, the bathroom. He even hoisted me up onto the kitchen counter and—"

"Okay, let's stay on point," Kiki cut in. "There's a Gucci boot box filled with cash in my bedroom. I need you to go to Sarah Ann Duckworth's office and pay my invoice."

"Consider it done. Where is it?"

"Five-eighty Broadway in SoHo. It's near Prince Street."

"Not a problem. That's the same building I go to

for airbrush tanning. In fact, maybe I'll stop in and see if Sally can—"

"There's no time for that!" Kiki shrieked. "Because after you pay Sarah Ann, you need to bring the rest of the money to me. Not to mention some basic essentials. When you go to my apartment, pack a weekend bag. You know what I need."

"This is so like a Lifetime movie. You're the heroine on the run, and I'm the best friend you can count on. I hope this involves a handoff at Grand Central Station. That would be so exciting."

Kiki swept the lobby with a circular gaze. Nobody knew she was here. And she fully intended to keep it that way. "Forget the train station. I'm *not* leaving this hotel. Maybe all of this will blow over if I just disappear for a couple of days."

"Well, it's going to take more than a weekend bag. Think of all the stress you're under. I say you need the entire beauty regimen, some lounging wear, and a few sexy outfits, too. I mean, you *are* staying at Affair. A girl should be prepared."

"The last thing on my mind is romance of any kind. Even if the most amazing man in the world walked up to me right now and professed his undying attraction, I would tell him to go jump in the Hudson River."

From: kiki@misstexas95.com
To: breckin@withthisring.com
Subject: I Must Be Insane!

Breckin!

Did I say move this shotgun ceremony to New York? You must think I see little people in salt and pepper shakers. A summer wedding here would be absolute madness. Honestly! First of all, everybody is in the Hamptons. And second, a Manhattan summer can be just as ghastly as a Texas one. I'm talking scorching, sticky heat. That would mean crescent moon underarm stains for men and too much facial shine for women. Roman tends to sweat, too, and I don't want him looking anything less than his absolute cutest! Why don't you research yacht rentals in Miami? Maybe everybody could fly there. It would be so P. Diddy.

Air Kisses,
Kiki

Chapter Four

"You can't mean that," Suzi-Suzi said.

"Oh, I'm absolutely serious," Kiki answered.

"So let me get this straight, even if George Clooney showed up at Affair in the next five minutes, you wouldn't be interested."

"Precisely," Kiki insisted.

"You are a sick, sick woman," Suzi-Suzi said. "What about Tim McGraw?"

"The country singer?"

"Oh, my God!" Suzi-Suzi squealed. "I think he's so sexy. But only when he's got the cowboy hat on. Have you seen him without it? All the magic dies. It's like, from country music superstar to . . . 'Aren't you my life insurance salesman?' "

Kiki laughed. "Not interested."

"Okay, Bruce Willis. I think he's a really hot bald guy. I could so get into some Bruce Willis."

"Again, not interested," Kiki maintained. "Besides,

he's way too pleased with himself whenever he plays that damn harmonica. Since when is that an instrument anyway? I might as well get up on stage, ding the cowbell, and expect people to give me a standing ovation."

"There's got to be *somebody*," Suzi-Suzi whined.

"Excuse me, is there anything I can do for you?" a male voice inquired.

Kiki was inspecting a nail and didn't even bother to look up. "No, I'm fine, but you might want to make a condom run for those two on the couch over there."

"What?" Suzi-Suzi asked.

"Nothing," Kiki said. "I was just talking to some guy who works at the hotel."

"Actually, I *own* the hotel," the man corrected.

Officially annoyed now, Kiki glanced up at the rude intruder with the self-esteem complex. "Can't you see that I'm on—"

But the moment she took him in, the words died right there in her throat. Standing before her was an astonishingly gorgeous specimen of man. And she suddenly realized who he was. Fabrizio Tomba. Of course. The owner and mastermind behind Affair. The boutique hotel was intended to be Manhattan's sexy little secret. But the media coverage had been intense. Word on *the* new place for a rendezvous had spread fast, and Fabrizio had become the face of the establishment, basically the personification of good, safe, illicit sex. Pictures didn't do him justice. The ones that turned up in *New York*, *Gotham*, and other magazines with factory-like regularity paled in comparison to the real thing.

Kiki reminded herself that he was never alone in those photos. There was always a different woman holding his arm, sitting on his lap, or sticking her tongue down his throat—models, actresses, heiresses, the latest reality show starlets. He was quite the player. But Kiki could see why so women were so eager to say, "Game on."

Slyly, she drank him in. Usually, she had nothing to say for pretty boys. They took longer to get ready for an evening out, routinely swiped her best beauty products, and could never pass a mirror without introducing themselves and chatting too long. But Fabrizio was pretty with a purpose. In fact, he bent the word to the breaking point. His phenomenal good looks reminded her of the late JFK Jr. Zero effort. Just good genes, better manners, and the kind of drop-dead physicality that serves as a simple, breathtaking reminder to mere mortals of the world. There was such a thing as tourist-class attractiveness. And then there were the beautiful people.

Fabrizio stood patiently, his tiger brown eyes—big and inquisitive—locked onto hers.

Kiki tried to hide the fact that she needed to swallow. Instead, she took a quiet breath. The live-and-in-person download of Fabrizio Tomba had hit her on all sorts of levels—none of them comfortable. It was instant, heavy-duty crush. And she secretly hated herself for succumbing so fast. Her next move was reflex: Act like a bitch. When in doubt, it was a girl's best default mechanism. "So you own the place. Congratulations." She gestured to the late-night Cinemax movie being acted out on the adjacent sofa. "Why don't you see about getting them a room? Otherwise, there's a fairly good chance that I might throw up in your lobby."

"That's surprising." His tone was deliberately casual. "Judging from today's headlines, I wouldn't take you for a girl with public-displays-of-affection issues."

Kiki knew that her eyes were open wide, that the look on her face was equal parts humiliation and barely disguised lust. If ever she needed to prove her acting prowess, then it was right now. He was casting her off as the media scandal girl of the moment. Somehow she had to rise above his insult, to metamorphose into a café society fashionista simply enduring a bad day in the columns. And pull it off with chameleonlike poise.

"Are you there?" Suzi-Suzi screamed.

Kiki let out a tinkling little laugh. That dismissed Fabrizio's tabloid dig. Then she raised her hand for his immediate silence. That dismissed the rest of him. "Suzi-Suzi, darling," she began in her best kiss-kiss, not-a-care-in-the-world voice, "forgive my rudeness.

I was interrupted by the owner of the hotel. He's been impressing me with his taste in reading material. Anyway, be a doll and do those little favors for me. Ring me back if you have any problems."

"Why are you talking like that?" Suzi-Suzi demanded.

"Lovely," Kiki sang. "Bye-bye." Then she snapped her phone shut, returned it to her purse, and peered up to see Fabrizio drilling his eyes into her. She felt the muscles of her stomach tighten. Oh, God, he was hot. And oh, God, did he know it.

"This hotel thrives on discretion for obvious reasons," Fabrizio said. "But waiting in the lobby for Tom Brock in that outfit after today's front page is pushing it. Don't you think?"

Kiki double-checked her immediate anger. First of all, she wouldn't wait around in a lobby for anyone other than Dr. Sherwin K. Parikh of the Tribeca Skin Center. And second, there was *nothing* wrong with her outfit. A little saucy, yes, but she had the body to pull it off. So there. "This will probably come as a shock, since you live your life in the tabloids, but not everything they print is necessarily true."

"I guess that means you know who I am."

Kiki grinned. Such an easy setup. "I have to admit that it did take me a minute. You're hard to recognize without a bimbo by your side."

He raked her up and down with an appreciative glance. "You're definitely the same girl from this morning's paper. Do you have any real clothes, or do you always dress in fabric swatches?"

Kiki had to give him credit. A come-on disguised as a soft-landing insult. Only the truly advanced pickup artist could pull off that move. But she had a better one. "Funny. If the hotel thing doesn't work out, you should consider joining the cast of *Queer Eye*. I hear they're real big on bitchy fashion humor."

Fabrizio's face registered the hit. For a microsecond, twin splotches of red stained his cheeks.

Kiki moistened her lips. Questioning a playboy stud's manhood was the ultimate abuse. And she loved dishing it out. Did that make her a dominatrix?

"So enlighten me. What part of today's news is fact, and what part is fiction?"

"If you must know, I met Tom Brock for the first time yesterday. In fact, I never even shook his hand."

"Not much for small talk, huh? You just like to get right to it?"

Kiki glowered at him. "No, not at all. The simple truth is that a charm fell off my bracelet." A thought struck her. "Wait a minute. I'll prove it." She began digging through her handbag. "It's a Juicy Couture bracelet, and the little heart charm came loose and landed under Tom Brock's feet." Where the hell was it? Suddenly, an image came to mind—the bracelet on her bathroom counter. Damn. "Okay, I don't have it with me, so you're just going to have to take my word that it exists. Anyway, just as I bent down to pick it up, this horrible photographer comes out of nowhere and starts snapping our picture. That's *all* that happened!"

Kiki hesitated. She wanted to go on, but a wave of emotion rolled over her. All at once, everything seemed to tumble down. Waking up to the shock of being cheap headline news. Enduring Sarah Ann's caustic scolding. Adjusting to her new status as paparazzi prey. Getting kicked out of Stella McCartney. Stressing out over the inevitable public scorn. The sum of it all was just too much.

At first, Kiki tried to stop the tears, but once they started, she just gave in to her inner drama queen. It would've been futile to do anything else. "None of that . . . I never even . . . I love their baby . . . She probably hates me . . . I just wanted . . . an omelet . . . They chased me . . . My brother's getting married . . . Now I have to cancel my birthday party . . ." In between the convulsive sobs, snatches of her stream of consciousness ramblings were intelligible.

Fabrizio didn't like to see a woman cry. The cloud scudding across his handsome face told her so. He swooped down to offer comfort, putting his arm around her, murmuring quiet assurances that everything would be okay.

Kiki felt herself react to the closeness. Fabrizio's touch was infinitely calming. And, oh, God, did he ever smell good. His cologne was strong in her nostrils. Spicy hints of cinnamon with an exotic blend of

wild grass and sandalwood. She knew the scent.
H.O.T. Always by Bond No. 9. With tax, the sticker
shock came to two hundred dollars a bottle. But talk
about truth in advertising. Her crying jag subsided.
Only for a moment, though. Then it cranked back
up again.

Slowly, Fabrizio moved to stand, gently guiding
her with him. "Come on. Let's go to my office. We
can talk there. Would you like some tea?"

Kiki managed a nod worthy of a sniffling toddler.

He squeezed her shoulder and gestured to a linger-
ing bellboy. "Tate, call the kitchen and have tea service sent to my office."

The young man responded with a rapid, "Right
away, sir," as if Fabrizio were a military commander
and the tea request the most important mission on
earth.

As they made their way past the amorous couple
on the sofa, Kiki could stand it no more. How long
could she be expected to hold in her disgust? *"Get a
freaking room already!"* she screamed.

The shock of her outburst startled the young
woman to the point where she lost balance, slipped
off her lover's lap, and landed in a heap on the floor.

And then, as if the primal scream had never been
unleashed, Kiki resumed her demeanor as wounded
little girl, walking timidly beside Fabrizio, even leaning on him for support.

In response, Fabrizio calmly motioned for Tate

again. "One more thing. Find out who that couple is and instruct the front desk to send a bottle of champagne to their room and comp them for tonight's stay."

Kiki ignored the attempt at damage control on her behalf and instead studied Fabrizio's hands. And hands were always a big thing with her. His were scrupulously clean, all long fingers and neatly trimmed nails, as if ready to go gloveless in an operating theater.

He ushered her past the front desk, down a short hallway, and inside a modestly sized office. The tea service sat waiting on a small black lacquered table next to an immaculate desk.

Kiki took in the room's almost obsessive absence of clutter. It could be that Fabrizio Tomba did no work at all, or quite the opposite, that he was a high performer and destined for exceptional achievement. She'd read once where one of the most common traits shared among top-producing CEOs was an iron-fisted discipline for a desk that never appeared overwhelmed.

While he poured the tea, Kiki sank into an Eames lounge chair. The chocolate leather was seductively soft and receptive to her form, like the well-used mitt of an all-star first baseman. She kicked back and embraced the quiet, the intimacy, the luxury of being taken care of.

"How do you like your tea?"

"Just honey and lemon." Kiki dabbed her eyes with a tissue, surprised to find no mascara stains, then remembering that she'd left the apartment without so much as a swipe of lip gloss. Oh, God, she must look awful.

He smiled as he passed her the Gold Band pattern Tiffany and Co. cup and saucer. "Why don't you start at the beginning? Tell me your side of the story. I promise not to tease this time."

A great-looking man was inviting her to talk about herself? Alert the media. Usually, guys like Fabrizio just blathered on about themselves. Without preamble, Kiki launched into her whole sordid tale, miraculously getting through it with no tears and a minimum of cursing.

When Kiki finished, he just sat there at his clean desk, those incredible brown eyes wide with unfaked interest in the insanity that had been the last twenty-four hours of her life. "So the only person who knows that you're here right now is your friend, Suzi."

Kiki practically swooned. Not only did he encourage a woman to talk about herself, but he actually paid attention to what she had to say. Oh, God, she was already one-third of the way to being in love. "Yes, but her name's Suzi-Suzi."

"That's what I said."

"No, you just said Suzi. Add a hyphen and another Suzi. Two first names. Kind of like Mary Jane or Betty Lou, only it's Suzi-Suzi."

"Glad we cleared that up."

"It can be very confusing. You should hear her trying to place a catalog order over the phone. Completely ridiculous."

"Yes, I agree." There was no obvious hint of ridicule, but, of course, it was going on.

Kiki could read it in his eyes. And the ambiguity drove her crazy. Did he think the name was ridiculous? Or did he think she was? She sipped her tea and watched him, marveling at his mouth. He had the most incredible lips. "No cross-examination? Does that mean you believe my version of the incident?"

Fabrizio shrugged, then grinned. "I never put much stock in that story to begin with. I know Tom. He'd never cheat on Kirsten."

Kiki lengthened her spine and put the teacup back onto the saucer with a distinct clank. "What is *that* supposed to mean?"

Fabrizio looked puzzled. "Just that he's dedicated to Kirsten and the baby. He's not going to throw that away for—"

"So I'm not worth leaving a marriage for?" Kiki cut in hotly. "Is that what you're trying to say?"

"I thought nothing happened between you and Tom."

"Nothing did!"

"Then what's the point?"

"The point *is* . . . that . . . Tom Brock . . . or any other married man with children for that matter, should consider himself damn lucky to leave his family for me."

Fabrizio laughed as he spoke. "You're absolutely right."

Kiki rose from the chair. "Don't patronize me!"

Fabrizio laughed harder now. "Will you please tell me what this argument is *about*?"

"You insinuated that I was cheap," Kiki said flatly.

His smile wasn't mocking. It was amused. Clearly, he liked her. "Maybe you should write for the tabloids. You misread situations, too. All I said was that Tom Brock wouldn't cheat."

"But the implication was that—"

"*Nothing* was implied," Fabrizio insisted gently. "But if you need the ego boost, I'll say it." He cleared his throat. "You, lady, are one hot number, and a smart man would ditch his wife and kid to start a new life with you."

This infuriated Kiki. "So you actually think that I'm some kind of home wrecker?"

Fabrizio buried his face in his hands. "I think my only way out of this is by helicopter." He resurfaced with a lazy smile. "You know, if I make a run for the roof, you'll never catch me in those heels."

Kiki gave him a diffident sniff. "Who says I'd bother to give chase?"

Now it was Fabrizio's turn to be offended. But he did so in the style of a great pretender. "What? I'm not good enough to go after?"

This pushed a reluctant smile past her lips. It took a nanosecond to realize how frustrating she must be to him. "You probably think I'm insane."

"I refuse to answer on the grounds that it may incriminate me."

Kiki tilted her head to one side. "Fair enough."

"Truce?"

"Truce." It was over. Their first fight. Now Kiki was back in the real world of wondering if he would ask for her phone number. "I need a place to hide out for a few days," she announced casually. "So I guess the question is this: Can I stay at Affair if I'm not actually having one?"

A faint smile played around Fabrizio's lips as he consulted the sleek iMac sitting atop his desk. "Normally, we have strict rules about such things." He winked at her. "But I'll make a special exception in this case."

"How accommodating. I appreciate the five-star service, Fabrizio."

"Call me Fab," he said, clicking the mouse like mad.

Fab. Taken at face value, the name fit. Perfectly.

Suddenly, worry lines creased his forehead as he stared at the screen. "I might have some bad news.

Looks like the hotel is booked solid." Obviously not one to give up easily, his search continued.

Kiki felt the disappointment in the pit of her stomach.

"Wait. Disregard that," Fab said, decidedly more upbeat now. "We have one room available." He started to laugh. "Pretty ironic, though."

"Why's that?"

"It's called the Mistress Hideaway."

Kiki gave him a little snarl. "Hilarious." One beat. "How much? The *Post* was right about one thing—I'm out of work, and as much as I loathe to admit it, I'm a girl who needs to be budget conscious."

"The rate's five hundred."

"*A night?*" She could see the bottom of the Gucci boot box already. Why couldn't Fab operate a Marv's Motor Inn like her future sister-in-law?

He looked up, still amused by her. "Tell you what. I'll cut the rate to two fifty. Even though you've already cost me a comped room and a bottle of Cristal." He started to type. "You should check in under an alias. The tabloids probably have flacks working the phones to check every hotel in the city for a Kiki Douglas. Any ideas?"

"Jennifer Aniston."

Fab did a double take.

"I've always wanted to be her," Kiki explained. "Love the hair."

His fingers danced over the keyboard. "Okay. Jennifer Aniston it is. Welcome to Affair, Miss Aniston." He gave her a bold, flirtatious stare that stretched on long enough to ease the situation into sexual gear. "And if there's anything I can do to make your stay more pleasurable, please don't hesitate to ask."

From: kiki@misstexas95.com
To: breckin@withthisring.com
Subject: Word of Caution

Breckin!

We must make a pact and vow to stick together throughout this wedding. No matter what. I say this because we are surrounded by people with questionable judgment. Here's a cheat sheet:

1) My brother is marrying a woman he met five minutes ago.
2) His bride-to-be's family runs a cheap motel chain.
3) One of the bridesmaids engineered a legal attack that allowed a vile rich man (similar to my ex-husband; okay, it WAS my ex) to totally take advantage of a defenseless young wife (that would be me) in a divorce settlement.

Would YOU trust the opinions of these people? Brace yourself. It's just you and me, darling. How is the yacht research coming along?

Air Kisses,
Kiki

Chapter Five

True to its name, the Mistress Hideaway was tucked away in a discreet corner of the hotel, the half corridor to its entrance directly accessible by stairwell for added discretion.

Fab escorted Kiki to the suite personally, and as they entered the small haven that was no larger than four hundred square feet, he said, "If these walls could talk . . ."

Kiki took in her temporary home. "They would probably be saying *Get me a bigger room*."

Fab placed the old-fashioned room key on the small writing desk. "Don't be such a diva. It's cozy."

"*Cozy?* That's happy talk for claustrophobic." Even as the words of her thumbs-down review sliced the air, Kiki studied the room. In all honesty, there was a great escape quality to it. The exposed beams and brick walls of the hotel's past life as a warehouse gave it a certain charm. Then there were the light brown walnut flooring, the Moroccan rugs, and the oversized bed with huge pillows dressed in Egyptian white cotton.

Fab proceeded with the mini-tour. "You've got a plasma screen TV, DVD player, stereo, high-speed Internet access, fully stocked minibar, and twenty-four-hour room service. Joie is our in-house restaurant. The chef is incredible—I poached him from my favorite bistro in Paris. There's a spacious walk-in shower. The bathroom is stocked with Sisley products. And the terry cloth bathrobe hanging on the door is yours to keep." He paused a moment, opening his hands to the surroundings as he glanced around. "I believe that's it."

Kiki could sense his imminent departure, and a sudden urgency to delay the inevitable surprised her. "Not quite. You never told me what these walls would say if they could talk."

"Let's just leave it at this: Many famous marriages would be in trouble."

Kiki's eyes went wide. "I want names. And you can trust me. I won't tell a soul." She pantomimed locking her lips and throwing the imaginary key over her shoulder.

"Presidents, movie stars, heads of industry. That's all you'll get out of me."

Kiki crawled onto the bed and rolled over on her back. It was the body language of bored teenager. But the short cutoffs riding farther up her thighs hinted at something else. She sighed. Clearly gossip wasn't his thing. "You're no fun."

"Oh, but I can be." His voice went down an octave. From sexy . . . to sexier. In the game of counter-attack flirtation, he was a Jedi master.

Kiki's lips were slightly parted, and as she did something barely legal with her tongue, Fab moved closer to the bed. Her stomach did a couple of revolutions.

And then the ring of her cellular blasted the exotic/erotic moment to smithereens.

Kiki jumped to answer. It could be Sarah Ann Duckworth calling with a way out of the public relations nightmare. Or her agent, Keith Bush, dialing in with news about a job. But the screen merely revealed that Suzi-Suzi was burning up the wire. Kiki picked up. "Remind me to talk to you about your bad timing."

"Yours isn't so hot, either," Suzi-Suzi snapped. "I'm thirty minutes late for a catalog shoot because I've been running all over the city for *you*." Big sigh. "But I'm here in the lobby with all of your stuff. Where do you keep your luggage? I couldn't find a single piece, so I packed everything in garbage bags. I look like a girl who just ran away from a homeless shelter."

Kiki smacked her own forehead. "Oh, I forgot to tell you. I keep my Vuitton pieces in Mrs. Manheim's apartment. There's no room in my closet, and she has loads of space."

"Listen, I have to run. Are you coming down or not?"

"Just tell the front desk to bring everything to Jennifer Aniston's room. That's my alias."

"Love that. In fact, I can't wait to say it. Oh, before I forget. Sarah Ann said that she appreciates the payment but can no longer represent you."

"Shut up!"

"I'm serious. Something about signing on Kirsten Brock as a client. I know it sucks, but you'll figure it out. Hey, I'm dashing. I'll call you later."

Kiki held the dead mobile to her ear as the import of Suzi-Suzi's news began to resonate. "I can't believe it," she murmured, as much to herself as to the dreamboat standing next to her in the five-hundred-dollar-a-night closet.

"What?" Fab asked.

She tossed the phone onto the bed and looked at him. "My publicist just dropped me from her client roster." Kiki delivered this news with a gravity presidential advisors might employ on the topic of national security.

"Sounds like a good thing," Fab reasoned. "I don't think she's up for the job. Have you seen today's paper? You're getting some really bad publicity."

Kiki was in no mood to laugh. The frisson of irritation that came next effectively snapped whatever was left of the sexual tightwire that had tensed up the room just minutes before.

Fab seemed to read the mood change. "I'll leave you to get settled."

"Do I seem that *un*settled?" Kiki asked archly.

"Relax. It's an expression, not a judgment. Maybe you want to take a nap or soak your feet from all the running around in those heels."

"A foot massage would be nice."

Fab nodded dutifully. "I'll check with the spa. They stay booked, but I have some pull." He scribbled a number onto the back of a business card and handed it over. "My mobile." For emphasis, he patted the Motorola device attached to his belt. "It's always with me. Call if you need . . . *anything*." Then he winked and started for the exit. "I'll have your luggage sent up as soon as it arrives." His last words were punctuated by the sight of Tate, the ubiquitous bellboy, standing on the other side of the door beside a rolling cart piled high with garbage bags and one Gucci boot box.

"Miss Aniston's . . . things, sir," Tate said.

Fab cleared a path for the bellboy's entry.

"I'll say one thing," Fab remarked, smirking. "You're full of surprises. I figured you for designer luggage." And then he was gone.

Kiki stared at the cart in disbelief. It appeared as if Suzi-Suzi had packed up the entire apartment. "I'm sorry about this. Just put the bags anywhere. It doesn't matter."

"No problem, Miss Aniston."

"Don't be silly," Kiki told the young man. "You can call me Jennifer." She tipped him and sent the boy on his way, feeling pangs of loneliness the moment she heard the deafening sounds of complete solitude. What was she going to do with herself in this little box for three days?

She spent about ten minutes organizing her belongings, then grew bored with the project. Hmm. There was always her new book endeavor, *First Runner-Up . . . But Still a Winner*. Oh, God, she loved that title. Maybe she should fire up the laptop and crank out a chapter on, say, picking up the pieces and soldiering on after getting dumped by your publicist. Yes! Exactly the kind of material that would speak to women everywhere.

But Kiki didn't feel very much like writing. Oh, she wanted to get out of here! How could this be? In the room only fifteen minutes and already stir-crazy. This promised to be a *very* long three days. A change of scenery might help. She snatched the key and ventured out to roam the halls, hoping to encounter a famous married person going in or out of a room.

But her floor was as quiet as a monastery. Well, except for the whip snaps and moans coming from the room she just passed. Probably a politician. Most of them secretly longed to be punished sexually. Must be some sort of perverse contrition for all the tricks they slipped past the voting public. Hmm. A provocative observation. Perhaps she should write another mini-polemic, this one about politics in general. "Kiki Goes to Washington." A great chapter title! And her savvy take on issues of the day would probably surprise a lot of people.

On the way back to her room, Kiki encountered another hotel guest waiting for the elevator. The woman appeared older, possibly late forties, her head and face swathed in a flowing Hermès scarf, her eyes eclipsed by large Christian Dior sunglasses. But no matter the disguise, Kiki knew swelling from plastic surgery when she saw it.

Desperate to know what work she had done and, more importantly, who performed it and how much it cost, Kiki approached. "Hi, I'm Jennifer Aniston. We must be neighbors. I'm staying in the Mistress Hideaway just down the hall."

The woman responded with a curt nod as she pressed the button again to call the elevator.

"Don't worry," Kiki went on. "I'm nobody's mistress. Never have been. Hey, I couldn't stand my own husband, so chances are it's not going to work out with some other woman's." She laughed a little. "That reminds me of a friend of mine. She's a mistress. Loves it. Gets him about one week a month, and that's quite enough for her. Of course, holidays are always a problem. I imagine that's a really lonely time for mistresses. Don't you think? Someone should do something special for them during that time of year. I don't know. Maybe a Christmas brunch. That would be nice."

"Yes," the woman answered crisply, avoiding eye contact. "I suppose it would be."

"So what brings you to Affair?" Kiki pressed gingerly, taking her voice down to a hushed whisper. "I'm just here to get away from it all. Pretty boring, huh? I mean, I wish I could say that I had Jude Law stashed away in my room. But it's just me. Needed a little rest and relaxation. What about you?"

"I really don't feel like speaking to anyone right now," the woman said. If looks could kill, then the hotel staff would be planning a funeral service for the elevator. The *Extreme Makeover* victim was staring daggers through it.

"Maybe later then," Kiki said cheerily. "We could have a cup of tea together. By the way, I didn't catch your name."

"I can't believe you don't recognize me, *Jennifer Aniston*," the woman said savagely. "I'm Courteney Cox."

Kiki giggled nervously. "I'm sorry. That's just my hotel alias. My real name is—"

The woman snorted. "I know who you are." She jabbed the elevator button again. "Is this goddamn thing broken?"

"I think it's just slow," Kiki said easily. "This used to be an old warehouse." One beat. "You know, I'm always surprised by the number of viewers who remember Jeannette. She never got much screen time, but people really connected with her."

"Who the hell is Jeannette?"

"My character from *All My Children*," Kiki said. "I assume that's where you recognize me from. Of course, I was also first runner-up in the 1995 Miss America Pageant."

"All I know is what I read in today's *New York Post*. You should be ashamed of yourself."

"It's all lies!" Kiki paused a moment. "Well, most of it anyway. But the parts about me and Tom Brock? *Total* fabrication. They should've had Jackie Collins's name on the byline."

"Women like you make me sick."

Kiki was taken aback by the venomous look spewing from the stranger's practically swollen-shut eyes. The rebuke stunned her. "Women like *me*? I don't understand."

All of a sudden, the elevator doors creaked opened.

"Women like you never do." She stepped inside, jammed a finger onto the instrument panel, and then she was gone.

Haunted by the encounter, Kiki just stared blankly at the closing doors, listening as the elevator made its descent. Finally, she meandered back to the room, feeling more anxiety than she had before leaving it in the first place. As if she needed additional problems to tackle. But this human conundrum would drive her insane until she solved it.

Women like you make me sick.

The bitter words turned over in Kiki's mind. What did she mean by that? Kiki had always considered herself a true feminist, a champion for the female race in general. After all, that's why she was writing the book. To give something back. Even in high school, Kiki had demonstrated the sensitivity to be inclusive. Most beauty queens operated in a rarefied orbit. But Kiki believed in reaching out. Example: Lindy Wiatt. She was teased unmercifully for being fat and ugly. But Kiki recruited her as a personal assistant. Getting ready for pageants could be so hectic, and what a godsend to have someone at the ready to fetch Diet Cokes, make an emergency hair spray run, and keep the makeup case fully stocked and in tip-top shape.

Suddenly, a dark memory surfaced. Hmm. Thinking back, there had to be a better example than Lindy. After all, the girl had tried to run over Kiki in the school parking lot. They said the attack had been stress-related and triggered by extreme dieting. At first, Kiki had felt *so* guilty. But how was she to know that the seven-day celery and water fast she recommended to Lindy might trigger such a random act of violence? *Cosmopolitan* had raved about the diet. Luckily, Lindy had been back on the job in time for the Miss Fredericksburg Hospitality Pageant. Nobody had a better system for maintaining makeup brushes. Lindy had kept them as clean as surgical instruments. Today she was assisting neurologists with complicated brain surgeries! Maybe working with Kiki had inspired her to help others.

The jingle of Kiki's cellular rang like sweet music. It couldn't be Sarah Ann. Bitch! But it might be Keith. Feeling hopeful, she rushed across the room to see. No such luck. Bastard! To no surprise, SUZI-SUZI CALLING lit up the screen.

Kiki deep-sixed the hello formalities. "Why did you pack for a year abroad? You do realize that I'm only going to be here for three days, don't you?"

Suzi-Suzi sobbed into the receiver. "I've got the worst luck in the world!"

Kiki climbed into the bed and got comfortable. Probably trouble with Chad, the married boyfriend. And that could mean a marathon phone session. "I'm here, sweetie. Tell me all about it."

"That shoot was for a sexual fetish catalog! They wanted to paint my body with latex. They wanted me to squash bugs in high heels, too!"

"Oh, my God!" Kiki screamed. "How disgusting! What is going on in America? Sex used to be so simple. Remember the innocent days when freaky meant vibrators and fur-covered handcuffs?" She hesitated, allowing Suzi-Suzi a chance to compose herself. "Well, what did you do?"

"I told them to just *forget* the idea of painting latex on me. But I did stomp on some bugs. What else could I do? I needed the money."

"You don't have to explain to me," Kiki said, trying to sound supportive. "You know, I don't get it. How does a guy get turned on by watching a girl kill bugs? I mean, what happened in this man's childhood?"

"I know. It's completely retarded. Like those people who dress up as stuffed animals to have sex."

"The plushies!" Kiki said. "Or is it the furries? I can't remember. *CSI* did a show about it once."

"This is so wrong!" Suzi-Suzi shouted, her voice brimming with frustration. "I just want to model something normal for once. A push-up bra, an ugly sweater, a nurse's uniform—*anything!*"

"Maybe you should consider leaving the agency. They goofed and let you sign those horrible modeling releases. Ever since it's been one bad gig after another."

Suzi-Suzi expelled a defeated sigh. "Tell me something I don't know. But where else can I go? Let's be honest. I'm almost thirty, and it's not like anybody's tapping me on the shoulder to say, 'Damn, girl, ain't you Heidi Klum?' At the end of the day, I feel lucky to be with PLK Management."

"I hate to hear you talk this way."

"Kiki, please. I don't have an inferiority complex. I'm only being realistic. I've accepted the fact that I'm a third-tier model, but I just want some decent assignments."

Kiki considered the situation. "Maybe you should try commercials. I know a girl who made ten thousand dollars from a Dr Pepper ad. And all she did was hold on to a cute guy while he drove a Jet Ski."

"It sounds like a good idea, but PLK only books for print work."

"So? You're in New York. There are *hundreds* of agencies. Wait a minute. That reminds me! I met this guy once in the recovery room at Bliss Spa. His name's Doug something. Gay, fabulous, *flawless* skin. Anyway, he runs an agency for Broadway talent. All commercials. I mean, the theater doesn't pay anything. Those people have to supplement income. He even books for overseas work. Wouldn't it be great to fly to Japan for a commercial job? It'd be just like that movie with Bill Murray, *Lost in Translation*. I just know that Doug would *die* to sign you."

"You really think so?" Suzi-Suzi wondered aloud, her voice rattling with self-doubt. "I've never been in a Broadway show. I don't even go to them. Except for *Mamma Mia!* I've seen that twice. I love ABBA. Does that count?"

"Sure!" Kiki sang, doing her best to rev up Suzi-Suzi's confidence. "At the end of the show, everybody gets up to dance in the aisles during 'Dancing Queen.' By that measure, you're practically *in* the show. Put it down on your resume—'starred in *Mamma Mia!*' Nobody will ever know."

"That is *so* brilliant!" Suzi-Suzi said. "And so true, too. I mean, last time I was totally rocking out in the lower orchestra. In fact, one of the chorus boys pointed at me and gave me this big smile."

"See. It's not a lie. Maybe a slight exaggeration. But nothing more than that."

"So how do I get in touch with this Doug person?"

"Oh, God, I have no idea. I can't remember his last name or the name of his agency."

"*Kiki!*"

"Calm down. I know a girl at Bliss. He's a regular there. She'll know who I'm talking about and give me all the contact info."

"I feel so much better about things now. It's like I suddenly have a new career or something."

Kiki nestled back against the pillows, feeling quite pleased with herself. Basically, she'd just rescued Suzi-Suzi from a near breakdown. This would make another great chapter for the book. Just as she opened her mouth to say something, Kiki heard the distinctive break of someone else's call-waiting.

"Ooh—Chad's beeping in. I better go. He gets mad when the phone rings into voice mail. Call me later." And then the line went dead.

For several long introspective moments, Kiki just

lay there, wondering what to do next. Glancing over to the nightstand, she noticed Fab's business card. It practically glowed radioactive. She reached out for it, fingering the raised lettering and embossed graphics. Then she flipped it over to see his cell number scrawled on the back.

The mere thought of him made her body itch, the so-vivid memory of Fab's impossible attractiveness crawling all over her like a hot rash. God, he really was extraordinary. Everything about him—his proud aquiline nose, his sensuously deliberate mouth, his strong, square jaw. And even covered up in his regulation Armani, Kiki knew that the body was the stuff of punishing five a.m. workouts. She could tell by his broad shoulders, the triangular shape of his chest, the discipline of his trim waistline, and his shapely butt that deserved its own cable channel.

Kiki had to wonder, though, about the character of a man who lived such a charmed existence. The success was on the cover of *Fast Company*. The looks were instant legend. The media was covering his every move. The women were falling at his feet. Certainly he believed some of the hype. After all, he called himself Fab. But how many deals had he struck with the devil to become Mr. Perfect?

And how many hearts had he broken along the way?

From: breckin@withthisring.com
To: kiki@misstexas95.com
Subject: Re: Word of Caution

Kiki,

Hello, doll! I'm still tickled that we're back in touch. What a glorious blast from the past. I must say, though, I've never taken my wedding planning orders from a bridesmaid. A horrifying mother of the bride? Yes. Scratch that. ALWAYS. Except for Angela Binder. Remember her? She was the bitchy yearbook editor all through high school. I did her wedding two years ago, and she didn't even INVITE her mother. Something about a confrontation on Maury Povich about Angela's stepfather. I didn't ask. The point is, no bridesmaid has EVER marched right up to play General Schwarzkopf. Leave it to you to start a new trend. But are you sure that you're on the same page as Roman and this girl from New Jersey?

Big Hug,
Breckin

Chapter Six

Kiki's finger wavered on the cellular keypad. There had to be a good reason to call him. Hmm. Well, the music selection left something to be desired. That was certainly a worthy issue to raise. Feeling emboldened by the legitimate concern, she dialed.

"Fab Tomba." The voice was in efficient business mode but still sexy.

"Hello, I'm staying in the Mistress Hideaway and would like to speak with the *owner* of this hotel."

"Yes, speaking. How can I help?"

Kiki could sense him smiling into the receiver. "I'm in the mood for some music, and the only choices here are Frank Sinatra, Michael Buble, Luther Vandross, and Barry White."

"Ah, you must be a hip-hop girl. I'll have the latest Snoop Dogg CD brought up in a flash."

"No, I'm more of a metal chick. You see, I have

anger issues, and I like to thrash around the room breaking stuff. Metallica is more my speed."

"Not a problem. Consider the matter handled." And then he signed off without a goodbye.

Kiki just held the phone to her ear for several long, tormented seconds. Something about their exchange left her unsettled. Paranoid thoughts began to consume her. Had she just been dissed? Basically, the man had hung up on her. She could probably call housekeeping for extra towels and get better conversation. Maybe Fab was just busy, though. He *did* have a hotel to run. Still, it seemed rather abrupt.

For at least fifteen minutes, Kiki merely lay there, silently driving herself insane as she deconstructed the micro-moment for all of its real and imagined subtextual meanings.

All of a sudden, three fast knocks rapped the door.

Kiki's heart lurched. It was him. She knew it. That's why he ended the call so quickly. Because he wanted no unnecessary delay between finishing his task at hand and standing outside her suite.

But she opened the door to find Tate on the other side of it—holding a big stack of Metallica CDs. What looked to be the band's entire catalog, too.

Kiki relieved Tate of the multidisc joke, snatched a twenty-dollar bill from the Gucci boot box, and sent him on his way. She flipped through the hard rock collection. No flirty Post-it. No teasing little note on Affair stationery. No communication at all.

She continued obsessing over the situation. Did he really think that she enjoyed listening to Metallica? Suddenly drowsy, she closed her eyes for a few minutes. When she opened them, it was dark outside. How long had she been asleep? She checked the clock on her cellular. Quarter past eight. Oh, God, she must have been dozing for hours! Scandal fatigue could really take the energy out of a girl.

Kiki indulged in a hot shower, tossed on a Junk Food Cookie Monster baby doll tee with a pair of low-waisted velour sweatpants emblazoned across the ass with the words HE'S TRASH—DUMP HIM, and slathered onto her face a generous heaping of Borghese Fango mud.

Feeling a little pissed off, she loaded the stereo with one of the Metallica discs and blasted "Enter Sandman" at top volume, hoping some of the other guests would call the front desk to complain. That would teach Mr. Fabrizio Tomba!

But the self-imposed sonic assault only served to irritate Kiki further. Unable to stifle her frustrations another second, she twisted down the volume and called the front desk herself.

"Good evening, Miss Aniston. How can I assist you this evening?"

"I need a message delivered to Mr. Tomba," Kiki announced tartly.

"Of course."

"Please tell him that the color is dull on my plasma TV, that the bath towels feel like sandpaper, and that if he had an ounce of sophistication, then he would stock imported gummi bears from Spain in the mini-bar and not the domestic kind."

"I'll see that he gets this straightaway, Miss Aniston."

"Thank you."

"My pleasure."

Kiki used her thumb to wipe off the Fango mud smudged on the telephone mouthpiece, banged the receiver back into the cradle, and turned up the music again. Even louder this time. Only at the track break did she hear a pounding on the door. Maybe the politician was done being dominated and wanted some peace and quiet.

Kiki peered through the peephole. To her astonishment, she saw Fab. There was no point in scrambling to make herself presentable. It's not like he even bothered to call. And why waste a perfectly good Fango treatment only minutes into its topical benefits? So, hair balled up in a scrunchie, face plastered with mask, she swung open the door.

Fab noted her appearance but betrayed no reaction. "In the immortal words of Paris Hilton, 'That's hot.' "

As Kiki smiled, she felt the drying mud crack a little.

He gestured to the dining cart behind him. "I hope you haven't eaten. I brought dinner. Takeout from Spice Market."

Kiki yanked him into the room. "That's my favorite restaurant, and I'm starving."

Fab laughed, reaching back to navigate the cart inside. "I brought a pitcher of blood-orange *mojitos*, too. If you get me drunk and take advantage of me, though, please be responsible. Safe sex only."

"I did notice the emergency seduction package available in the minibar. But don't even think about charging that to my room."

He lifted three silver domes to reveal mushroom egg rolls, fried chicken wings in lime and fish sauce, and egg-drop soup with a tomato puree. "You like?"

Kiki grabbed a wing. "Me like *a lot*." She tore into it while he poured the first round of drinks. "Do you handle all complaints with such a personalized touch?"

He gave a quizzical look as he passed over a crystal highballer. "What complaints?"

Thank God her face was Fango green. Otherwise, it would be scarlet with embarrassment. "Um . . . I woke up from a long nap and was kind of groggy. I might've called the front desk. But disregard that. I was a little out of it." Greedily, she gulped down the *mojito* to the halfway point, hoping to get even more out of it. While she had been terrorizing his staff, he had been plotting out a romantic dinner.

Fab took a bite of egg roll. "You know, now that

you mention it, there was an odd complaint tonight. A woman on this floor, actually. Something about scratchy towels and bad gummi bears."

She waved off the teasing accusation. "Was that me? God, I don't know what I said to that poor man. Like I was saying . . . I was half asleep."

Fab laughed a little. "Should I come back in twenty minutes? Give you a chance to rinse that stuff off your face and change clothes?"

Kiki shrugged. "What's the point? You've already seen me like this." She finished the rest of Fab's egg roll. "This is *so* good. I love Spice Market."

Fab grinned. "I've never seen a woman in full beauty prep before. It's kind of cute."

Kiki found this announcement illuminating. "Never?"

Fab shook his head.

"I take it you prefer short relationships."

"Why do you say that?"

"Because if a man sticks around long enough, women get over the whole he-can't-see-me-without-makeup thing."

Fab rolled the cart closer to the bed, sat on the edge of the mattress, and began serving up the egg-drop soup. "But we just met today. So what does that say about us?"

Kiki took a seat beside him and splayed out her left hand. "It means you better start shopping for a ring, because this could be serious."

Fab laughed again. "You're funny. Why do you act in *soap operas*?" He spat out the last two words like sour milk. "You should be on a sitcom."

"What's wrong with soap operas?" She sounded defensive. She *was* defensive.

"I suppose the ones that come on at night are okay. But the daytime shows are a joke. Nothing happens. And no real time goes by. They drink the same cup of coffee Monday through Friday. And I hate those long pauses when people just stare at each other and say nothing. Nobody does that."

"Well, it's good steady work and a great training ground for other things. I'd sign up for another soap in a heartbeat."

"Way to go, baby. Aim high."

Kiki finished her drink and looked at him. "You have *no* idea what you're talking about. And just so you know, there's a cure for AGS."

"What's AGS?"

"Average Guy Syndrome. It's this terrible affliction that many men have."

Fab smiled, playing along. "What are the symptoms?"

"Pretending to be an expert on subjects you know nothing about."

"I see. This sounds serious."

"Oh, it is."

"And you think I have it."

"Oh, I'm sure of it."

"Is there anything I can do?"

"Well, for starters," Kiki began silkily, "you can shut the fuck up about soap operas."

Fab laughed and poured another round of *mojitos*.

"And by the way, getting me drunk won't make your condition any less unattractive."

"Hey, all I'm saying is that you could be selling yourself short."

All of a sudden, Kiki grew pensive. Just hours ago she had been giving the same speech to her best friend. Suzi-Suzi thought PLK Management was her personal Mount Everest. And Kiki would dance naked in Times Square if *All My Children* called to say Jeannette had survived the plunge from the cruise ship by floating on a piece of driftwood. "This business can be brutal when you reach a certain age."

Fab seemed to pick up on her vulnerability. "America is youth obsessed. I'll give you that."

"But it's different for men. You can age gracefully. Producers don't scrutinize you for lines around the eyes or react to a few extra pounds by writing you out of a swimsuit scene."

"But how responsible are you for that?" Fab asked, his challenge gentle yet firm.

"For sexual politics and the age-old double standard? I think you overestimate my influence on the world."

"But we all make our own place in it."

Kiki stared at him. "And what's mine?"

Fab regarded her closely, curling his lips into a half smile. "It's not easy talking existentialism to a woman with a green face, but I'll give it a go."

"Please do. I'm anxious to hear."

He hesitated. "Do you mean that? Because it sounds like you're giving me permission to walk the plank." With that, he reached for the pitcher and refilled her glass with more blood-orange *mojito*.

Kiki took a generous sip, beginning to feel the tingle of the alcohol. "No, I'm inviting you to share your perspective."

"You won't take it the wrong way and torpedo the evening?"

"Now, I can't promise that."

"I didn't think so." And then he pretended to drink straight from the pitcher before topping off his own glass.

She laughed at him. "Hey, you swam out to the deep end. Not me."

"This is true." He took in a deep breath. "Okay, here goes . . . I think that you've trapped yourself into believing that trading on your beauty is the only road to take."

Suddenly, Kiki realized that the easy banter, flirty games, and silly arguments were morphing into something far more substantial. They were engaging in heavy-duty emotional intercourse. Obviously, he wanted that. And she was glad that he did.

"If the tabloids are to be believed, your Miss

America days happened ten years ago," Fab went on. "But it seems like you're still zeroed in on being the pretty, sexy girl. Maybe that's why you walked down the aisle with that old rich guy. Maybe that's why you're still going after the starlet roles on soaps. What amazes me about you is that you're so smart. You're so funny, too. But making those qualities really work for you doesn't seem to be in your master plan."

Kiki sat there, completely stunned. Being part of a careful, psychological exploration with a man was a new kind of intimacy for her. An awkward silence lingered. Definitely a who-goes-next moment. She waged an internal debate on how much to reveal to him, since they had now merged into major league getting-to-know-you. All of a sudden, she felt high up, as if on a tightwire.

Finally, she spoke. "I'm not a good actress." It was simple. It was matter-of-fact. And it was true. She cocked her head to one side. "That's why I got breast implants. Nice boobs can compensate for lack of talent. Just ask Carmen Electra."

"What about training?" Fab asked earnestly. "Even the best actors continue developing their skills. Both Charlize Theron and Halle Berry worked with a coach on the movies that won them Oscars."

"I've tried classes," Kiki said, downing the remainder of drink number two and feeling more relaxed than ever. "But I can't do those silly exercises. Like pretending I'm a tree that's about to be cut down. I mean, what's that about? I suppose the real culprit is my own lack of drive. Being the pretty, sexy girl has always come easy for me. It's the only thing I've ever really been good at. And it's the only thing most people have ever paid attention to."

"Don't you think Charlize and Halle felt the same way at some point? For a long time they were just beautiful scenery in movies, but they worked hard and dug deep. And look what happened."

Kiki gazed adoringly at Fab, and she really liked what she saw, beyond the more obvious hot-guy appeal. There was an optimistic sparkle in his eyes, an Up With People quality that was sweet, refreshing, and totally against type. Where was the midnight rambler that the society columnists gushed about? They had him pegged as a serial dater, the kind of guy who turned up missing if sex didn't materialize quickly, preferably right away, definitely by the third date. Yet here was a perfect gentleman, content to offer motivational platitudes to the ambition-challenged as a substitute to foreplay.

"So why couldn't you win an Oscar one day?" Fab asked.

Kiki laughed lightly, equally amused, enchanted, and mystified by his belief in her. "God, you really are a frustrated Tony Robbins."

He averted his gaze and concentrated on his soup, saying nothing.

Worried that she might have hurt his feelings, Kiki talked fast to explain. "It's just that I don't think I want it bad enough. The whole acting thing. I'd be fine with a decent supporting role that paid well. I'm not a *good* actress, but I'm competent. I can deliver decent line readings and hit my mark. I've never had a story arc to call my own, and that's okay. I usually just play the best friend. My function is to react while a major character confides a secret or yammers on about being in love with two men at the same time."

Fab grinned and gestured to the pitcher of *mojitos*. Kiki nodded yes.

He did the honors for round three, drained his faster than a gunslinger in a hot saloon, pushed the dining cart away, and leaned back onto the bed, propping himself up with his elbows. "I have to admit . . . I was wrong about you."

Kiki chased some of her drink down, too, the tingle officially turning to buzz. "What do you mean?"

"I figured you for this impossible princess type who has to be the center of everyone's universe."

Kiki stretched out to join Fab. "Hey, I'm too busy being the center of my *own* universe."

Fab's eyes locked onto hers, left, and then locked again.

"I'm writing a book," Kiki blurted, as much to Fab's astonishment as to her own.

His brow shot up with real curiosity.

She was practically head over heels now. For a

man to be half drunk, lounging on a bed with a woman, and expressing unfeigned interest in a subject that had nothing to do with getting naked . . . well, it was pretty amazing.

"What kind of book?"

Kiki felt a certain shyness creep up. It was one thing to share her secret dream with Suzi-Suzi or Danni. When it came down to each other, no one in their group ever stood in judgment. How could they? The truth was, all of their lives were a bit of a mess—Kiki with her current, multilayered crisis, Suzi-Suzi with her so-called modeling career and married boyfriend, and Danni with her paradoxical status as a Christian stripper.

But Fab's opinion could possibly have an impact. Who would've thought that Manhattan's reigning playboy had the capacity to deep-think? Give him limited access and arm him with a half-fact/half-fiction tabloid piece, and the man could spin analysis worthy of Freud.

"An autobiography?" Fab pressed, still waiting for an answer.

Kiki waved off that idea. "Oh, God, no. Don't you find all these people writing memoirs annoying? Everybody thinks that their life will make such an interesting book, and it's just not true. The remainder tables at the bookstores are proof of that. Mine would have a pinch of autobiography. But not the whole thing. I mean, I'm not going to devote an entire chapter to the time somebody stole my Wonder Woman lunch box."

Fab nodded agreeably, smiling. "So a bit of autobiography and what else?"

"It's kind of difficult to pin down," Kiki murmured. "Basically, the angle I'm taking is postmodern observations from a pretty girl's perspective." She giggled. "Hey, maybe I could lead a new wave of feminism."

Fab seemed genuinely enchanted by her revelation. In fact, his face appeared to be lit from within. "How much have you written?"

"Oh, not very much," Kiki said. "I've jotted things down here and there. I'm really just conceptualizing it right now. But who am I kidding? I'll probably never finish. I mean, how many people have said, 'I'm writing a book' and never made it to the last page?"

Fab threaded his fingers behind his head and kicked back, stretching out completely. Through the sheer fabric of his white, French-cuffed Gucci shirt, his washboard stomach was evident. So were the trails of dark tangled hairs that started just above his navel and gathered thickness on their way down to . . . *there*. "Tell me," he whispered intimately, "I'm intrigued. What kind of observations does a postmodern pretty girl have?"

Kiki eased back onto one elbow. She was facing him, their bodies parallel, and when he casually shifted to the same position and reached out to lazily claim a few of her fingers, the gesture had a certain effect on her central nervous system. "There are so many," she managed, a bit breathlessly. "I wouldn't know where to start. Give me a subject."

"Marriage." He dropped the hot topic without warning.

"Okay . . . *marriage* . . . well, I've done it once, so obviously, I'm for it . . . you know, in theory. But you made that comment about me marrying for money . . . which . . . okay, it's true . . . to a degree . . ."

Fab laughed.

"*But* . . . and this is where the pretty, sexy girl gets maligned in our culture . . . everybody thinks that we're gold diggers. Well, you know what? We are. But not exclusively. What about the women who are successful in their own right? They want a rich husband, too, because when they *do* get married, they want to quit working and stay at home with their babies. To me, that's just greedy. I mean, they're already self-sufficient, but they're still trying to land a rich guy. Meanwhile, girls like me are out there barely hanging on. *We* need the rich ones."

Fab bobbed his head to the beat of her twisted logic. "That's an interesting take. I'd keep reading."

Kiki beamed. "And you're not even the target audience."

"Don't be so sure. Some men might read your

book just to glean some insight into the general psyche of the pretty, sexy girl."

"You really think so?"

Fab nodded yes. "Do you have a literary agent?"

"No. I have a television agent, Keith Bush. I assume that he's still my agent. You see, he never returns my calls."

"That should change after today," Fab said. "You're front-page news."

"Ugh—don't remind me. Of course, that *is* the reason I'm here. And I might not have met you otherwise. I guess I shouldn't complain."

Fab's thumb caressed the inside of Kiki's palm. "You don't hear me complaining." He was moving things forward. It was a come-on. But it didn't feel like one. And *this* is how men like him woke up with women like her whenever they put their minds to it. After a few beats of silence, he added, "You should take advantage of this media situation. Why not turn lemons into lemonade? Put your idea for the book down on paper. I know some agents. I'll put you in touch."

Kiki rose up. "Are you serious?"

"Very. The natural progression of a scandal like this is that for about five minutes, everybody wants to be in business with you. So be ready and make sure that it's something *you* want. Otherwise, you'll end up on a reality show like *Big Brother*."

She nodded severely, appreciating his counsel.

"But how does this kind of notoriety have anything to do with being an author?"

"It doesn't," Fab said matter-of-factly. "But you've captured the interest of the media. Publishing can be a crazy business. Sometimes getting a book deal has nothing to do with being a writer. I'll make a few calls tomorrow and find out how you should proceed."

Kiki felt downright giddy. She looked at Fab, and suddenly, he was a Popsicle that she wanted to lick from top to bottom. He actually *believed* in her. She reached out to rest one hand against the side of his face in a way that was heartfelt yet still invited more. "Where did you come from?" She knew her eyes were shining as she said it.

"Downstairs," he deadpanned. "I own this joint. Remember?"

In one rapid-fire movement, Kiki straddled Fab's hips and pinned his arms over his head. "Okay, mystery man. You've put me on the shrink couch tonight, and I know *nothing* about you."

Fab craned his neck to take in the scene, her hands trapping his wrists, her knees locked onto his hips. It was as if he couldn't believe what she was doing to him. "Kiss me," he whispered. "And maybe I'll tell you where I was born." His mouth lolled open with great expectations.

Boom! Kiki's heart took off. That quick. That automatic. She eased down to meet his lips. There was desperation in the move. A certain panic. Because she knew that where there was a beginning, there was also an end. But for now she simply grabbed hungrily at the moment, ravenous for the sensation, for the taste, of Fab Tomba.

The kiss went further than she intended. Her legs twitched weakly, and as she lay plastered against him like Scotch tape, she could feel his arousal swell against her stomach. Kiki pulled back from his mouth but lingered around his neck, completely dazed, eyes half closed, breath coming in soft little pants. "Oh, my God," she murmured.

"*That* was an incredible first kiss," Fab whispered.

She rose up just enough to make eye contact, then collapsed on top of him in a fit of laughter. "You've got Fango mud all over your face."

Her cellular rang.

Kiki silently cursed the intrusive device even as she instinctively reached for it.

With good humor, Fab began to flake off the dried mud.

Kiki giggled, saw DANNI CALLING on the screen, and picked up with a hushed, "I can't talk right now. I'll call you—"

But sound of Danni sobbing cut her off midsentence.

Kiki's stomach dropped. Something was very wrong. Suzi-Suzi could wail about almost anything. The final episode of *Sex and the City* had sent her to bed for three days. But Danni was always solid as a rock. "Where are you?" Kiki asked, her voice calm but firm.

"I'm at Lenox Hill Hospital," Danni cried.

From: kiki@misstexas95.com
To: numbersgeek@aol.com
    vshelton@kleinschmidtbelker
Subject: Potential Fashion Debacle

My Fellow Bridesmaids,

Let's just get it out in the open, shall we? I'm the official outsider of this group. If choosing the sister of the groom isn't a decision arrived at by gunpoint, then tell me what is. That being said, allow me to be the voice of radical honesty. I consider myself to be somewhat of a professional bridesmaid. I'm in FIVE weddings this summer alone. Agony! And the idea of yet another ghastly bridesmaid dress is more than I can endure. The mere thought has driven me to put two pharmacists on speed dial (a girl needs options, and why limit yourself to one antianxiety medication?). Anyway, how about a pact? We must agree NOT to march down the aisle looking like Barbara, Louise, and Irlene Mandrell from the tragic 80s. Fab dresses only!

PS Vivien, this will be a challenge because you're so tall. But think of all the drag queens who manage to find dresses that make them look fantastic. No worries.

All My Best,
Kiki

Chapter Seven

The cabdriver eyeballed a strange look into the rearview mirror.

"It's a treatment mask," Kiki explained, not shy about showing her annoyance. "Deeply cleansing. Now please just get to the hospital as fast as you can. This is an emergency."

She sank back against the seat, worried sick about Danni and biting nervously at a nail as the taxi raced toward Seventy-seventh Street on the Upper East Side. First, Kiki had no idea why the girl was at Lenox Hill. And second, Danni had a phobia about hospitals. Her Achilles' heel. A million years ago, she had been engaged to a dreamy surgeon who called off the wedding *after* she showed up at the church. Ever since, Danni had suffered mild panic attacks anytime she walked inside a hospital, a doctor's office, or even a living room while someone was watching *ER*.

Once more, Kiki tried Danni's cellular, praying the call wouldn't ring into voice mail again. But it did. She hurled the phone back into her purse, then fished it out again to dial Suzi-Suzi. More voice mail. "God!" Kiki screeched. "Does anybody answer their phone anymore?"

Her face was cracking under the dried Fango mud. It hurt to speak, and her lips felt as parched as the Mohave Desert. Actually, she was supposed to sponge off the mask before it began to dry. But Kiki, in an effort to keep stress-induced breakouts to a minimum, sometimes allowed the product to set like concrete. Besides, tonight the mask was pulling double duty as a slam-dunk disguise. No creepy photographer would ever recognize her in this goop.

Kiki zipped down the window, grateful for the whipping summer wind. "Fab Tomba, Fab Tomba, Fab Tomba," she muttered against the hot breeze, his name tripping off her lips with all the sweetness and effortlessness of powdered sugar. The total recall of that first kiss ran like instant replay in her mind. Oh, God, it had been fantastic. Correction. *Beyond* fantastic. As first kisses go, the only way to describe it was . . . well, off the charts.

Kiki's body still hummed from the sensual memory. When her mouth had been crushed against his, there hadn't been a muscle, a nerve, a cell, not so much as a nanosecond of a buried impulse, that didn't sing with blissful harmony for the here-and-now and the what-would-be. If a simple kiss carried that kind of impact, then the sixty-thousand-dollar question was this: What would making love to him yield?

She smiled to herself as the image of him leaving the suite with a slight smear of Fango mud on his face tattooed her brain. Part of Kiki had felt obliged to tell him. But the more devious part of her won out in the end. Maybe it was the secret knowledge of him unknowingly walking around with war paint from that cosmic kiss. The idea made her glow with happiness.

Finally, the cab jerked to a stop in front of Lenox Hill Hospital. Kiki paid the fare and dashed inside through the emergency room entrance, ignoring the odd looks as she arrowed directly toward a tired-looking nurse behind the main reception desk. "I'm looking for Danni Summer."

The nurse checked records and pointed in a vague direction.

Kiki followed the ambivalent finger. She darted in and out of semiprivate rooms until she found Danni, sharing recovery space with a patient coughing so violently that Kiki swore the woman might hack up those weapons of mass destruction that were never found.

"Oh, my God!" Kiki exclaimed, thunderstruck by Danni's condition. "What happened?"

Danni stared back miserably, her right leg elevated, her left shoulder in a sling. "Occupational hazards." Her voice was late-night hoarse.

The one-woman leper colony started up again.

Kiki gave her a half-empathetic, half-disgusted smile before closing a flimsy curtain. Not the obliteration she longed for but better than nothing. She took a deep breath and returned her focus to Danni, wincing at the sight. Her friend's pain was palpable.

"Don't worry. I just need some rest," Danni croaked. "The injuries are fairly minor."

"*Minor?* You look like you got hit by a bus."

"It's just a damaged rotator cuff from hanging on the pole. My knee was swollen, too. The doctor said that was from dancing on high heels. He drained some water from it. That relieved most of the pressure. But it still hurts."

Kiki reached out to brush a tendril of hair away from Danni's eyes. "Sweetie, you *have* to slow down. All of this dancing is too hard on your body. I mean, if you're not careful, you could really develop a serious injury."

Danni managed a brief smile. "The doctor told me the exact same thing. He must be feeding you these lines."

"I haven't even *seen* a doctor," Kiki said sharply. "The only medical person I've encountered is a narcoleptic nurse."

"Well, he's around here somewhere," Danni replied. And then, sotto voce, "He looks just like George Clooney. I think I'm in love."

Kiki adjusted Danni's pillows. "So much for your fear of hospitals."

Danni grinned, somewhat dreamily now. "Oh, Dr. Wonderful gave me a sedative to calm me down." She appeared to be fading by the second. "Your face is green. Did you know that?"

Kiki took Danni's hand and squeezed gently. "Yes, sweetie, I know my face is green."

"I can't stop dancing, Kiki," Danni murmured. Her eyelids fluttered. "It's like a sports injury, you know? I just have to tough it out and get back on the field. There are so many Bon Jovi songs that I haven't choreographed yet. Like 'You Give Love a Bad Name.'"

Kiki brooked no argument. "We can talk about all of this later, sweetie. Why don't you go to sleep?"

"Call . . . Suzi-Su," Danni muttered, trailing off, falling in and out of consciousness.

"I will," Kiki promised. But it suddenly dawned on her why Suzi-Suzi had been unreachable. This was the one night of the week that Chad slept over, and Suzi-Suzi unplugged the phone to give him the full, unencumbered-by-the-outside-world Stepford wife treatment. Kiki sighed. Friends. Couldn't live with them. Couldn't live without them. Couldn't institutionalize them.

As Danni drifted into a deep sleep, Kiki stood

there and began a soliloquy about Fab. She was dying to talk to someone so badly that even a zonked-out person would do in a pinch. She blathered on about his kindness in discounting the hotel suite, his surprise appearance with the Spice Market dinner, his uncanny ability to psychoanalyze and seduce at the same time.

"Please . . . tell me you don't mean . . . *the* Fab Tomba," Danni murmured. For a split second, her eyes opened, then closed again.

Kiki clung to the idea that Danni was still conscious enough to finish this train of thought. In fact, right now that hope and that hope alone was setting the rhythm of Kiki's heartbeat.

"He used to . . . date . . . Tiffany Lynn . . . a dancer at the club," Danni whispered before slipping back into oblivion. Only this time she stayed there.

Kiki yearned to counteract the sedative. Maybe Ritalin? Or shock treatment? She wanted chapter and verse on everything Danni knew about Fab. But the idea of getting it tonight was officially a dead issue. "Why does everything happen to me?" Kiki wailed.

And then a crazy idea burned up her brain stem. She glanced at the clock on the wall. By stripper standards, the night had only just begun. Danni might be down for the count, but this Tiffany Lynn person was probably getting warmed up to set the Champagne Room on fire.

A wave of guilt rolled over Kiki. How could she

even entertain the notion of leaving Danni alone in the hospital? Hmm. Well, when you really thought about the situation, it wasn't *so* terrible. Not like Danni's condition was life-threatening. Please. The girl was already yammering on about returning to work. And she *was* under a doctor's care—a dead ringer for George Clooney, no less. By comparison, Danni was in better shape than Kiki!

All guilt cast aside, Kiki commandeered Danni's cellular and scrolled through the stored numbers until she found a listing for CLUB. That had to be it. She dialed.

"Camisole," a female voice smacked while the driving bass of Usher's "Yeah" thundered in the background.

"Is Tiffany Lynn working tonight?" Kiki asked.

"Sure. Come party with her, honey. Get a private dance. Bring your man. He'll love it. Or just stop in alone if that's your thing."

Kiki rolled her eyes. What a sales pitch. The girl had obviously been listening to too many Dale Carnegie tapes. "Thanks." And then she hung up, kissed Danni on the cheek, and dashed out.

Luckily, the so-called gentlemen's club was on the East Side and only a short cab ride away. Why did they call these places *gentlemen's clubs* anyway? A better choice would be *an oasis for pigs* or *haven for horny losers*. Hmm. Maybe a subject worthy of tackling in her book.

A thick bouncer with biceps for brains blocked the entrance and shook down Kiki for a thirty-dollar cover charge. "Hey, baby, what's up with the face? Is it Halloween? Nobody told me."

"Nobody told you it was 2005, either," Kiki shot back. "Acid wash went out in the eighties."

The already drunk Wall Street types filing in behind her cackled like high school boys who had just heard a good your-mama's-so-ugly joke.

Camisole marketed itself with illusions of grandeur, using "The Manhattan man's first choice in upscale adult entertainment" as a positioning line. But at the end of the day, the parlance meant nothing.

A strip club was a strip club. Music thrashed. Strobe lights flashed. Lasers scanned. Mirrors amplified. Smoke billowed. And herds of young executive males—highly successful and highly stressed—were in great moods because hot girls were naked.

Prince's hard-charging "D.M.S.R." exploded from the speakers. "Never mind your friends/Girl it ain't no sin/To strip right down to your underwear." Rock's diminutive royalty rasped the lyrics over a beat that tested the mettle of the state-of-the-art sound system.

On the stage, two dancers walked slowly back and forth, looking bored. Basically, they were doing nothing. But the girls were nude. So in the great American pecking order of amazing routines, this ranked right up there with the best of David Copperfield— at least with the crowd gathered here tonight.

A fast-moving barmaid with an empty drink tray stopped to give Kiki a strange look. "Nice makeup. Very She-Hulk. Can I get you anything?"

Kiki smiled, shaking her head. "I'm just looking for Tiffany Lynn."

"She's up there," the waitress said, pointing at the stage. "The blond one."

Kiki maneuvered her way to the lip of the performance platform. Up close, Tiffany Lynn was more than a dime-a-dozen exotic dancer. The girl was truly beautiful. Funny that the mention of Charlize Theron had only hours ago tripped off Fab's lips, because this woman could easily be her twin.

Tiffany Lynn arched her back and popped a hip to one side in time with the Prince beat, sending impressive muscle ripples down her stomach. Then she pushed her perfect breasts forward, as if to prick the eyes of the men who wanted her.

This move provoked a macho chorus of whoops and whistles from the crowd. But if Tiffany Lynn appreciated the reaction, it didn't show on her vacant face. She just paced the area until the song ended, hypnotizing the regulars with the mechanical rhythm of her wild-side walk.

Kiki stood waiting as Fab's ex stepped down from the stage. "Tiffany Lynn!" she called out.

The girl with the porn star name turned to Kiki and did a double take. "Do I know you?" Her voice was soft, kind, and almost sang with a musical intonation.

"I'm a friend of Danni's," Kiki said.

Tiffany Lynn's piercing baby blues widened with authentic concern. "Oh, I've been so worried about her. How is she?"

"Nothing too serious. A damaged rotator cuff and a swollen knee."

Tiffany Lynn shook her head. "I've told her to go easy on those pole moves. She's not a gymnast." One beat. "What's that stuff all over your face?"

"A treatment mask. It's a long story. Listen, there's something I want to talk with you about. Can I buy you a drink?"

Tiffany Lynn shrugged easily. "Sure, why not? But just coffee for me. I've got an essay due tomorrow."

Kiki tried not to stereotype, but certainly the phrase *I've got an essay due tomorrow* belonged under the heading "Things You Don't Expect a Stripper to Say." "You're in school?"

Tiffany Lynn nodded. "Yeah. I go to NYU. I have a class with one of the Olsen sisters. I don't know if it's Mary-Kate or Ashley. But she's very sweet. I'm sorry. I didn't catch your name."

"Kiki."

"Nice. You don't hear that one very often. Guys will remember that. Are you thinking about dancing, too? Camisole's a great club. The manager's a pretty decent guy. Be warned, though. He does hit on all the new girls, but just lie and tell him you're a lesbian. That's what I did. He left me alone. Plus, he's great at working around your schedule. I only show up one week a month. With private dance money and tips, I make enough to play full-time college girl the rest of the time."

"I don't want to work at the club," Kiki said.

Embarrassed, Tiffany Lynn covered her mouth and giggled. "I'm sorry. I just assumed. Most girls who approach me want the 411 on dancing here."

Kiki decided to just come out with it. "I was hoping for the 411 on Fab Tomba."

Tiffany Lynn hesitated. "I'll need more than a cup of coffee for that conversation." She spun around to extend her lithe, honey brown body over the bar. "Hey, Kirby, who do I have to sleep with to get two shots of tequila around here?"

The hot bartender with the neatly trimmed goatee gave her a wink and a crooked smile. "Me, I hope." Then he showed off, wowing them with an intricate move worthy of Tom Cruise in *Cocktail*. As the beat of Destiny Child's "Lose My Breath" boomed inside the grown-up playground, his worked-out body moved in perfect synchronization. There were twists, turns, spins, bottles flipped midair, and at the end of the spectacular, two hits of Mexican 1800 Tequila swirling hurricane-style in side-by-side shot glasses.

Tiffany Lynn knocked one back like it was the antidote for a deadly disease. "This girl wants to know all about Fab," she told the liquor magician.

Kirby balled up a fist and smacked the business end of it into his other hand. "He broke this angel's heart. If he shows his pretty-boy mug in here again, I just might break him."

Now it was Kiki's turn to need a drink. She made the tequila disappear fast. The potent liquid burned a trail down her throat and sent a telegram to her brain: QUIT WHILE YOU'RE AHEAD.

"Hey, Fab's not *that* bad," Tiffany Lynn said. The qualifier was proof that romantic feelings could still be bubbling near the surface. "Don't listen to him. Kirby's like a big brother to all the dancers. None of the guys we date are good enough."

"That's because they're all losers and assholes," Kirby said, wiping a spill off the countertop. He zeroed in on Kiki. "You must be the latest on his hit list. I guess that's why your face turned green."

Kiki wondered if the real green monster might be the bartender. Did he have a legitimate beef? Or was Kirby just envious because Fab had scored with Tiffany Lynn? After all, no man wanted to get typecast in the thankless role of platonic protector. Especially among a group of beauties who took their clothes off at the drop of a drumbeat. A diabetic would have an easier time working at Dylan's Candy Bar on Third Avenue.

"Just be careful," Kirby said. He gave her a ray-gun gaze. "Keep your eyes open and don't fall too hard too fast."

Kiki downloaded the suggestion. It sounded less like jealous talk and more like good advice.

"I don't think he's such a bad guy," Tiffany Lynn said. "The trouble with Fab is that he's so easy to fall *for*. Come on. He's as hot as can be, he's nice, and let's not even *talk* about the way that he kisses."

"Yeah, let's not," Kiki agreed.

"When I was with him, though," Tiffany Lynn went on, "I just felt like there was a part of him that I couldn't reach. You know? He was looking for some quality that I didn't have. And I wanted to change for him, but I didn't know how. That's stupid, right? To want to change for some guy. At the end of the day, you never really can." She shrugged. "What can I say? I wanted him for the long haul, but he was a great three-week boyfriend. A girl could do worse."

"I think he's sort of a sport dater," Kirby went on, now and then tossing a glance to Tiffany Lynn, who stood there offering occasional nods of confirmation. "Novelty girls are his thing." He tilted a head toward the obvious object of his desire. "She was the newest and hottest dancer at the club. Just in from California. Everybody was talking about her. Then he dumps her for that chick who made it to the final two on *The Apprentice.*" Kirby shrugged. "I don't know. High profile babes must do something for his ego." He halted, regarding Kiki for a moment. "So what's your story? Besides the green face."

I'm the tabloid scandal girl of the moment. Kiki kept the words to herself. But she was definitely thinking them.

"Wait a minute!" Tiffany Lynn exclaimed, staring lasers at Kiki as she pieced together the who's-that-girl puzzle in her mind. "You're Kiki Douglas!"

She shrank from the positive ID and hoped nobody within earshot heard or gave a damn.

Kirby just stared blankly. Clearly, the name carried no meaning to him, a man who probably dealt in point spreads and batting averages, only trafficking in celebrity gossip when a story got so big that it came out of the water faucet and proved impossible to ignore.

"She's the girl from today's *Post,*" Tiffany Lynn informed him. "You know, the one with Tom Brock . . ."

"Ah." Suddenly, a ripple of awareness skated across Kirby's face. He nodded, smoothing the hairs on his goatee as he said, "What can I say? My case is rested."

"Fab didn't seek me out, though," Kiki said. "We met by accident." But the words sounded lame once they reached the air.

123

Kirby knew this and shared a secret look with Tiffany Lynn, shaking his head with when-will-they-learn wisdom while he served up a second dose of the good stuff. "Hey, maybe he's changed. Maybe it's true love. The fact that you're Topic A from Trump Tower to the subway john is probably a coincidence."

In response, Kiki swallowed the tequila faster than a badass in a biker bar. Then she slammed the shot glass back onto the counter with an almighty crash. "Just shut up and pour, bartender."

Chapter Eight

"When you think about it, Fab's really not that hand-some," Kiki slurred. "I mean, come on, he's practically ugly."

"This girl is hammered," Kirby said. "She's so hammered they need a new word for it."

Kiki was sandwiched between Camisole's bartender and one of the club's most popular strippers (certainly Fab's favorite) in a taxi barreling toward the Meat Packing District, and, ultimately, Affair.

Right now she was brimming with love for her two new best friends. They were marvelous. "Party in my suite!" Kiki roared, collapsing into a fit of drunken laughter.

Tiffany Lynn gave her a sisterly pat on the knee. "Honey, there's not going to be any kind of party. We're going to get you into your room, put you in bed, and let you sleep this off."

"No!" Kiki shouted. "Party in my suite!" Quite

suddenly, perhaps weakened by the outburst, she slumped against the rock that was Kirby's shoulder for several long, disoriented seconds.

Then a great idea sprang to mind. Hmm. Maybe she wasn't so drunk after all. "Hey, let's find Fab so you can beat him up." She peered at Kirby as she suggested this. "I've got his mobile number. We should call right now to set up the smackdown." Frantically, she looked around. "Where's my purse? Who's got my purse?"

"It's right here," Tiffany Lynn assured her. "But the battery's low on your cell. Let's call him later."

"Okay," Kiki agreed. She held onto Kirby's Popeye arm with both hands. "Do you really think you could beat him up?"

He laughed. "Fab Tomba? I think *you* could."

Kiki smiled. "Okay. If you say so. I just would feel bad if you got hurt or something. That's all."

"What?" The question hit the air as he puffed out his chest. "You don't think I can wipe the floor with that guy?"

"Nobody is wiping the floor with anybody," Tiffany Lynn cut in. She reached over to pull roughly at Kirby's hair.

He winced. "Shit! What'd you do that for?"

"Because you're not helping the situation," Tiffany Lynn hissed. "You're not going to beat up Fab Tomba."

"But I could," Kirby shot back. "Trust me. He doesn't want a piece of this."

"What are you—twelve?" Tiffany Lynn asked.

"I'm just saying," Kirby went on. "I could kick that guy's ass from here to Long Island and never even break a sweat."

Tiffany Lynn let out a frustrated groan. "Why are we even having this conversation? It's stupid."

"She—" Kirby began.

But Tiffany Lynn stopped him cold. "*She* is drunk and has no idea what she's saying."

"Oh, yes, I do," Kiki answered, even though her eyes were closed. "I know what I'm saying, I know what you're saying, and I know what he's saying. And if the cabdriver could speak English, then I'd know what he was saying, too."

But Tiffany Lynn ignored Kiki to continue fussing at Kirby. "How many shots of tequila did you give her?"

"I don't know," he mumbled. "A lot. She told me that she could handle her liquor. I guess she lied."

"Oh, you think?" Tiffany Lynn sighed.

Kiki found herself drifting in and out of sleep as she snuggled against Kirby. "I feel so bad for you," she murmured. "I really, really do."

"How come?"

Kiki yawned. "Because. None of the dancers at the club will go to bed with you. They've got you pi-

geonholed in this older brother role. And then you
have to stand there while they parade around naked
and pretend not to want them. I saw you watching
Tiffany Lynn tonight. How could you not? The music
was hot. She was doing her thing. It must be
torture."

An awkward silence descended inside the car.

"Tiffany Lynn, let me ask you something. What's
so wrong with Kirby?" Kiki asked.

"There's noth—"

"Now I realize that he's not Fab. But you just have
to get over that." Kiki bulldozed on, feeling a second
wind now. Somehow the alcohol clarified this unre-
quited thing between her new friends. Maybe she
could help.

"What does that mean?" Kirby asked. *"He's not
Fab."* His voice mocked her.

"Oh, please," Kiki scoffed. "You know what I
mean. Fab is gorgeous. Accept that and move on."

"Just a few minutes ago you said he wasn't that
handsome," Kirby pointed out.

"Okay, *now* who's hammered?" Kiki rolled her
eyes. "I never said that. In fact, my mouth couldn't
even form those words. Fab Tomba is the most beautiful man I've ever seen." She patted Kirby's bulging
bicep. "But you're pretty hot in your own right. And
you should be proud of that. Face it, though, there's
only one Fab."

"I don't care about Fab Tomba!" Kirby yelled.

"You're the one who's obsessed. You can't stop saying his name."

"That's insane," Kiki sniffed. "I've hardly mentioned him all night."

Kirby gave up.

Tiffany Lynn giggled.

"Let's get back to the two of you," Kiki said. "Why aren't you da—"

The driver negotiated a sharp turn, careening his passengers to one side of the vehicle.

Kirby and Tiffany Lynn recovered quickly.

As for Kiki . . . not so much. A terrible nausea hit, exploding like a dirty bomb in the center of her chest. She couldn't see, think, or move. It took every bit of foggy concentration not to lose the contents of her stomach. This was democracy in action. No matter how high-end the booze, it could deliver low-end results.

The car stopped moving.

Tiffany Lynn handled the fare business.

Kirby eased Kiki out of the backseat and onto the street. Her knees buckled the moment her feet hit the pavement. Standing up required an industrial strength that the liquor had atrophied somewhere back on the Upper East Side.

But Kirby was right there, his arm clinched around her waist. "That's it, party girl. Nice and easy."

Kiki slumped against him. The class was Vulnerability 101. And right now she was at the top of it.

129

Thank God for the nice guys of the world. She met Kirby's kind eyes and managed a loopy smile, silently apologizing for the tequila psychosis.

His look was instant forgiveness as he half walked, half carried Kiki inside the hotel, Tiffany Lynn flanking her on the other side. When they entered the luxurious lobby, Kirby whistled softly. "Swanky. Maybe we should get a room and sleep it off, too."

"Sleep what off?" Tiffany Lynn countered. "I'm not drunk, and you're not either."

Kirby shot up his eyebrows. "Forget the sleeping it off part then. Let's just get a room."

"I don't think so."

"Oh, you *should*," Kiki chimed in. "And why won't you give Kirby a chance? Is it because he's a bartender?"

"What's wrong with my job?"

"How old are you?" Kiki asked.

"Thirty-four."

"You need a grown-up job," Kiki said matter-of-factly, the worst of the nausea receding as they scooted her inside the elevator. "And I think I speak for all women when I say that nobody wants to be married to a forty-year-old bartender. That's just ridiculous."

Tiffany Lynn nodded in agreement.

Kirby glowered. "Which floor?"

"Five," Kiki answered.

He pressed the corresponding button, then spun

back to finish the argument. "And who said anything about getting married?"

"Oh, I totally see the two of you married," Kiki said. Her voice rang with such absolute certainty that a casual bystander would believe that the only thing left to decide was which band should play at the reception. She reached out to clutch Tiffany Lynn's wrist. "I can be one of your bridesmaids! I'm already in five weddings this summer. I mean, what's one more?"

The stripper and the bartender exchanged uneasy glances. But hints of longing were there.

Finally, Tiffany Lynn said, "I can't *marry* him. We haven't even been on a date yet."

"Or slept together," Kirby put in. "And it's important that a couple be sexually compatible. I read that in *Maxim*."

Kiki jabbed him in the gut with her elbow. A small price to pay for saying something so stupid. "Okay, I'm not even a lesbian, and *I'm* sexually compatible with her." She giggled at her own joke, then stumbled.

Kirby caught her in the nick of time. And the shy half smile on his face said that he already knew the answer to the compatibility question. Raising it was just a ploy.

The elevator doors opened.

Kirby secured his arm around Kiki's waist and ventured out for the final gauntlet to her room. Without preamble he said, as much to the corridor as to Tiffany Lynn, "We should go out sometime."

Kiki grinned, feeling quite the matchmaker. Where would these two be without her? Not here together. That's for sure. Tiffany Lynn would probably be home sweating out an essay for an eight o'clock class she always skipped. And as for Kirby, well, his scenario would probably have something to do with Tiffany Lynn's photograph in the Camisole calendar and a very busy right hand.

"So what do you say?"

Tiffany Lynn wavered. "Maybe. I can't decide right now."

"You know, it would be so much easier if you'd just admit that you want me," Kirby said.

Kiki was *thisclose* to driving her heel into the idiot's foot.

"Actually, that would make it harder," Tiffany Lynn said. "Because I don't." She went through the motions. But it was all mock defiance.

There seemed to be an invisible parrot on Kirby's shoulder, giving him guff for playing big brother all these months. He stopped walking.

Kiki read the smirk on his face. It said the bartender had a new game plan. Platonic Kirby had left the building.

"If I kissed you right now," he said in a low voice, "you'd come up for air and *run* downstairs to get us a room. That's how much you want me."

Kiki had to give Kirby bonus points for all-or-nothing courage. If lost, this was precisely the kind of challenge that could fuck up a man's confidence for life.

Tiffany Lynn watched him watch her. The movie-star gorgeous face was burning, but it was doing so under pressure of the good kind of embarrassment.

"You're blushing," Kirby said. The observation was first-grade simple. But saying it out loud was an advanced fail-safe for upping the ante on the blush in question.

Tiffany Lynn's cheeks were already red. They got more red. "If this kiss is going to be so amazing, then why would I waste all that time running downstairs? Kiki's about to pass out any minute. We could just use her room."

Wait a minute. *Her* room? Suddenly, Kiki felt a little less drunk. She willed herself to sober up and fight for her right to crash properly. But before she could pull a midnight Norma Rae, Kirby steadied her against the wall and left her there to do her own balancing act.

Then he went charging into battle. Call it the Secret Crush War. All hail Kirby the Conqueror, cupping Tiffany Lynn's face in his hands and moving his lips to hers. She opened her mouth a fraction . . . halfway . . . all the way. Her body was hard against him, his body harder against hers. And the first kiss thundered on.

Kiki's heart soared as she watched the new lovers embracing like stars in a big-screen clinch at the end of a romantic movie. She always cried at those moments. Matthew McConaughey and Kate Hudson got her every time in *How to Lose a Guy in Ten Days*. Kirby and Tiffany Lynn were pushing her emotional buttons, too—but in a different way. The realization had just hit her: Kiki would be spending the next few hours sitting *outside* the Mistress Hideaway.

At least they had the manners and self-control to furnish her with pillows and blankets from the room. Better accouterments than most girls got from their college dorm roommates when this sort of thing went on.

Kiki was just getting comfortable when a shirtless Kirby flung open the door to toss a note and a bag of candy at her feet. "This was on your pillow." And then he was gone.

The candy triggered Kiki's initial smile: Haribo brand gummi bears—imported from Spain. She read the note:

Dinner was delightful. How about tomorrow night? A woman like you should never eat alone . . . F

She was practically swooning as she ran a finger over the raised lettering on his personal correspondence card, then over his handwriting. His penmanship was neat and sophisticated, not the chicken

scratch you got from most guys who only seemed
able to scribble BUY BEER on a piece of scrap paper
and tack it to the refrigerator.

Kiki had a certain weakness for men who wrote
little notes. Excluding BUY BEER reminders, of course.
E-mail had basically ruined the art of the letter.
Hmm. This would be good fodder for her book. How
e-mail and Post-its had rung the death knell of written communication between men and women.

No matter the alcohol haze, Kiki's excitement over
the gesture was tempered by the warnings put forth
by Tiffany Lynn and Kirby. But then she read the
note. Again. And found herself completely won over.
Again. Oh, God, she loved the closing. Simply *F*. Not
Sincerely, Fabrizio Tomba. Not *All the best, Fab*. Just *F*.
Actually, it was rather intimate, as if they were already lovers. She began to slowly drift away with
that thought in mind.

And then Tiffany Lynn emerged from the suite, a
crestfallen Kirby close behind her. "I may be a stripper, but I'm *not* a tramp! What was I thinking? I can't
have sex with you in Kiki's room! That's moving way
too fast. You'll just have to wait until we get back to
my apartment."

Kirby brightened. "I can do that. Actually, that's
what I wanted in the first place. This was actually a
test to prove that you're a true lady with dignity."

Kiki addressed Tiffany Lynn. "Actually, a *true* lady
with—"

"We better go," Kirby said quickly, taking Tiffany Lynn by the arm and rushing toward the elevator. "Kiki's exhausted. And drunk, I might add. She needs her rest."

"The sheets are fine!" Tiffany Lynn called out. "There was only a bit of groping before I came to my senses! But new linens are being sent up anyway!"

Hours later, the shrill ring of the cellular blasted Kiki awake with a start. Almost instantly, the party damage made itself known. Her head was throbbing. Her mouth was desert dry. And she was very confused.

Kiki reached out for the mobile—if only to silence the goddamn thing. That's when she saw the note on the nightstand written in big, girlish cursive. She read that first.

Don't worry—the sheets are fine! Not that you ever would've noticed. You were completely gone. Who knows? Maybe you WILL be in my wedding. Last night was fabulous. I can't believe this guy has been under my nose all this time. It's totally like that Vanessa Williams song, "Save the Best for Last." Thank you! Please call soon. We want to stay in touch. Love, Tiffany Lynn

Okay. Kiki felt more up to speed now. The last twelve hours were beginning to download. The kiss with Fab . . . Danni at the hospital . . . Camisole . . .

Five hundred shots of tequila . . . Tiffany Lynn and Kirby . . . The kiss with Fab. Hmm. That seemed to be a recurring theme as far as matters of importance.

Meanwhile, the cellular screamed on and on.

Finally, Kiki just answered, not even bothering to look at the ID screen. "Hello?"

"Oh, thank God you're there!" It was Suzi-Suzi. "Whatever you do, *don't* read today's *Post*. Just stay away. It'll only upset you."

Kiki plopped down against the mattress. It was exhaustion. It was defeat, too. "Why even tell me that? You know I'm just going to run out and find a copy anyway." She sighed wearily. "So what are they saying now? Am I having Tom Brock's baby yet?"

"Nothing that serious," Suzi-Suzi murmured. "It's pretty much a rehash of yesterday's garbage. They did put the bit in about you saying their baby looked like a monkey."

"I never said that!" Kiki screamed. As frustration began to mount, she could practically feel her blood pressure tick up, up, up. Out of sheer self-preservation, Kiki made an instant decision. "Suzi-Suzi, I don't want to hear any more. You're right. This *is* upsetting. But I can't control it, so why allow it to make me crazy?"

"You mean you're not going to read it?" Suzi-Suzi asked. Her tone was incredulity to the nth degree.

"Well, of course, I'll read it. In fact, I'll probably

go find a paper as soon as we hang up. But for now, let's talk about something else. *Anything* else."

A few beats of silence went back and forth.

Suzi-Suzi was the first to break it. "Well, I'm finished with Chad. Completely. We are *so* over."

Kiki stifled a groan. Why did the subject have to be *that* particular anything? No matter how grim the talk, at the end of the day, Suzi-Suzi always ended up staying with him.

"Okay, so I'm trying to be a decent wife and make him a nice breakfast this morning," Suzi-Suzi began.

"Uh—he has a wife for that," Kiki said. "You're the mistress. I hope you were at least doing this naked and in high heels."

"*Anyway.*" Suzi-Suzi pressed on. "I'm making scrambled eggs and end up burning my hand on the skillet."

Kiki winced. "Okay, Chad is *so* not worth a burn. He's not worth scrambled eggs, either. Didn't you have any cereal?"

"Would you please let me finish!" Suzi-Suzi demanded. She paused a beat. "So, of course, I stop what I'm doing to put ice on it, take a Vicodin, and call the plastic surgeon because you never know about scarring. What if somebody wants me to do hand modeling for jewelry or dish soap or something like that?"

"Yeah, that would be anybody's first concern," Kiki said.

Suzi-Suzi charged on. "Well, here I am, injured *and* dealing with a potential career crisis. Meanwhile, Chad is freaking out because I stopped making his breakfast. Can you believe that?"

"Yes," Kiki answered simply. "After everything you've told me about this man, I can definitely believe that."

"Okay, so I'm like, 'Well, I guess I should just get back to slaving over the stove and you can drop me off at the burn center after you've had a chance to digest your precious little meal.' And he's like, 'Yeah, that sounds like a plan.' Ugh! I just wanted to scream. Actually, I did scream. Then he said he'd grab a bite on his way to the train station. And he just left. You know what? I don't even care."

"You shouldn't," Kiki said. It seemed like the appropriate response—agreeable and supportive. But Kiki knew better than to put stock in Suzi-Suzi's postfight hyperbole. First, she knew her friend very well. And second, any girl who had to state emphatically that she didn't care was right smack-dab in the middle of caring.

Suzi-Suzi talked fast. "I don't know how his wife puts up with him six nights a week. God, I'm so glad she doesn't know about us. If she did, I bet she'd call and ask for another night of freedom. Maybe more. He has a key to my apartment, you know. I should get the locks changed. What do you think?" But Suzi-Suzi didn't wait for an answer. "He's been acting weird lately, too. Did I tell you that he cries after he ejaculates now? That's his new thing. And I'm not talking about getting a little emotional and shedding a few tears. This man sobs and wails and carries on like someone just melted down his golf clubs to make a garden sculpture. It's so weird. And I don't think I'm *that* great in bed. I mean, I can hold my own. But make a man have an absolute breakdown? That seems like Jenna Jameson territory. Anyway, sex with him has turned into such a downer. It's not like he ever had that much stamina anyway. Chad's lucky to last through a long commercial break. And that's a marathon session. But now at the end of it, I have to run around fetching him tissues and making him hot tea. One minute he's my lover, and the next minute he's a weepy old woman who just lost her cat. This is *not* a sexy situation anymore."

Kiki heard a click.

"Ooh—this is Chad beeping in. But who cares? He can call all day if he wants to. I'll never pick up. Well, maybe I will once. You know, just to see what he wants." One beat. "If that's the case, though, I might as well find out now. I'll call you later." And then Suzi-Suzi was gone.

Kiki's phone was ringing again before she could put it down. "Hello?"

"Kiki?" The female voice was vaguely familiar. "It's Misty Dallin. Did I catch you at a bad time?"

"No," Kiki lied. "How are you?" When it came to

Misty Dallin, there was no good time. Theirs was a friendship sealed in the crucible of growing up in the same Texas town. And even then it had been ambivalent at best. Now Kiki was stuck in her wedding. If only she had done something terrible to Misty a long time ago. Like steal her boyfriend. She would probably be free today. Hmm. Being a slut could sometimes reap positive benefits well into the future.

"I'm calling with some bad news," Misty began.

Kiki experienced instant relief. The wedding had been called off. Thank God! Actually, Kiki wasn't surprised at all. Misty had been planning to marry the producer of a girlie show at one of the big casinos in Reno. Any man (except a good plastic surgeon) who inspected boobs for a living was guaranteed to be bad news.

"I have to cut you from the bridal party," Misty said. At first, her voice seemed tentative. But there was definite ice in the tone when she haughtily added, "Your services are no longer required."

For a moment, Kiki just sat there, stunned, the cold dismissal echoing inside her head. *Your services are no longer required.* That's the kind of line you fed a temp who wasn't working out.

Misty wasted no time in offering the explanation Kiki was waiting for. "This Tom Brock business is all over the Internet. Everybody's talking about it. I want my wedding day to be all about me, so I just don't think it's a good idea for you to come. Certainly you understand."

Kiki was livid. "Listen, Misty, I've already bought a nonrefundable ticket to Reno, paid for my ugly bridesmaid dress, and sent a fat check for your *honeymoon fund*, which, I might add, is a really tacky way to rack up on cash gifts!"

Misty drew in a shocked breath. "You bitch! Those bridesmaid dresses are *beautiful*!"

Kiki didn't regret a single word now. Screw the fact that she was out the better part of a thousand dollars for this joke of a marriage that would last two years, tops. The only words Misty picked up on were the critical ones about the dresses. How could people be so self-absorbed?

"Those dresses are an act of fashion terrorism!" Kiki hissed. "And, frankly, I feel lucky to have been spared. As for the other girls, I hope they join a good support group. Because they're going to need it!" With that, she banged down the phone.

Hot tears rolled down her cheeks. Oh, God, she was so mad! She could feel an angry fire balling up in the center of her chest. And the emotion had nothing to do with stupid Misty Dallin. No. That twit was already forgotten. The most upsetting part of all was the realization that the scandal had left the island of Manhattan.

Kiki's humiliation had officially gone national.

From: kbush@wma.com
To: kiki@misstexas95.com
Subject: Possibilities

Hi Kiki,

Nice ink today in the *Post*. You know the old saying—there's no such thing as bad publicity. Here's proof: Had a conversation with the producers of VH1's *The Surreal Life*. They're casting now for a new season and think you could be a great addition. Not sure about any others you might be shacking up with. The only definite name so far is a kid from *Eight Is Enough*. Can't remember which one. As your agent, I advise you to move fast on this. There's only one scandal girl slot, and I've heard that they're talking to Tonya Harding's people, too.

Keith

From: kiki@misstexas95.com
To: kbush@wma.com
Subject: Re: Possibilities

Dear Keith,

Let me be perfectly clear: I would rather go on the *Fear Factor* bug/entrails/indeterminate organism diet for the rest of my life than race Tonya Harding to the finish line for a stupid reality show gig.
PS You're fired.

Air Kisses,
Kiki

Chapter Nine

Scrubbing off the Fango mud was backbreaking work. Kiki hunched over the vanity for what seemed like an eternity. The mask exfoliated in loose flakes. Scraping old paint off a windowsill would take less effort.

As she rubbed, rubbed, and rubbed some more, it occurred to Kiki that, despite her best efforts to convince herself otherwise, money woes were still front and center.

Finally, she erased every green speck, the results better than she expected. Her face was blemish free, healthy looking, as smooth as a baby's bottom, and flushing with a pink glow. But the state of her finances? Not so rosy.

Even with the deep discount, staying at Affair was beginning to add up. The room charges alone would be a tidy sum. Extras still had to be factored in, too. And last night's whirligig ride? Hardly cheap. Cabs, strippers, and booze could drain some serious dough. The same could be said for greedy bitches. After all, paying off Sarah Ann Duckworth had cleaned out more than half of the Gucci boot box stash.

And what about the American Express bill? Hello! It was still floating around unpaid. Ditto last month's rent. Anxiety began to build as the impossible situation crystallized in Kiki's mind. Then she felt it. Right in her gut. Her stomach all of a sudden had no bottom.

The regrets began to pile up. Like that pithy e-mail she'd sent to fire Keith Bush. In a scramble, she powered her laptop and zapped a second missive to calm the waters.

Keith, I can't believe you haven't called me. Wasn't that last e-mail I sent hilarious? I'm always joking like that. Find me a good comedy! Your client always and forever, Kiki

Well, she might go crawling back to Keith Bush, but he could forget about this *Surreal Life* business. Hmm. What about a guest spot on *Law & Order*? That show needed to cast several extra speaking roles for every episode. Not exactly a dream job but the money would tide her over, and it had nothing to do with elbowing Tonya Harding out of the way for a gig.

Yes! That was a fantastic idea. And Kiki was perfect for it. Of course, the casting people would take one look at her and say *Dead hooker* or *Hooker's friend*. But that's because the show had those types in every script. How hard could it be to stretch out on a sidewalk and pretend to be a corpse? Or wear a micromini, smack gum, and deliver lines like, "I knew that john was bad news. He gave me the creeps. I told Angel to stay away, but she needed the bling to buy her kid braces."

Until then, though, Kiki needed to find an income Band-Aid. Maybe her father could throw some extra money into her monthly care package. A million years ago, Kiki had a trust fund. Inherited at twenty-one. God, whose idea was that? Just because she could legally buy a drink didn't mean she could manage a large sum of money. She shopped, she traveled, she "invested" in a jerky boyfriend's loser business, she let another jerky boyfriend "play the market." It hadn't taken long for the inheritance to disappear altogether. Luckily, her father understood that succeeding as an actress took time. That's why he didn't mind sending out the occasional monthly check. Okay, it was pretty much a regular monthly check. But whatever.

Kiki took a deep breath and called her father. She hated to ask her family for money. Especially at her age. In a perfect world, she would be firmly established by now. But life had dealt her one crushing blow after another. The Miss America loss. That beast of a starter husband. Those *All My Children* producers who killed off Jeannette. And now this media debacle surrounding Tom Brock. The fact that Kiki could soldier on at all was a testament to the indomitable human spirit. So a little gift from Daddy Sonntag was hardly a handout. Really. If anything, it was a celebration of her plucky nature.

"Hi, Daddy!" Her voice climbed up the scale to little girl intonation the moment he answered.

"Kiki, baby, how are you?" He sounded happy to hear from her. But fatigued as well.

"I'm okay," she said. "I've been better, though. But I'm hanging in there. You know me." It was true. And just cryptic enough to wedge an opening.

"I hope it's not money trouble bringing you down because I can't help you there anymore."

The import of her father's words automatically weighed down the almost weightless cellular. Suddenly, the mobile felt as heavy as a brick in her hand.

Her father blathered on. Something about depleted mineral reserves, falling stocks, and capital needs for the winery. She basically stopped listening once she realized that her monthly checks were now a relic of the past. The question begged itself again: Why did everything bad always happen to her?

"What do you think about your brother getting married?" The edge in his voice told Kiki that her father seemed to be struggling with the idea. That was strange. Usually, anything Roman did (pee

147

standing up, graduate from college, work for the family business) qualified as the best thing to happen since Viagra passed the FDA trials.

"I'm happy for him," Kiki managed to say mechanically. But she didn't have time to be happy for Roman. She was too busy worrying about herself. "I have to go, Daddy. I'll check in later." And then she hung up in a snit, a move driven more by fear than mere selfishness.

As she lay there on the bed, completely dejected, an internal thunderbolt hit, rocking her solar plexus. *Danni.* Oh, God! Kiki had completely forgotten about Danni. Hmm. But she could wait. The girl had hospital drugs and a George Clooney look-alike at her disposal. She was fine. In fact, Kiki would gladly trade places with her.

Suddenly, it dawned on Kiki that she was filthy. All those cab rides. The hospital visit. That barfly stint at Camisole. Ugh. If Kiki were a germ-phobic, then she would definitely be in a straitjacket by now. This much was true: The wild night needed to be washed away.

Maybe the answers to some of the endless problems ahead would come to her under the steam jets. The Mistress Hideaway shower was one of those built-for-two numbers. Sexy? Perhaps. If you liked that sort of thing. But Kiki was more into sheets with a decadently high thread count. Anyway, the main problem with the shower was that she couldn't get it nice and steamy. This was supposed to be luxury? Beyond annoyed, she stepped out, wrapped a towel around her body, and called Fab's cell. Indeed. The owner *should* be aware of such failings.

"Fab Tomba."

"I'm trying to take a shower, and I feel like I'm in Antarctica! It won't get hot and steamy!"

He sighed with amusement. "Good morning, Kiki."

"Oh, good morning," she chirped. "By the way, thanks for the candy."

"My pleasure. You raised a quality concern. It's my duty to satisfy."

Kiki melted a little bit. There was topspin on his phrasing of *satisfy*.

"So," Fab began, his voice lazy, almost teasing, "as I understand it, you're having a problem getting hot in your room."

Kiki stood there dripping wet in the towel, feeling half clean and all the way foolish now for calling. "Well, I wouldn't put it *that* way."

"And which way is that?"

Kiki felt a flush rise from her neck to her cheeks. "You make it sound like I have some kind of . . . sexual issue."

"Oh, I would never suggest that," Fab said earnestly.

"Because I don't."

"Of course not. Quite the contrary. You appear to be very . . . accommodating in your approach to that area of life."

Kiki blanched. "I'm *accommodating*? Exactly what is that supposed to mean?"

"Nothing." Fab laughed a little. "We don't seem to be on the same semantic wavelength this morning."

Were they ever? She and Fab always seemed to be on the verge of a knock-down-drag-out. One wrong word, one misplaced phrase, one awkwardly stated sentiment, and there could be blood on the walls. His. Hers. Theirs. God, Kiki hated it. But she loved it, too. The source of the tension was truly delicious.

"No," Kiki said, unwilling to let it pass. "I want to know what you meant by *accommodating*."

"What do you think I meant?"

"I don't know. But it sounds insulting."

"That's an interesting reaction."

"Okay, I'm in no mood to be psychoanalyzed again. As it relates to someone's approach to sex . . . *accommodating* is a loaded term. I mean, the slut in high school who gives blow jobs in the parking lot could be described that way."

"This is a small hotel, Kiki," Fab began. "No incident, no matter how minor or seemingly insignificant, escapes my attention. I'm aware that you slept *outside* your room during the wee hours. I'm also aware that extra linens were requested for your suite."

"Oh, really?" Kiki remarked, somewhat gleefully.

"How very Orwellian of you." She paused a beat. "But as it turned out, I slept in my room like a baby, and the extra linens weren't necessary. Luckily, there are some girls out there who know how to hold out for a little romance. So I suppose you know that I ran into one of your old girlfriends last night."

"Yes, I saw the security tape. And I'm happy for Tiffany Lynn and the barmaid."

"Kirby's hardly a *barmaid*," Kiki shot back. "Actually, he thinks *you're* a bit on the girlie side."

"That's just because I once refused his challenge to an arm-wrestling contest."

"What's wrong?" Kiki trilled. "Afraid to lose?"

"No. Afraid to hold hands with him. One thing might lead to another. I should just confess now. I never went to Camisole for the dancers. It was the bartender all along."

Kiki smiled. He did it every time. Made her blow a gasket one minute and repaired the damage the next.

"I think it was all those fancy moves," Fab went on. "You know, the ones that prove he spends hours and hours with the *Cocktail* DVD on slow-mo."

Kiki laughed.

"And believe me," Fab continued. "I'm not the only guy who's noticed. It's only a matter of time before Camisole is exposed as a gay bar."

Now Kiki completely lost it. "Would you please stop?" she begged, barely getting the words out. "Oh, my God. If Kirby knew you were saying this, it would be *so* over for you. By the way, I need to find him a new job. Any ideas?"

"Let's see . . . what to do with a lifetime bartender who can juggle and bench-press a Toyota . . . NASA! I've got a friend there. He can start tomorrow as a rocket scientist."

"*Fab!*" Kiki scolded. But she was giggling throughout her mock protest. "I'm serious. I adore Tiffany Lynn. And don't think you've escaped a serious cross-examination about her. But I'll wait to do that face-to-face. Anyway, I think she and Kirby make a darling couple. I want them to get married so that I can be in their wedding, which is really saying a lot because I'm *so* beyond the whole bridesmaid thing. But for Tiffany Lynn I would get back in the mix."

"Didn't you just meet her for the first time last night?" Fab asked.

"Yes, but there was tequila involved, which totally fast-forwards a friendship," Kiki said. "Anyway, we've got to get Kirby on a better career path. Strip club bartender is *not* husband material."

"And dancer in a strip club is wife material?"

"Excuse me, but Tiffany Lynn is enrolled at NYU. That girl has her shit together." Kiki drummed her fingers on the bathroom counter, concentrating on the Kirby occupation conundrum as if it were hard science. "Is there anything for him here at the hotel?"

"You want me to hire Kirby to work at Affair," Fab said, the implication in his tone suggesting that the bartender stood a better chance of winning the Kentucky Derby on a donkey.

"What's wrong with that idea? It's not like you couldn't use the help managing this place."

"So now you want him to join my management team?"

"Well, it should be a move *up*. Otherwise, why bother?"

"Why bother is right. Does this man even have a resume? Did he graduate from college? Does he have any—"

"Okay, okay," Kiki cut in, exasperated. "I'll do my homework first. But don't think this subject is closed. Because it's not." She sighed heavily. "Where do we stand on the steam issue? If you ask me, the hotel should treat to a day at Bliss Spa for making me put up with such substandard amenities." Hmm. That reminded her. Mental note to call Bliss about the agent contact info for Suzi-Suzi.

Three knocks rapped the door.

Kiki scooted over to answer it, quickly slipping into the white terry cloth robe with the AFFAIR logo embroidered on the back. Maybe Fab had arranged for room service to be sent up. That would be lovely.

But what stood waiting on the other side was something even more lovely—Fab in the flesh, with an oh-so-pleased-with-himself grin curling his lips, mobile in one hand, the *New York Post* in the other. Ugh. Okay, that last part—not so lovely.

Kiki tried to appear put out. Granted, acting *was* her profession. But she had nothing on, say, Hilary Swank. The ripple of delight she felt at finding him there was no doubt shining through. "What?" Kiki posed with faux annoyance. "You show up with no coffee? No breakfast?" She waved him inside the tiny suite as she snapped her cellular shut. "And you say *I* rely too much on my looks."

Fab plopped the newspaper onto the writing desk and made a beeline for the bathroom.

Kiki glanced down at the tabloid. The headline TEMPTRESS ON THE RUN screamed back. Photos of her running barefoot down the sidewalk and getting thrown out of the Stella McCartney boutique dominated the front page.

"You do realize that most guests who stay here are too busy to complain," Fab called out.

Kiki stormed into the bathroom, determined to show him firsthand the hotel's fatal flaw. To make her point, she turned on the jets full blast. And waited. No steam. Ha! Gazing back at him in triumph, she rolled her eyes skyward.

Fab merely smiled. "With *two* people in this shower," he began, sounding very much the all-knowing American to dense foreigner, "as it was, I might add, originally designed to provide room for, steam levels are more than adequate."

"That's discrimination," Kiki said. "And I should file a class action lawsuit on behalf of all single guests

154

who have ever had the misfortune to darken the doors of Affair."

Fab hardly clamored to get his legal team on speed dial. If anything, the threat seemed to amuse him, much like a child's magic show might. "Since the grand opening, we've had two single guests," he informed her. "And you're one of them."

Instantly, Kiki thought of the mystery woman she'd encountered the day before. That nasty tone and those caustic words ricocheted in her memory.

Women like you make me sick.

How rude! And what did that mean? *Women like her*. God, it was driving her mad. Obviously, this bitter person had lumped her in with a group of undesirables. Kiki just had to get to the bottom of the issue. "And who might this other person be?" she asked, adopting a tone of mildly casual interest.

"You mean the single guest?"

She nodded.

Fab's eyes narrowed with exaggerated suspicion. "I'm not at liberty to say. But why do you ask?"

"Just curious," Kiki sniffed.

"*Kiki* . . ."

"Oh, please. You sound just like Ricky Ricardo from *I Love Lucy*."

Fab's stare continued to penetrate.

"Okay, I give. There's a woman on this floor who said the most vile thing to me, and I want to confront her about it. I think she's here alone." She picked up

155

on the faintest twinkle of recognition in Fab's eyes. "And I think you know exactly who I'm talking about."

If Fab did know, then he betrayed nothing.

"Can you give me her room number?"

"Absolutely not. And that's assuming I knew who you were talking about. Guest information is *strictly* confidential."

"Well, how am I supposed to find her?" Kiki whined. "I suppose I could knock on every door. But there are some kinky people on this floor that I'd rather *not* meet. Did you know the man across the hall was into S and M? From what I gather, he likes to be dominated. He must have a very alpha-type wife who emasculates him. *Elle* did an article about it once. You know, I was just telling my friend Suzi-Suzi that sex has become so ridiculously complicated. I mean, honestly! How do you take a man seriously after he tells you that his fantasy is for you to pee on him?"

Fab shook his head. "No matter where you take this conversation, I'm not giving you the room number."

Kiki reached for a washcloth. "Drop this outside her door. That way I'll know, but you will have told me nothing."

"Speaking of S and M, maybe *you* need the good spanking." He tossed a glance toward the shower.

"Are you just going to leave the water running like that?"

"See," Kiki demonstrated, waving a hand in true spokesmodel fashion. "It's been going all this time and no steam."

Fab gave her a look. It was sexy. It was almost lewd. It was just right. Simmering. Spicy. Bubbling up but not boiling over. Oh, God, even the way he just stood there was a turn-on. It was sick. "You want steam? I'll give you some." And all of a sudden, he proceeded to strip.

At first, she couldn't believe it.

But then Fab was down to his Burberry boxer briefs.

And all she could do was take in that body. So naturally lean and muscular. Shoulders as broad as an Olympic swimmer's. She gulped on air as his fingers found the waistband of the briefs and slowly began to inch them down. Kiki's heartbeat took off in what could only be described as . . . exquisite panic. For the passion to unleash. For the pleasure to come. "I should call security," she breathed.

"To lock me out?"

Kiki dropped her robe. "No, stupid. To lock you in."

From: kiki@misstexas95.com
To: crownjule@aol.com
Subject: Winter Weddings

Julia!

I figure any girl who gets Roman, my DARLING brother, to commit to marriage must be a prize, so I'm assuming that you're an absolute doll. Since we're practically family, may I be honest? I'm only mildly thrilled to be in the wedding. I say that because I'm already in four others this summer. Scratch that. Three others. The point is that it's just a bad time for me. So much is going on. I can't even begin to go into it. Anyway, I've got two words for you—winter wedding. They can be enchantingly romantic. I was flipping through *In Style* not long ago, saw pictures from a December ceremony, and literally started to weep. Just imagine how beautiful it could be! Sit tight. I'll have Breckin work up some ideas.

Air Kisses,
Kiki

Chapter Ten

Sometimes a man could be right. Granted, this happened with all the frequency of leap years, lunar eclipses, and a Madonna interview during which she *didn't* wax lyrical on Kabbalah. But it did take place on occasion.

The steam was rising.

Kiki stood there, flattened against the shower wall, waiting for Fab to move, to talk, to breathe. Anything but prolong the delicious agony of the most important question on earth—the one that only Fab had the answer to: What would he do to her first?

His eyes were hooded. His expression was hungry. But his self-control was . . . well, *annoying*.

The incongruity stunned her—that simultaneously she could be so turned on and so irritated. Okay, a girl wanted a man to take his time. But this one seemed to have all the look-don't-touch discipline of Gandhi on a hunger strike. At some point there

Kylie Adams

needed to be thrashing limbs and heavy panting. And that time was right now.

"Fab," she whispered, surprised to hear her own voice breaking. "*Fab*," she murmured again. God, she loved the sound of his name. "What are you doing?"

He inched toward her, until his face was close to hers, a face with beard stubble that would rub so wonderfully against her smooth skin.

Kiki couldn't wait to feel it.

"I'm deciding," Fab announced, practically breathing the words directly into her mouth, his fingers tracing the contours of her arms.

"Deciding what?"

"How I want to take you first." His thumb was on her lower lip, slippery on the wetness there, washed by the currents of the steam jets going full blast.

Kiki put out her tongue to touch his finger. The messages from her body were coming fast and furious. The impossible anticipation in her stomach. The rush of blood in her taut nipples. The greedy ache to be satisfied at her very core.

His finger hovered at her mouth . . . waiting.

Kiki eased her lips apart to take it deeper.

And then Fab pulled back, moving his hand behind her neck, drawing her even closer.

Her blood was on fire. She could feel him now—hot and hard against her thigh, rigid as rock, bigger than any man had a right to be. Kiki wanted to touch him, to feel him. She longed to hold him for the very

160

first time with both hands. Her fingers began the seemingly endless trail down.

But Fab stopped them.

Kiki pushed back, her eyes pleading.

And then Fab bruised her lips with his, crushing his body against her . . . but still stopping her from doing what she craved.

For the moment, it was enough. Kiki shut her eyes tight, as if doing so would seal in the desire and keep it fresh until the end of time. She moaned softly as their teeth clashed gently, as their tongues waged a glorious erotic battle, as their mouths became one.

Fab's grip on her wrists grew more firm, just as his kiss grew more urgent. And through it all the hot water rained down, sloshing against their merged bodies, generating steam all around them.

Kiki felt everything. The power of his muscular chest heavy on her breasts. The thump of his heart beating through his skin. The pulse of his erection straining against her leg. Oh, God, she was burning. In a sexual sauna of boiling ice. Quite suddenly, and fighting every desire to do anything but, she attempted to draw back from his mouth.

But Fab resisted. And the kiss throbbed on and on.

Kiki realized that this was war. A war they were both winning. A war she wanted to fight seven days a week and twice on Saturdays. And never once ask for mercy. That was a personal promise.

It took every bit of willpower to tear her lips away from his. "Fab . . . *please*." Her begging was life-or-death, but Kiki didn't know exactly what it was for. She only knew that she wanted *more*.

More of him.

More of that.

More of this.

Fab's eyelids sank down over smoldering eyes that were suddenly heat-seeking missiles zeroing in on a target.

And then Kiki got her answer. His first order of business would be her breasts. She watched him watch them—the two white triangles of surgically enhanced perfection.

Kiki was proud of the job. Unlike so many women who went in for implants, she'd resisted the urge to go too big. Unlike Jacinda, her actress friend who made the decision—while fading on the operating table no less—that a DD cup size would be the cat's meow. Now she couldn't wear designer anymore, suffered from back trouble, and had to strap herself down to use the StairMaster. Even worse, her boyfriend ended up leaving her for an Asian model who was built like a little boy. Poor Jacinda.

Fab made a move.

Suddenly, all thoughts of Jacinda's fake-boob Waterloo got kicked out the door. Kiki released a shuddering sigh as she witnessed the greedy act of Fab's hands claiming her breasts, pushing them together, bending down as if in homage to the eighth wonder of the world.

He nuzzled there, his unshaven cheek tantalizingly rough against her silken softness. "God, your tits are spectacular." His tongue ran over the shell pink cones that capped his new discovery, teasing them one at a time.

Kiki's hands found the back of Fab's head and pulled it closer, just as she wondered about the other plans he mind might be dreaming up.

Fab's tongue became Fab's teeth. And he bit down on the petal tips. Soft and loving. Hard and threatening.

Kiki groaned out her delight.

His eyes were shining at her twin marvels, and the lusciously arrogant way the impossibly tight buds sprang back against him seemed to render him spellbound.

A passionate realization roared inside her. This was one for the sensual memory files—a moment Kiki knew she would access one night while pleasuring herself.

Fab was a man of unforgettable firsts. The first time she saw him. The first time she kissed him. The first time she . . .

"Oh! Ooooooh!" Kiki moaned, ecstasy blanketing her mind.

It happened without warning. Fab slipped two fingers inside her, his touch firm and insistent. The shock sent a shudder down her body. She arched her back and thrust her pelvis at the magical intruder that was his hand.

"I can't believe how wet you are," Fab whispered.

"Trust me," Kiki murmured. "It's not the shower." It was official. She was melting for him. The most precious part of her had become a flood tide. Another first. Usually, it took time to heat the kettle. But this man got her whistling quicker than any other man could put his lips together and blow.

His fingers dipped deeper inside, pausing, separating, ruling her with an almost rude boldness.

"Fab, please." Kiki cried out the words, but their meaning got lost in the translation. The truth was, she had no idea what she desired. Her brain was an order screen with bad electrical wiring. She wanted him to go faster. To go slower. To be more intense. To do it with tenderness. To whisper sweet entreaties. To bark out dirty commands. There was only one thing she knew for sure—that Fab triggered a wanting beyond the ken of any reality she'd ever known.

"I can feel you pulsing on my fingers," Fab murmured. "Can you feel it?" And as he waited for the answer, his lips feasted on her neck with a sudden, ruthless, ravenous aggression.

Kiki barely nodded. That was already old news to her. Okay, Fab's fingers could turn her into a Jacuzzi fountain. So what? She was more interested in another part of his body. And her heart hammered against her ribs as simple anticipation became magnificent obsession.

"Fab, please." Oh, God, those same two words again. She sounded like Faith Hill in *The Stepford Wives* before the combustion. But Kiki knew what she wanted now. She was just afraid to say it out loud.

His body tightened like the strings of a bow. He withdrew his hand and replaced it with something else—the dream at the end of her illicit rainbow, pulsating with purpose and radiating heat, hovering right at the mouth of the cauldron she'd become. "Please what?" Fab asked.

Kiki's realization was instant. He was playing with her, mocking her, at the most terrible, wonderful moment. Bastard. Quite suddenly, she felt a return to form. The spark came back. No longer would she be the pliant native girl to his Tarzan. The collision of bodies might've started his way. But it would end her way. "Please . . . Fab . . . tell me that you have a condom."

He looked at her, his face a masterpiece of astonishment. It was the last thing he expected to come out of her mouth. *Please, Fab, make love to me.* That's what he wanted to hear. But it wasn't the medieval era, he wasn't the marauding conqueror, and she wasn't the girl from the village he just burned. Arrogant greedy man. For a minute there, he almost had his own scene from one of those bodice-ripper novels.

Fab's hand swooped overhead to a shelf that housed sample-sized shampoo, conditioner, and body wash products by Kiehl's. He fished around, suddenly producing a Mylar-wrapped Trojan Magnum. In a single sweeping movement, it was ripped open with his teeth and slipped on—all while using just one hand.

Kiki raised an eyebrow. "Impressive. I take it you didn't learn that in the Boy Scouts."

"No, but the first girl I tried it on was a Brownie once upon a time. Does that count?" Fab grabbed a fistful of her wet hair in a way that wasn't rough . . . but masterful. And he moved in until their lips were millimeters apart. Without warning, he plunged inside of her.

Kiki's body shook with the force of his momentum. She felt full—wrapped tight around him. It was exactly where she wanted to be. Breath rushed from her lungs as he increased amperage, his chest crushing against her breasts.

She reached down to cup the steel that was his butt, amazed by his hard muscle. If there was an ounce of fat on this man, she hadn't found it yet.

Fab's fist was still twisted tightly in her hair, his other hand caressing her neck, his tongue plundering her left ear in between desperate breaths and worshipful murmurs, invoking God, her name, and the occasional, "Oh, Fab!"

Kiki's muscles quivered with the effort of holding her stomach tight. In fact, her body was shaking with the strain as Fab continued to thrust up and down, side to side, in a fantastic rhythm that was building fast . . . to the *moment*.

And then he began to speed-whisper into her ear. "I'm going to be honest. I could come any second now. I'd like to think I'm that guy . . . you know, the one with the stamina who can wait until his partner's there, too. Usually, I *am* that guy. But I was so hot for you today I could hardly stand it. I thought about you all night. I couldn't even go to sleep. I did, finally. But I had to do something first. I won't say what. It's too embarrassing. But let's just say you stepped into a fantasy role usually reserved for Catherine Zeta-Jones. So take all of that into account, plus the fact that I've got a management meeting that was supposed to start ten minutes ago. Don't get me wrong. I know you're busy, too. God, you're writing a book. That has to take up a lot of time. By the way, I talked to my friends. The agents I was telling you about. They all want to take a look at your stuff. I've got the details on how to write a proposal in my office. Think about it. Between my work and your work, we're two very busy people. So I think I should just come. That way we can both get on with our day. But I'll be back tonight, and it will be all about you. I promise. What I was—"

"Fab, *please*! Shut up! God, I've never heard a man

talk so much during sex in my life. It's like you're channeling Lorelai Gilmore or something."

Fab Tomba had already lost his famed cool. But in the howling cry into the steam clouds that came next, he lost it even more—and he shot into her like a runaway river.

What saved Kiki from the cruel eternity of waiting for tonight was Fab's last brilliant move, a corkscrew motion where he bucked down and reared up with such amazing force that her feet went flying up from the shower floor in perfect concert with her bottom banging against the tile. The zenith of sensations overwhelmed her. Oh, God! Celestial choirs. Flights through the sky. Phosphorus starbursts. This is what a mind-melting orgasm felt like.

Fab collapsed, still inside her but completely spent and fighting for breath. Kiki grinned lazily into the mist, struggling with the weight of his body.

"Sorry," Fab murmured, stretching his arms against the wall like pylons and trapping her between them. "My legs are so weak right now. I think my knees literally buckled." He made no move to exit her. "I just want to stay inside you for a little bit longer." He sighed the sigh of the deliriously satisfied. "It's a great place to hang out."

Kiki shut her eyes. Oh, God, she wasn't quite done with the little points of pleasure. Then she let her head fall back and sucked in a slow steady breath as the final erogenous pulses dissolved. Okay. *Now* it was over.

In celebration, Kiki cupped his cheeks and kissed him full on the lips. "I can't *believe* I beat out Catherine Zeta-Jones in your self love fantasy. I'm dying to tell Suzi-Suzi and Danni. *Dying*."

From: kiki@misstexas95.com
To: numbersgeek@aol.com
    vshelton@kleinschmidtbelker
Subject: Saving Graces

Girls, girls, girls!

And I'm not talking about that ghastly Mötley Crüe song. I'm talking about us! I have a plan in motion that you're both going to adore. I've already teased Julia with this brilliant concept—a winter wedding. First of all, I'm swamped and, quite frankly, I think one more wedding might turn me into Mariah Carey. Remember that incident when she was walking around Times Square with the Hello Kitty boom box? Well, that could be me! Anyway, winter weddings are a hidden jewel. Why is everyone so hell-bent on tying the knot during the summer? And in Texas! Horrors! The heat will be unbearable. And there's always some old man with flop sweat who wants to dance with every woman under the age of eighty. And I've already mentioned that I wany my brother to be at his most scrumptious (sweat on the upper lip is a bad look for a wedding). Anyway, I'll keep you posted on developments.

PS This will also be particularly fabulous if either one of you suffers from underarm flab. It's a winter wedding. No sleeveless worries!

Air Kisses,
Kiki

Chapter Eleven

"That is *so* romantic." Suzi-Suzi sighed wistfully. "I wish Chad would masturbate and think about me. But he never does that."

"Never masturbates or never thinks about you?" Kiki asked. She was lounging in her suite, basking in the afterglow of her trip with Fab to the waterfall at the end of the world.

"Oh, didn't I tell you? Chad *never* touches himself," Suzi-Suzi said. Her voice took on a serious tone.

"But that's ridiculous," Kiki argued. "Of course, he does."

"No, he *never* does," Suzi-Suzi insisted. "That man does not like a hand on his . . . you know . . . tallywacker. I tried to give him a hand job once, and he totally freaked out. Like a little girl who just saw a big spider or something. Anyway, a hand is a hand. And that includes his own. He swears up and down that he never pleasures himself. At first, I didn't believe him. I thought every man *had* to do it or his thing would fall off, or he'd get red balls or something."

"I think it's blue balls," Kiki corrected.

"*Blue?*" Suzi-Suzi countered. "I thought that's what happened to them in really cold weather." She groaned. "Whatever."

"Now I'm intrigued," Kiki murmured. "Why do you think he's so scared of a hand on his penis? You know, Chad's got some serious sexual hang-ups. Between this and the crying after he comes . . ."

"I know!" Suzi-Suzi thundered. "I tried to look it up on the Internet, but I couldn't find anything. Now I *know* it's weird. I mean, everything's on the Internet these days. That's where I go to get my horoscope."

Kiki stretched luxuriously. God, it felt so good to have sex. Especially after such a long dry spell. It'd been months and months. Now she felt like a nymphomaniac, because getting Fab back into this room as soon as possible was her very reason for living. Hmm. As goals go, this was hardly one that Stephen Covey would endorse as representing one of the Eight Habits.

Suzi-Suzi blathered on. "My life is way too complicated. Why does God punish me? I pray for simple things. I want a boring modeling job like, say, bathing suits or nursing uniforms, and I want a guy who, after he shoots his spunk, doesn't act like me whenever I watch *Terms of Endearment*."

"Hey, why not hire a sex therapist," Kiki suggested.

"Chad would never go for that," Suzi-Suzi grumbled. "I can't even get him to agree to couples counseling."

Kiki chuckled. "That's a new one. Couples counseling for a married man and his mistress."

"Oh, not just us," Suzi-Suzi said. "I told him that his wife should be there, too. We're all in this together, and it's time to start dealing with the issues."

Kiki gazed out the window for a moment . . . to make sure that there was an outside world and that she wasn't living in the same alternative universe as Suzi-Suzi, who truly had no idea that having a married boyfriend was . . . well, just *wrong*.

"I suppose I could fib about the sex therapist," Suzi-Suzi muttered. "You know, just say we're going to a friend's place for dinner, casually bring up sex during the conversation, and just let things go from there."

Kiki pulled a face. "Uh, sweetie, I don't think Chad's going to announce to someone he just met that he cries when he ejaculates and that he's got a phobia about hands on his tallywacker."

"Oh, well, I'm sure that I can work it in," Suzi-Suzi said earnestly.

"Don't you think he'll be furious at you for bringing it up?" Kiki asked.

"Oh . . . I never thought of that." One beat. "I should definitely wait for him to bring it up. And I still think the pretend dinner is the way to go. Where do you find one of these sex therapists? The only one I've heard of is Dr. Ruth, and I imagine she's quite expensive." Suzi-Suzi gasped. "Speaking of money, I need a job. Did you ever find out the name of that agent?"

"No," Kiki said, her voice drenched with instant apology. "I thought about it this morning, but then before I knew it, I was having sex with Fab. I'll find out today. I promise."

"Do you realize how lucky you are?" Suzi-Suzi gushed. "I mean, Fab is a great lover, and he doesn't cry in bed. That is *so* rare. At least in my experience."

Kiki yawned and stretched. "Do you ever just sit around and think about all the guys you've ever slept with?"

"I try not to," Suzi-Suzi said. "I've been with some really kooky men. Normal on the outside, but get them in the bedroom, and it's, like, 'Paging the psych ward.' Did I ever tell you about the guy who could only get an erection if I dressed up like Batgirl?"

"Yes," Kiki replied. "That was Chad last Halloween."

Suzi-Suzi was silent. "Oh, that's right!" One beat. "Okay, this is ridiculous. We *totally* need a sex therapist."

"I don't know," Kiki mused. "It's just kind of interesting to reflect. There's a wild new trend now in publishing. Women are writing sexual memoirs detailing *everything*. I'd never do that, but it might be interesting to have to relive each guy in order to write about him."

"Oh, my God," Suzi-Suzi cut in. "I saw this woman on one of the morning shows who wrote a whole book about her anal sex experiences. She was completely in love with her own butt. By comparison, Chad seemed almost normal."

Kiki gave the subject some philosophical focus. "You know, on second thought, I would never write a book like that. *These are the people I slept with.* I mean, it's so self-indulgent. And there's no insight. Nobody's learning anything that can improve their life. I don't even think it's that entertaining. It's like the sex version of some old person who wants to tell you what they ate that day. Pointless really."

"I suppose you're right," Suzi-Suzi agreed. "But your book would be way better than mine. They'd make yours the next *Red Shoe Diaries*. Meanwhile, Chad and I would end up on Comedy Central."

Kiki giggled. "I don't know about *that*. I suppose there have been a few memorable ones." Her mind tripped back. "In high school I had this boyfriend my junior year—Jaron. Oh, my God. *Phenomenal* kisser. I wanted to make out with him all day. And I did. We were always getting caught under a stairwell or outside in the parking lot. He had a Dodge Colt that was so small, but it didn't matter." She windmilled her legs in the air to get a few Pilates moves in for the day. "College was like, whatever. Most guys I knew stayed drunk those four years. When I took that acting class, though, the first year I moved to New York, there was this guy named Yaz."

"*Yaz*," Suzi-Suzi repeated dreamily. "I *love* that name. Why can't I date a Yaz?"

"Oh, you would *definitely* want to date this one. Not just a stud. A super stud. He could do it like nobody's business. But you know, it was almost *too* much. He just went on and on and on. Finally, I'd be like, 'Enough already! I'm getting sore, and I don't want to miss *Beverly Hills 90210*.' I dated a Chad once, too. He was okay. That man was *obsessed* with my breasts. Flattering up to a point. And then it's like, hello, there are other parts to my body. Wait a minute. Now that I think of it, he had a weird thing after he came, too. He would leave really really fast. Like a fireman who just heard the three alarm bell or something. Maybe that's just a weird sex thing with guys named Chad . . ."

Suzi-Suzi remained silent.

Kiki blabbed on. "There was this guy Johnny, too. He was the IRS agent who helped me straighten out that mess after I didn't file for three years. Pretty much blah as a lover, but he sure did love to cuddle."

"That sounds nice," Suzi-Suzi murmured from a million miles away.

"What are you doing?" Kiki demanded.

"Oh, sorry. I jumped online to look up sex therapists, and there are *so* many in New York. If all these people make a living at this, then we're in a city with some *serious* sexual problems. Ooh—here's a woman who does hypnosis sexual therapy. That sounds like fun. While he's under, maybe she can get him to stop slobbering so much when he kisses."

Kiki rolled over onto her stomach. "Okay, I am *such* a terrible friend. Do you realize that I have completely spaced out and forgotten about Danni?"

"Oh, please," Suzi-Suzi said, dismissing the subject altogether. "I talked to her before I called you. She's back at home, has a date with the George Clooney doctor tonight, and can start dancing again sometime next week. Danni Summer is fine. *We* are the ones with problems."

Kiki felt better now. She had just parted her lips to reply when a second call beeped in. The number didn't ring any bells. "I've got another call. Let me know how the hypnosis thing goes." She clicked over. "Hello?"

Heather Vandercamp was on the line. Another summer bride, and a quasi-friend from a hundred years ago who really dug deep into the past so she could have eighteen bridesmaids. Ridiculous with an upper case "R." "Kiki, how *are* you?" The voice was all faux distress. "It's Heather in Seattle. I had to call as soon as I heard."

Ugh. The Tom Brock Affair. God, she kept forgetting about it. Of course, it did happen to be the reason why she was ensconced here. "Heather, please," Kiki said reassuringly. "That situation is a complete joke. I barely know Tom Brock. I am friends with his wife, though."

"*You're* friends with Kirsten Brock?" The tone suggested that such a development ranked up there with other impossibilities like a straight husband for Liza Minnelli or an Oscar for Pamela Anderson.

"Of course," Kiki lied. She kept her tone breezy. "We've been laughing about this. As soon as the maelstrom dies down, we'll be able to go shopping again."

On the other end of the line, Heather Vandercamp was silent. Then she got to the point. "That's good." But clearly she didn't think so. "Kiki, I have some disappointing news. My mother is convinced the wedding has gotten too big. It kills me to do it, but I have to go on a bridesmaid diet." She laughed a little. "In other words, lose a few."

Kiki just lay there, fuming, the theme from *Jaws* playing inside her head. So the bridal sharks were circling. First Misty Dallin and now Heather. "Are you telling me that I'm out?"

"Deciding who to cut was *torture*," Heather said.

"And there were so many girls to consider—my sisters, my cousins, my closest friends, girls at the office." She sighed heavily. "I wish I could have *fifty* bridesmaids."

Kiki couldn't take another word. "Heather, get over yourself. On my who-gives-a-shit meter, your stupid wedding registers a flatline. That's how little I care about it. *My* concern is the nonrefundable super-saver airfare to Seattle that I already purchased. And that god-awful dress I bought. Not to mention the gifts, which I ordered way in advance from Tiffany and Co. so they could be monogrammed. By the way, personalized items *can't* be returned. And I don't believe for a second that your mother is making you cut *bridesmaids*." She put all her emphasis on the plural. "It's probably just me. I bet you have seventeen in the ceremony now."

"Actually," Heather said tartly, "it's still eighteen. I brought in an alternate to take *your* spot."

"Bitch!" Kiki screamed.

"Scandal whore!" Heather shot back.

Kiki hated to go nuclear on a blushing bride, but the girl had gone too far. "Heather, you should be smart about things and plan a wedding in direct proportion to how long the marriage will last. I give it just a few months, a year at best, so you should really consider one of those late-night Vegas chapels with the Elvis impersonators."

Heather drew in a shocked breath, then recovered

to snipe, "Is that what *you* did when you married that rich man who escaped from the nursing home?"

"Walter might've been old and disgusting, but at least he wasn't gay! Darling, you've been watching too much *Will and Grace*."

"Kippy is *not* gay!" Heather shrieked. But it was obvious that this outraged defense had scratched her throat more than once.

Kiki gave a tinkling little laugh. "Kippy is prettier than you are and manages an Ann Taylor store. Do the math, sweetheart. One plus one equals queen . . . *of denial*." And then she hung up, obliterating Heather Vandercamp from her life.

The moment Kiki rose up, her eyes fell on the *New York Post* hanging halfway off the nightstand. Damn the Internet. There was no such thing as *local* news anymore.

Quite suddenly, she felt like a caged animal, locked up in this tiny suite, waiting zombie-like for something interesting to happen—a phone call, a meal, another visit from Fab.

Of course, this couldn't go on much longer—the whole hibernation bit. Today's news was mainly a rehash of the day before yesterday's news. And as for yesterday, nothing really happened. Okay, so they booted her out of Stella McCartney. It's been covered. Ancient history. No way this nonsense could last *another* news cycle.

Kiki swiped on some lip gloss and dressed quickly. It wouldn't be wise to leave the hotel, but she could camp out in the lobby for a refreshing change of pace. Besides, Fab might wander by. And that alone was reason enough for a location switcheroo.

The elevator creaked down to the first floor.

Kiki stepped out to an ugly scene between Fab and a gorgeous younger woman. Luckily, he hadn't seen her. She scooted off to the side to keep it that way. With interest that stretched on to infinity, she sized up the situation.

The Girl: Twenty-one years old, tops. And that would be ancient, too. Probably younger. *Hopefully*, old enough to vote. She had the same exotic features as Fab—the dark hair, the dark eyes, the insanely effortless beauty. Somehow she'd managed to squeeze into a tight little baby tee with I'M BORED WITH YOU emblazoned across her chest. The shirt came up short above a skirt that should've been a belt, exposing enough bare belly to prove the bitch could drop and give you five hundred crunches and never stop smiling. Definitely Miss Universe–worthy—by way of a vice rap for prostitution, of course. In those nosebleed high heels, the only thing missing from her hooker act was the lamppost prop. How could a woman walk around dressed like that? It was disgusting.

The Boy: *Her* boy. At least a short time ago he was, all wet and steamy in the shower. Now he was red faced, agitated, and front and center with a tramp who made the back alley girls rounded up in the vice squad paddy wagon look like a cotillion raid.

If feelings matched skin tone, then right now Kiki would be a raging jungle green. But this time it had nothing to do with Fango mud and everything to do with jealousy.

"You're not staying in this hotel," Fab was saying. He beamed a look to kill over the girl's shoulder at a smug, smirking party-boy type lurking several steps behind.

Kiki recognized him. It was Zac Toledo, basically the male version of Paris Hilton without the trust fund. The columns tracked his moves. And they were easy to track because they didn't change up very often. He club-hopped, he danced, he slept around.

"We were here last night," the girl hissed. "The bed's already been broken in, so what does it matter?" She challenged him with wild, angry eyes.

Fab's face became a kaleidoscope of feelings revealed: hurt, anger, guilt, regret, disappointment. The whole gamut.

"Don't worry," the girl went on bitterly. "I'm sure Zac didn't do anything to me that you didn't do to my classmate, Tiffany Lynn." She grinned, because she knew that her verbal cruise missile had hit its target. And blown him to smithereens.

Fab conflicted metamorphosed into Fab devastated.

That's when Kiki knew for certain. That's when her heart started to break, too. Because he was as easy to read as a child's big-letter storybook.

Fab loved this girl.

From: kiki@misstexas95.com
To: breckin@withthisring.com
Subject: Cinderella's Castle!

Breckin!

I'm SO over the winter wedding idea. That can be SUCH a dreary time. I mean, the weather is totally unpredictable, some people go through holiday depression, and let's face it, there is no busier time than the Christmas season. Who has time for a wedding? Guess what I'm thinking? You never will. Disney World! Oh, my God! It could be so fabulous. Julia can get married in Cinderella's Castle, and Roman can be her prince. Okay, I'm swooning just thinking about it. Find out more on Disney World. It's not just for kids anymore. Haven't you seen the commercials?

Air Kisses,
Kiki

Chapter Twelve

The cackle came courtesy of Zac Toledo, a postcard-perfect image of LA cool in his distressed/paint-splashed Grail polo and destroyed-wash Chip & Pepper jeans.

Fab lunged toward him, like a lion pumped up for a fresh kill. "Hey, buddy—you might want to wait outside."

Zac disregarded the suggestion in that infuriating way that only twenty-year-old boys who think they're God's gift can.

The girl pressed her hands against Fab's chest in a begging attempt to stop him from removing Zac by force. "Screw Affair!" she shrieked. "We don't have to stay here! I don't even *want* to stay here anymore! There are a thousand hotels in this city! Every last one of them better than this hellhole!"

"Serafina!" Fab yelled back. "What are you doing? This guy's a jerk, and he's just using you."

"Well, if anyone should know about a guy using girls, then it would be you," she fired right back.

"This isn't about me," Fab said.

"Exactly," Serafina snapped triumphantly. "It's about *me*. Which means it's none of your business."

"You're my sister," Fab said quietly, his voice close to being sinister. "It will *always* be my business."

The floodgates of relief opened up, and Kiki got washed away by the most wonderful feeling in the world. Not his *lover*, but his *sister*! Oh, thank God! For a minute there . . .

Kiki swept into the Tomba sibling dustup like a fairy godmother, giving Fab a secret look that translated *Let me handle this.* She smiled at the girl, who, up close, was practically Fab in glorious female form. "Serafina—what a lovely name. For an equally lovely girl." She put out a hand.

Serafina warily accepted it. "Who are you?"

Kiki glanced around. There were guests lurking about, taking in the family drama as if it were a new reality show. Hmm. Never can be too careful. "I'm Jennifer Aniston."

Serafina pulled a face. "No, you're not."

"Yes, I am, dear. Check the register if you must."

"You're that skank from the *Post*."

Kiki hooked an arm around Serafina's shoulder, dug her nails into her flesh just enough to let the girl know that *skank* was not appreciated, and gently led her away from Fab. "That's all a terrible misunderstanding. Sort of like that skirt you're wearing. Of course, you didn't *mean* to put it on and walk out the door looking like you'd do anything for fifty dollars and a dime bag of pot."

Serafina stopped in her tracks. "Excuse me, but I don't even know you. So why are you in my face?"

Kiki simply gave her an empathetic smile. "I, too, have a brother."

Serafina thawed slightly. "Is he overprotective? Does he basically track your every move like some stalker? Does he think every guy you've ever dated is an asshole?"

"Not so much," Kiki answered. "He's younger, and we don't even live in the same region."

Serafina gave her a dumb look. "So what's your point?"

"My point is this . . . brothers have a finely tuned radar for creepy guys. It's not *any* guy that he wants to keep you away from. Just the bad ones. Think about it. If you were with a quality, stand-up guy, then Fab would feel *relieved*. Not only would you be with someone fantastic who'd look out for you, but you'd be off the market for the Zac Toledos of the world."

The look on Serafina's face said she was listening. Sort of. "How do you know Zac?"

"Oh, honey," Kiki said, laughing the laugh of the weary. "Zac is not a person. He's a type. Trust me. I know all about the Zac brand of boy." She snapped her fingers in a homegirl Z-snap formation. "Been there. Done that. Got the soundtrack." Then she leaned in conspiratorially. "Explain this to me. What guy with half a brain in his head would bring a girl to her own brother's hotel? Okay, it'd be one thing if Fab owned the Waldorf. You know, a place so big that you could easily keep missing each other. But Affair?" Kiki shook her head in disbelief. "Please. This hotel is so small that Fab probably knew what you were up to before you even got out of the cab! Was it Zac's idea to come here?"

Serafina nodded.

"Figures," Kiki sniffed. "He probably thought you could get a free room."

Serafina shot a cool glance over to Zac, ignoring Fab entirely. "Guys can be so lame."

"Yes, they can. If we had more time—say, the rest of the afternoon—I'd tell you about my ex-husband, the two guys who sank my trust fund, the pervert who thought I was clueless about the hidden camera in his bedroom . . . or we could just sit quietly and discuss Ben Affleck."

This got a laugh. A real one. "Did you date him, too?"

"No, but sometimes a girl just has a feeling."

Serafina beamed a glare at Fab. "He treats me like I'm still in eighth grade."

"Just think about what I said," Kiki advised. "If

you were with a decent guy, you wouldn't be getting any static from big brother over there."

Another look to Zac. This time Serafina melted a little. "Zac is cool, though. The columns mention him all the time. And he's *so* cute."

"He is now," Kiki agreed. "I'll give you that. But wait until the heroin addiction sets in. We'll be having a different conversation one year from now." She paused a beat to allow this jaw-dropper to sink in, then moved on. "So you have classes with Tiffany Lynn? She's a friend of mine."

"Really? Are you a stripper, too?"

It was all coming back to Kiki now—how annoying younger siblings could be. "No, I'm an actress."

"Do you play strippers?"

"I haven't yet, but I'm not opposed to the idea," Kiki replied sunnily. "Especially now when I really need the work."

Serafina smiled shrewdly. "Do you subscribe to the way-to-a-man's-heart-is-through-his-family theory? Is that the reason for this big-sister act?"

"First of all, it's 'the way to a man's heart is through his stomach.' And I can't cook. So there goes that. But believe me. Fab's not the motivation here. When I see a beautiful young girl with bad taste in guys walking around poorly dressed, it's my *duty* to get involved. I was runner-up for Miss America in 1995."

"I was only eight that year, but I remember watching." Serafina's eyes went wide. "Wait a minute. Are you the one who did the dramatic monologue from *St. Elmo's Fire*?"

Kiki gave her an upbeat nod. Finally! A viewer who remembered *something* besides Miss California.

"News flash: It's really better to sing," Serafina said.

Kiki blanched. This girl did *not* need bitch training wheels. She was definitely ready for prime time.

"I think I'll go upstairs and pack now. *Obviously*, Zac and I are changing hotels."

"So after all of this spectacle and drama you're going to stay with that . . . night creature?" Kiki asked.

"*If* I decide to kick Zac to the curb, I'm not going to give my brother the satisfaction of thinking he had *anything* to do with it." Serafina punctuated the grand announcement with a bounce of her hair. She started off, then swung back around. "Mind if I give *you* some advice on the subject of men? As it relates to my brother, of course."

Kiki saw a gleam of something in Serafina's dark eyes. And it wasn't kindness. She steeled herself as she nodded.

"Don't get too comfortable in the role of girlfriend. Or whatever it is you are to him. Fab tends to bore easily. And I don't think a *runner-up* has what it takes to hold his attention for very long."

"Don't count on it," Kiki shot back. No way was this little strumpet going to get the best of her. "Chances are, when you're crying on Fab's shoulder after Zac dumps *you*, I'll be the one handing you tissues."

Serafina's Tomba-perfect lips parted in surprise. The look on her face said the last word was *always* hers. Now the qualifier *almost always* had to be employed. She stomped away in a huff.

Kiki made a beeline for the front desk to join Fab.

"Thanks for stepping in," he said, drinking deep on a Red Bull. "I was about to kill her. Or him. Maybe both of them." His neck was pulsing with aggression.

Kiki questioned the lightning jolt of Red Bull at a time like this but said nothing. "She's at that age where you can't tell a girl *anything*."

"Serafina's *always* been at that age."

"Zac's nothing but a phase," Kiki said. "But the more you object the more attractive he'll seem to her."

Fab shot up his brow. "Then maybe I should go tell her I'd like him to be my brother-in-law."

Skillfully, Kiki robbed the Red Bull and finished it off. He didn't need anymore. She did. "Now there's a plan."

Fab gave her a meaningful look. "The day started off much better than it's become."

"And you're surprised?" Kiki asked silkily. "Our shower scene is going to be pretty hard to top."

"Is that a challenge?"

Kiki threw down the gauntlet. "That depends. Are you up for it?"

He smiled at her, took back the Red Bull can, realized it was empty, and crushed it into his palm. "Oh, don't worry. I'll rise to the occasion." And with that he took her hand, leading her toward the stairwell, and, ultimately, directly into it. He was silent the whole way. Until the door closed.

"I'm getting addicted to you," Fab said.

Kiki felt it. The vivid brightness of the crucial moment. The rush of the push forward. The tempering that comes from not holding back.

Hungrily, Fab pressed his mouth to hers.

She breathed to the rhythm, and his deep knowingness of the beat made the most delicious music as the heat and wetness of her tongue melted into his.

Suddenly—and painfully for her—he pulled back, outlining her mouth with the cool satin of his fingertip. "I'm not getting any work done. I might have to evict you."

Kiki pretended to be hurt. She did her best breathy bombshell voice. "Me? I'm just a girl who expects good service when I stay at a hotel. That's all." Somewhere in heaven, Monroe was smiling down.

Fab sucked gently on her lower lip for a few seconds, then let go. "How do you like us at Affair so far?"

"You're very . . . what's the word . . . *accommodating*." She grinned at their inside joke, turning her head to throw a glance to the first set of stairs. Several flights up was her room and her bed. Soon to be their bed. Kiki started up.

But Fab stopped her. He shook his head. "I can't wait that long." His hands began to work fast on the hook, button, and zipper of his slacks.

There were manners to uphold, conventions to be followed, rules that a woman lived by . . . if she wanted a man's true and total respect. Saying no to a stairwell blow job was certainly one of them. But those thoughts were for tomorrow or the next day. Any other time than right now.

Kiki looked around, still horrified by the danger of what he wanted her to do, yet fearful that the moment might pass without her taking advantage of it.

It was a simple one, two step. Fab's zipper went down; Fab's cock went up. Fully erect and hot, straining in anticipation, rearing for attention. His eyes were smiling. So were his lips. Both were saying *Look what you've done to me*.

Kiki eased down onto the third step and reached out to grip him. She used both hands, amazed by his pulsating pride, thrilled by his continued expansion against her fingers. And then her mouth widened in welcome as she took him into it.

Fab let out a low growl of satisfaction.

Kiki thought nothing she'd ever heard could be more reassuring. She locked her lips around him, the desire to please a force all its own—overpowering, raging, enslaving. Her mind captured the finer points of the seedy scene—a decadent public encounter that couldn't wait a few steps or an elevator ride—as her mouth captured him, alternately teasing his engorged tip and swallowing his long shaft.

The sudden clatter of feet reverberated all around them. Someone was coming down the stairs.

Kiki's face went hot with alarm. She released him quickly and stood up to compose herself.

"Shit!" Fab cried, laughing as he struggled to force the erection back into his pants. Just in the nick of time, he got the zipper up, but the teeth of the metal were working overtime at the strain.

Kiki giggled uncontrollably. Even fully clothed, Fab's arousal was so apparent that only one word could accurately describe it—*obscene*, at least to the public-at-large.

Fab broke into a casual whistle and turned to face the wall.

And then the mystery woman rounded the last flight, incognito in her scarf and sunglasses, stopping at the very top to survey the situation. The expression on her face indicated that she came to the correct conclusion about what had been going on.

Kiki was swamped by embarrassment.

The woman let out a gasp of disgust and marched back up the stairs.

"Wait!" Kiki yelled. "I want to talk to you!" And she took off after her, leaving Fab to stare at the wall until the tent in his pants subsided enough to brave a public appearance.

"Hey, what about me?" Fab asked.

Kiki halted for a moment, peering down to see the wounds of abandonment on his face. "Think about your parents having sex." And then she lurched up the stairs.

"Oh, God! That's gross!" Fab exclaimed. One beat. Two beats. Three beats. "But I think it's working!"

By now Kiki was long gone, taking the steps two at a time in order to catch up. Finally, just as the woman reached her floor and slipped through the stairwell exit and into the carpeted corridor, Kiki reached out to stop her, gasping, "It's not what you think!"

The mystery woman recoiled from Kiki's touch.

"Okay, maybe it was. But that's the first time. In public, I mean. I've done it before, obviously. Anyway, all that stuff in the *Post* was a total lie."

"Why are you telling me this?"

Kiki thought about her answer. "Because you think

I'm this horrible woman, and I'm not." She sighed, extending a hand. "Let's start over. I'm Kiki Douglas."

At first, the woman regarded Kiki's hand as if it were a jagged edge. Then she accepted it, shaking firm and fast. "Jackie Dickinson." The voice was troubled, and with it came a shadow of vulnerable entreaty sweeping across what was visible of the woman's face.

Kiki let a few seconds of silence pass. "Are you up for a cup of coffee?"

Jackie seemed almost grateful for the invitation. The sigh that came next was a lonely one. "Why not? I've had it with daytime TV. I just made a fresh pot, too."

Jackie was booked in the Playpen, a suite much larger than Kiki's Mistress Hideaway. It featured a separate Jacuzzi, separate seating area, and better views of the bustling Meat Packing District.

Kiki offered Jackie an awkward half smile as she sipped java from an Affair mug and wondered where to start. Did she swim the laps of perfunctory small talk or just dive into the deep end? Clearly they were both in hiding at this hotel. So they must have something in common.

"Okay, I know why I'm here," Kiki launched without preamble. "It was a simple case of try-to-get-away-from-the-asshole-photographers, and this happened to be the next door I walked through. I mean, it was completely random. I could've just as easily marched into a T.G.I. Friday's. What about you?"

Jackie gave her a studied glance. "I'm recovering from plastic surgery and don't want to be seen. The way I figure it, any friends I might run into here shouldn't want to be seen either."

Kiki suppressed a yelp of delight. The subject door had been opened. Time for the cross-examination. "Face-lift?" she asked in a knowing, clipped, almost surgical tone. She'd seen hours of *Extreme Makeover*, and *The Swan*, plus all the footage of Carnie Wilson's gastric bypass surgery. In some circles—all of them Third World, of course—she might be able to pass herself off as a medical professional of the self-improvement variety. You know, in a pinch.

Jackie shook her head. "Brow lift."

Kiki studied her carefully. The skin was baby pink. "Chemical peel?"

"Microdermabrasion."

Hmm. She concentrated on the area under the eyes. No dramatically visible lines there. "CosmoPlast?"

"Thermage."

Well, her eyeliner was *way* too cover-girl perfect. This was a no-brainer. "Permanent makeup?"

"Just Bobbi Brown."

Okay, she had the next one. A total bull's-eye. Those nice, plump lips. The woman was practically Lisa Rinna, Meg Ryan, Barbara Hershey, and Lara Flynn Boyle all rolled into one. And she seemed to take the less invasive approach when choosing her procedures. "Collagen?"

"Fat infusions."

Wrong again! Ugh. That trim waistline. Hardly anyone Jackie's age had one that enviable. They all had the dreaded little paunch. "Tummy tuck?"

"Liposculpting."

Wow. Her last chance. Think hard. Think shrewd. Think Joan Rivers. Ah. The smooth neck. So many women showed their age there. "Neck lift?"

"South Beach Diet."

Kiki grimaced. Shit! Zero for eight. Obviously, she needed to pay closer attention to those makeover shows. She made an instant personal pact: No more babbling with Suzi-Suzi while doing high-tech medical research.

Jackie's almost grin was all knowing. "Don't worry. Your turn is coming. I didn't look like you when I was your age, but that doesn't mean you won't need everything I did. Maybe more. You'll probably start earlier, though." She zeroed in on Kiki's perfect C-cup breasts. "Looks like you already have."

"Oh, I went to Brazil for these," Kiki admitted easily. "Dr. Mendez did them. He used a special teardrop implant that has natural give. It's very realistic, not like a rock at all." She pushed her chest forward. "Do you want to feel?"

Jackie drew back stiffly. "No thanks."

Kiki was mystified. Usually, everybody wanted to feel her breasts. In fact, Bill, the sweet UPS driver in her building, was *thisclose* to giving them as a present to his wife. He asked to touch them practically every time he delivered a package.

All of a sudden, Kiki regarded Jackie carefully. "May I ask you something?"

Jackie sipped her coffee. "Go ahead."

"The other day you said to me, 'Women like you make me sick.' What did you mean by that?"

"Well, just look at you," Jackie vented with mild disgust. "You walk around half naked with your pouty breasts and your perfect size two body and your fat-free ass. You're not a woman. You're a candy counter. It's bad enough that men compare every woman they're with to strippers and porn queens. But at least that's fantasy. You're live and in person. You make it harder for real women."

Kiki beamed brightly. She was still somewhere at the beginning. "I'm actually a size four. But you said *two*! That's one of the best things I've heard all week." Kiki nodded thoughtfully, considering the rest while she drank her coffee. "Now I must say, I resent the implication that I make things harder for *real* women. I *am* a real woman. When I won runner-up in the 1995 Miss America Pageant, our opening number that year was a routine to 'Sisters Are Doin' It for Themselves.' Get this straight—it doesn't get any more *real* than that!" Kiki sang a few bars of the funky feminine force anthem by Aretha Franklin and Annie Lennox. " 'Standing on their own two feet . . . ringing on their own bells . . .' "

Jackie seemed to be grooving just a bit, no doubt remembering the indelible hook of the song. Then, quite abruptly, she stopped herself. "I suppose you're going to tell me that you consider yourself to be a feminist." Her voice was mocking.

"Of *course*!" Kiki enthused, embracing the loaded term with all the comfort of a warm cashmere blanket on a chilly winter night. "I'm a feminist from my waxed eyebrows to my Jimmy Choos!" She tilted her head. "Where did it all go so wrong for feminism?" Her voice went up an octave as the ponderous thought entered the Playpen ether. Kiki nodded seriously, lips pursed in professorial assessment. "Personally, I think it was the underarm and leg hair. *That* was a tough sell."

Jackie, having just taken in some coffee, almost did a perfect spit take. "You're trivializing the entire feminist movement down to *body hair*?" The impression lingered that Jackie Dickinson had just heard the words of a complete simpleton failing miserably in an attempt to pass herself off as a public intellectual.

Undaunted, Kiki charged on, a fiery one-woman march. "You're editorializing. I didn't mean it that way *exactly*. Well, maybe a little. You see, every girl out there supports the *idea* of feminism. I think it's only a slim minority that dress butch, hate men, look down on girls who dress sexy, and sue whenever a guy at the office says, 'What kind of perfume is that?' But they're a *loud* minority, and they polarize the whole movement. Take my friend, Suzi-Suzi. She's a total feminist. But she's afraid of the label because of that fat pill-popper Rush Limbaugh. Didn't he come up with *feminazi*? Well, Suzi-Suzi loves the movie *Schindler's List*. She bawls her eyes out every time she sees it, and she doesn't want to have anything to do with the Nazis, so she says she's not a feminist. But deep down, she really is. And there's my new friend, Tiffany Lynn. You'd love her. She's a stripper but sweet as s'mores and smart as a whip. A *complete* feminist. Totally radical. She's flashing the goods because the pay is so amazing. She only has to work one week a month and can spend the rest of the time studying at NYU. All because men turn into ATM machines when they see a pair of boobs. Now if you ask me, *that's* an example of asserting your female power. Anyway, it all comes down to *owning* your sexuality. And girls helping one another. That's key, too. Everybody thinks Miss America girls are catty, that we're constantly scratching each other's eyes out. But we're really very supportive. Okay, there's the occasional bad apple. I remember a Miss Missouri who stole my tit tape. But she had a horseface and nobody knew how on earth she got in. I think her kleptomania was a direct result of her insecurity. And, I must admit, I still hate that bitch Miss California for winning the title. But that's just human nature. Everybody wants to win. I mean, I still hate Barry Waltman for beating me in the seventh grade spelling bee. I missed 'annul.' Spelled it with two 'Ls'. Can you believe that? If only Britney had been screwing up back then, I would've nailed it." Kiki drew in a deep breath and launched back in to more speed-talking. "I don't know. I guess the point is this—at the end of the day, we're all just . . . *girls*— the good, the bad, the young, the old, the pretty, the ugly, the virtuous, the slutty, the rich, the poor. You know? We're all just *girls*. By the way, I think you look fantastic. And I hope you went through all this agony for yourself and not for some jerky husband. I mean, too many girls out there waste energy fighting each other and not fighting against the age-old double standard. But, hey, I'm guilty of the same. I run around like crazy, killing myself on the treadmill, starving myself on the Leek Soup Diet, which, just as a quick aside, is *amazing*. You can drop five pounds in a single weekend." Kiki's voice slipped to a whisper. "Not to be gross, but if you go on it, don't make any special plans because you'll *definitely* need your bathroom time." She winked confidentially and charged back to make her point, sighing dramatically. "Where was I? Oh, the double standard. So here we are, just trying to keep up. You're trying to keep up with girls younger than you. I'm trying to keep up with girls younger than me. And for what? The fight can't be won! There will always be someone younger, prettier, thinner, whatever. Yet we still drive ourselves insane. Look at you. Tucked away in here like you're in the witness protection program, dealing with the recovery miseries of being nipped and tucked, hissing at me in the hallway like an alley cat. Meanwhile—and I bet all the money left in my friend Danni's Gucci boot box on this—your husband's probably out of shape, bald, and has hair growing out of his nose. Well, we don't see him frantically searching to his left, to his right, behind his back, and everyplace else to see what other men look like. To him, Richard Gere is Richard Gere. It's got nothing to do with him. But with us? We all think we have to be Cindy fucking Crawford." Kiki sank back, practically exhausted from the rant. "You know, the weight of the body image world is crushing. It's like that fifty-ton block the Road Runner drops on Wile E. Coyote."

In a sudden and surprisingly affectionate gesture, Jackie reached out to squeeze Kiki's hand. "I take it all back. I *like* you."

Kiki was flooded with relief. "Oh, thank God! I've been going crazy thinking you thought I was awful. I don't know why it mattered to me so much. There's just something about you that makes me yearn for your approval. Isn't that strange? You have a certain regal quality. Maybe that's it. If you ask me, your husband's a total idiot for not worshiping you."

Jackie smiled warmly. "You're right, dear. About *everything*."

From: breckin@withthisring.com
To: kiki@misstexas95.com
Subject: Re: Cinderella's Castle!

Kiki,

Okay, doll, can we stop and take a deep breath? You've got me researching New York weddings, yacht weddings, winter weddings, and Disney World weddings. I'm basically running in every direction but the one these nuptials seem to be firmly planted in, cupcake, which is . . . and fix yourself a nice strong drink before you read this . . . TEXAS! That's right. Your brother is having a FREAKING TEXAS WEDDING! I'm telling you this for these reasons:

A) You need to face reality and accept the fact that Texas is calling you home. Besides, everybody expects you here because they know you're out of work.

B) You secretly want Sydney's new love Alex to be bald and fat since you dated him a million years ago, but he's more scrumptious than ever, so you need to prepare yourself.

C) If I don't stop you now you'll have me running numbers on European weddings next.
PS Did you really play Tom Brock's . . . ahem . . . trombone? I WANT DETAILS!

Big Hug,
Breckin

Chapter Thirteen

Kiki returned to her Mistress Hideaway and opened the door to hear the screaming rings of the suite's phone. She smiled, imagining Fab in the stairwell making SOS calls on his cell. There was a mad dash to answer, followed by a breathlessly melodic, "Hello?"

"Is this Kiki Douglas?" Unrecognizable voice. Female, butch, tough, raspy (obviously a smoker), pushy. May or may not be lesbian. Kiki was *not* one to judge.

She ran the numbers . . . *journalist*. Her stomach did that elevator thing, and she experienced a moment of total and sudden fear. Oh, God! What should she do? Hang up! A brilliant idea. Wait a minute. No. If the dirt digger had the gumshoe skills to find her, then a dial tone would hardly get her off the trail.

Thinking fast, Kiki hatched a plan. Unfortunately, this wasn't one of those video phones, so her boobs couldn't help her. She would have to rely on . . . her acting skills. Yes! She remembered her finest moment as a thespian. A steamy love scene on *The Guiding Light*. A costar with terrible breath. Kiki had improvised the blocking and thrown her head back in a pantomime of ecstasy, skillfully avoiding the rancid fumes of the actor too cheap to buy a tin of Altoids. The director had even praised her for showing extra passion.

Kiki's next utterance loomed with monumental importance. She felt the mind-strain of the pressure. She felt paranoid and hunted down, too. The tabloid fever was redlining on the thermometer. And this was her sweating it out.

"I am maid," Kiki said in her best Pakistani accent. "I clean room."

A booming silence.

Kiki felt bathed in relief. Had the reporter bought the act? Well, she should have. Kiki did a *great* Pakistani accent. Especially for her first time ever adopting one.

"You expect me to buy that housekeeper shit? I'm calling for your reaction to the Tom Brock story. This is a chance to give people *your* side of it."

Damn. The bitch couldn't be fooled so easily. Hmm. A formidable foe. Definitely of the Woodward and Bernstein school of crafty, no-stone-unturned dogmatic reportage. Of all the rotten luck! Why couldn't a reporter from *Us Weekly* be on the line?

They would've completely bought her Pakistani routine and then just made up a quote. Suddenly panicked, Kiki slammed down the receiver. She began to count. Five, four, three, two . . . and it started ringing again.

Oh, God, it was the worst feeling in the world—to be hunted down like an animal. They probably had the hotel staked out. Somehow she had to trick them into believing that she wasn't here anymore. Yes! An elaborate sting operation. Like Jennifer Garner on *Alias*, only without all the kicking and falling out of airplanes.

To escape the seemingly endless and blistering phone jangles, Kiki raced into the bathroom and shut the door, crouching down, cellular in hand. No way could she do this alone. This was a job for the lace mafia. Suzi-Suzi, Danni, and the new gangster princess among them . . . Tiffany Lynn.

Kiki jabbed in the first speed dial code.

"I can't talk," Suzi-Suzi whispered after the second ring. "We're at the sex therapist's office, and she's got Chad under hypnosis."

"This is an emergency!" Kiki yelled.

"*So is this*," Suzi-Suzi hissed, still talking in a hushed whisper. "I just found out that in high school Chad got caught masturbating in the library with a *National Geographic*. That's why he cries. The semen emission triggers the pain of a repressed memory. That's also why he doesn't like a hand on his pecker. It's all related to the shame of the library incident."

Kiki gripped the mobile so tight she thought the casing might break. Her well-meaning friend always came through in the end, but sometimes it took a goddamn sledgehammer. "Suzi-Suzi, listen to me. The tabloid vultures are swooping down. They know where I am! I need your help."

"Oh, my God!" Suzi-Suzi cried softly. "Okay, hold on."

Kiki could hear her talking, obviously to the sex therapist.

"Excuse me, I have to go right now. My best friend's in a terrible bind. Keep working with him, though. And since you already have him under, suggest that he not slobber so much when he kisses. Oh, one more thing. When Chad goes down on me, all he does is lick like a baby kitten. A girl needs more stimulation than that. You know, some finger action would be nice. Maybe a more assertive use of the tongue, too." One beat. "I'm on my way." Click.

Kiki jabbed in the second speed dial code.

A groggy Danni answered, slurring her hello.

"You sound awful!" Kiki cried.

"No, I feel great. George Clooney gave me Vicodin. He's so wonderful. I think I love him. I've completely forgotten about the hedge fund guy. I can't even remember his name now."

"Thad Davis," Kiki filled in.

"Oh, yeah . . . Thad," Danni murmured, totally blotto.

"What is this doctor's real name?"

"I have no idea." Danni giggled. "I just call him George. He doesn't seem to mind."

Kiki spoke in a loud, modulated tone. "Danni, I want you to listen to me very carefully. I need you to pull yourself together and come to Affair as soon as possible. I'm in trouble, and I need your help."

"What's wrong?" Danni asked, still loopy but showing audible signs of sobriety.

"I'll explain when you get here."

Kiki signed off and raced into the main suite to grab the note Tiffany Lynn had left, wincing at the incessant jangle of the suite phone as she darted back inside the bathroom and slammed the door. Her finger worked fast on the keypad.

"Hello?" Tiffany Lynn on the first ring. Not whispering and not drugged. Good news all around.

"Tiffany Lynn, thank God you answered!"

"Kiki? How funny. I was just thinking about you. I hope you didn't have *too* bad of a hangover."

"OhmyGodthere'sbeennotimeforoneofthosebutifIdidhaveoneIhighlyrecommendgreatsexinashowerasacure-all," Kiki said, suddenly speaking in impatiently fused word strings. She sucked in a deep breath to slow down. "I need your help."

"Anything," Tiffany Lynn said. And she meant it. The girl was gold.

But a big problem hung overhead like a mushroom cloud. Kiki had the workers but no plan for them to work. Her razor brain began to cut. After a few long seconds of superconcentration, the sting started to take shape.

"I need a car," Kiki blurted. "Do you have a car?"

"I don't. I'm sorry," Tiffany Lynn said, sounding as crushed as a little girl who just found out that the My Little Pony factory had ceased all production. "Wait a second." Brighter now. "Kirby has a car." Hot damn. My Little Pony was back in business. "He keeps it at his mother's house in New Jersey."

"Will he let you borrow it?"

"Not a chance," Tiffany Lynn said automatically. "But I'll just make him come along. That way you'll have a car *and* a driver."

"You're a total lifesaver," Kiki gushed.

Tiffany Lynn giggled. "No problem. Now, it's not the fanciest ride. Can you deal with a Ford Taurus?"

"That's perfect!" Kiki yelped. She needed something hopelessly bland, the kind of car that would blur into traffic to such a degree that it might as well be invisible. A Taurus fit the bill perfectly. "What color?"

"Silver."

"Oh, my God. That's brilliant. I am *so* in love with Kirby right now."

Tiffany Lynn giggled again. "I don't know about that. It's pretty boring if you ask me. But it's spotless inside and out. He hand waxes it and shampoos the carpet every weekend. Kirby says the Taurus is the man's man car of today. Kind of like the Pontiac Trans Am was back in the eighties."

"Perfect. Just get to the hotel as fast as you can." Kiki hung up and felt her heart go bang. Oh, God, this *had* to work.

Within the hour, the *Mission: Impossible* team was packed into the tiny Mistress Hideaway suite: Suzi-Suzi, looking very Emma Peel in a form-fitting unitard; Danni, hobbling on crutches and fighting off sleep; Tiffany Lynn, knocking them all out in a simple college-girl-shops-at-the-Gap ensemble; and Kirby, playing impromptu bartender as he fetched Diet Cokes from the minibar for the girls.

Kiki experienced a dart of excitement. She felt just like John Forsythe from *Charlie's Angels*, dictating an assignment to the sexy undercover detectives. Tiffany Lynn could be Jill, the gorgeous one. Suzi-Suzi could be Kelly, the model. And Danni could be Sabrina, the smart one. Hmm. That left Kirby in the role of Bosley, the dorky one. Oh, well. Hopefully, he wouldn't mind.

She paced the floor in front of them, like an anxious cat testing the limits of a cage. "It has to be timed perfectly. Like an intricately choreographed ballet."

Kirby raised a hand. "Uh, you've got two strippers

in the room. All I'm saying is the ballet analogy might offend." He shrugged impossibly broad shoulders. "Just a thought."

"Okay . . . as I was saying," Kiki went on, "it needs to be like . . . an intricately choreographed . . . lap dance."

Kirby gave her the thumbs-up sign.

Tiffany Lynn beamed.

Danni stared back like a postsurgery lobotomy patient.

"Hold on a second," Suzi-Suzi cut in. "Let's back up. How did these bottom-feeders find out you were here in the first place?"

Kiki halted. It was a good question. But she'd had no time to consider it. "Actually, I have no idea."

"Well, who *did* know you were staying here?" Tiffany Lynn asked. "That's a good place to start."

Kiki nodded in agreement to her logical suggestion. "Okay, everyone here in this room . . . Fab . . ."

Kirby pretended to have a tickle in his throat as he coughed out the word "asshole."

Kiki paused to shoot him a warning look, then continued reciting the list of possible suspects. "My new friend Jackie Dickinson . . . Fab's sister Serafina . . . uh . . . that should be it. Everybody else thinks I'm Jennifer Aniston."

"I don't trust him," Danni said.

"Trust who?" Suzi-Suzi wondered.

"Fab," Kirby confirmed. "He sells Kiki out to the

tabs, and his hotel gets the kind of publicity you can't even buy."

"Now let's not jump to conclusions," Tiffany Lynn said, trying to provide the voice of reason.

"Oh, go ahead," Kirby said hotly. "Rush to your boyfriend's defense."

"He's *not* my boyfriend," Tiffany Lynn fired back. "I've been over him for weeks."

"Well, you were going to have his name tattooed on your ass cheek," Kirby sneered.

"I only *thought* about doing that," Tiffany Lynn clarified. "I also thought about putting Johnny Depp's name on my butt. Does that make *him* my boyfriend, too?"

Kirby stood up. "Just admit it. You're still hung up on the guy."

Tiffany Lynn gazed up at the ceiling. "This is so retarded." Then she looked at Kirby. "How can I be hung up on Fab if I had sex with you, like, an hour ago? What does it take to prove that I'm into you?"

"For starters, you can stop saying his name all the time," Kirby snapped.

"What are you talking about? I hardly ever mention it!" Tiffany yelled.

Kirby pointed at her. "That's a lie! I asked you how I was in bed, and you said his name."

Tiffany Lynn shook with frustration. "I said you were fabulous!"

"Exactly!" Kirby thundered. "*Fabulous*. What are

the first three letters in the word? F-A-B. You just had to get it in, didn't you?"

"Okay, I *love* these two," Suzi-Suzi announced to no one in particular. "They are *so* entertaining."

Kiki held up her hands. "Tiffany Lynn's right. It doesn't make sense to jump to conclusions and blame Fab. And I'm not just saying that because I had sex with him this morning."

She struggled to be heard. "Can we please focus for just a minute. This is a serious accusation." She put hand over heart. "I know . . . that Fab wouldn't do that to me. He just wouldn't. It could so easily have been a member of the hotel staff. I don't know. Maybe one of them figured out that I wasn't Jennifer Aniston."

"You think?" It was Danni, finally showing humor and signs of life.

"But it doesn't matter anymore," Kiki said. "The fact is, the media knows where I am. And that's why all of you are here. To trick them into thinking I'm somewhere else."

Kirby whistled. "I realize I'm just part of the crew here, but I see a big gaping hole in your plan, sweetheart."

Kiki took a mildly annoyed say-what-you've-got-to-say breath.

"We're going to all this trouble to send the media on a wild-goose chase after a fake Kiki, right?"

She nodded.

"If the snitch is here at the hotel, whether it's *that guy* or a member of *that guy's* staff, then you're still right back where you started from," Kirby lectured.

"But I won't be in the same spot," Kiki argued. "I'm going to *insist* on changing suites." She smiled haughtily, as if she'd just solved not only her problem, but any dilemma plaguing the Middle East as well.

Kirby gave her a dumb look, putting thumb and forefinger to the side of his face in a telephone pantomime. "Hey, Page Six, she's on the third floor now." Then he pretended to hang up.

The collective glances from the girls said it without saying it: The man's got a point.

Kiki blanched. Her swallow became a gulp. Then she gave Kirby a glare that said shutting up was the polite thing to do. "Let's just stick to the plan." She turned to Tiffany Lynn. "Are you sure you're okay with public nudity?"

Tiffany Lynn returned a no-big-deal shrug. "They're just boobs. Plus, it's for a great cause."

Kirby shook his head. "No, baby." He pointed to Suzi-Suzi's chest. "*Those* are just boobs. What you've got is one of the most amazing pairs of t—"

"Let's go, angels," Kiki cut in. "It's time to prep for the mission and assume our position."

Suzi-Suzi glanced down at her cleavage. "Okay, *not* loving the new guy so much anymore."

A short time later, Kiki was regal as she walked

in advance of the team. It *would* work. It *had* to work. And when it did, one thing was certain: In the next headline cycle, the incident would be solidified in the wet newsprint of New York gossip. And she had a visual on the most obvious cover banner:

KIKI'S GREAT ESCAPE.

From: kiki@misstexas95.com
To: breckin@withthisring.com
Subject: Postcards from Paris

Breckin!

You're probably going to think, did she even READ my last e-mail, but, darling, I did, and it opened up a pathway to paradise in terms of ideas. Yes, more ideas! You were being a snarky little shit, but now I'm convinced that a European wedding is the ONLY way to go. I vote Paris. Why? Because I adore the people there. Have you read FRENCH WOMEN DON'T GET FAT? It's my new bible. I take it everywhere. Paris! It will be so magical. We have to plan a trip soon to scout locations. Of course, this means the wedding can't happen until sometime in 2006. At least. And what if we find the perfect place, and it's already booked? So it could be 2007 or even 2008. I hope Roman and Julia won't be too disappointed by the wait. Do you mind breaking the news? I'm swamped with a million things. If they put up too much of a fuss, just tell them that long engagements are good for couples.

Air Kisses,
Kiki

Chapter Fourteen

Kiki was nervous. And when the ancient elevator spit her out and into the Affair lobby, she got more nervous.

Even in full costume, she felt exposed. There was always the chance that some tabloid urchin would recognize her, that her Agent 99 plan would add up to less than zero come execution time.

She scoured the area like a ghost town sheriff looking for outlaw drifters in the Deadwood Saloon. In the corner: two lovers going at it on a plush sofa that threatened to swallow them. At the front desk: a silver-haired executive checking in with a girl who was likely born the year he finally braved his first prostate exam. Near the entrance: the fidgety desperate housewife who needed an extra Xanax because she wanted her building's FedEx driver more than her own husband.

Basically, the usual suspects. No sign of the enemy—on a visual level. A gut check revealed the same—on a metaphysical one. Kiki relaxed enough to park herself in a club chair near the window that looked onto Fourteenth Street. From right here she could watch it unfold. Outside and in.

Jackie Dickinson had provided Kiki with all the accouterments to play the role of makeover recovery victim. Hermès scarf that covered the head. Dior sunglasses that eclipsed the eyes. Postsurgery salve that gooped onto the face and left it glistening like slime. The getup got looks. And then those looks looked away. After all, everybody wanted the after. Nobody wanted the before. So Kiki was more invisible than a *Maxim* girl on a gay cruise.

The scheme had spilled into her mind like an easy jigsaw. She put the corner pieces together first. And then the rest had fallen into place.

Kiki felt a rush of excitement. The moment of truth had arrived. She watched as Kirby's silver Taurus coasted to the entrance of the hotel and parked directly behind a gleaming black Escalade.

Danni hit her mark next, hobbling up the sidewalk on aluminum crutches and loitering just outside the door.

Right on cue, Tiffany Lynn appeared, moving through the lobby at a slow bump-and-grind until she stopped dead center, flung off the Affair terry cloth robe, and stood there, gloriously nude from the waist up, La Perla thong perfection from the waist down.

A torrent of attention began to build.

Tiffany Lynn vogued through her best poses, like a Cannes A-lister who lived for the superleaded fuel of being flash-bulbed on the red-carpeted stairs of the Palais.

The massive invasion was next. Paparazzi lurking outside became paparazzi busting inside. They played instant shutterbug music for the mystery blond goddess, occasionally raising hands to the ceiling in theatrical appreciation for the naked girl's considerable visuals.

"That's Kiki Douglas!" Danni screamed.

In a millisecond, the interest in Tiffany Lynn closed down. And stayed that way. Photographer nuts were cracking as the cash burned right in front of their eyes. The bigger get was getting away. Like a swarm of locusts they moved in the direction of Danni's voice.

Outside, Suzi-Suzi stepped into view, swinging the Raquel wig that made her look just enough like Kiki to whip the image stealers into a frenzy. She timed her moment beautifully, allowing them a view that lasted a heartbeat and a half before slipping into the backseat of the Taurus and diving down.

Kirby slammed the gas. The sedan took off with a screech. By the time the last picture pig stumbled onto the sidewalk, the Taurus was weaving in and out of traffic.

"The bitch got away!" A bottom-feeder with bad teeth made the most obvious announcement of the century.

And Kiki was reading his lips, smiling wickedly. A reprieve for the moment. She glanced around, surprised that Fab hadn't turned up in the lobby during Tiffany Lynn's traveling Camisole show. The thought lingered. Where was he?

Her cellular rang.

A secret twenty bucks said it was Suzi-Suzi calling from the floor of Kirby's Taurus. But Kiki lost the bet. And she was glad to end the gamble upside down. Because it was Fab on the line. And that put things right side up again.

His voice was dry. "I just got a call from the front desk manager. Apparently, *Girls Gone Wild: New York* is filming in my lobby. I'm guessing you had something to do with that."

"First sign of trouble and you think of me? I'm offended," Kiki purred.

"That easily? Funny, I never figured you for the overly sensitive type." In the background, construction workers made lots of noise.

Kiki waited for quiet. "You sound busy. Since when do you call from job sites?"

The building ruckus morphed into street noise. "I was just checking on a new project."

"Another hotel?"

"No, a nightclub this time. It's right next door to Affair. So I'm calling it Foreign Affair."

Now Kiki could see him strutting down Fourteenth Street. "Clever. Every girl dreams of having one of those. I predict brisk business."

"Let's hope. There's a lot of money riding on this." She sensed an odd timbre in Fab's voice, something that she'd never heard before . . . genuine nervousness.

"Wait a minute. Fab Tomba *hopes*? I thought he just *knew*."

"It's a risky venture." His tone was serious. "The Gansevoort has a rooftop bar, there's Cielo, Hell, PM, Soho House, Hogs and Heifers, the Maritime. Plus, Spice Market and Pastis have big bar scenes . . ." He trailed off. "Sorry. I don't mean to be a drag. It's just that I had a tense meeting with investors today. And I'm one of them." He sighed. "Can't you tell?"

"I wouldn't worry so much about competition," Kiki said. "Nightlife crawlers are like kids on a playground. Wherever you kick the ball is where they'll run."

Fab was gliding through the lobby now, cellular to ear, speed-walking toward his office. "Nicely put. I might have to steal that."

Kiki took off in hot pursuit. "Feel free. And remember—all you need to guarantee success is a brutal door policy."

Fab laughed. "Brutal, huh?"

"I take that back. Brutal is too soft. Make it *excruciating*."

"Nightlife as social masochism," he said wryly. "I'm intrigued."

"And keep your listing out of *Fodor's*," Kiki went on. "You'll never want tourists invading the island. That's a sure sign things are going downhill."

"You know, maybe I should offer you a six-figure salary to be my velvet rope bitch."

Now it was Kiki's turn to laugh. "Ten years ago, I would've said yes to that. When do you open?"

"Next month. That's the plan. But it looks like the contractors have a year's worth of work left."

"They probably do. That doesn't mean they won't finish on time, though." She stepped inside his office to find him at his spotless desk. "Boo."

Fab glanced up. There was hesitation. "This must be a new look." He closed his mobile. "Don't get me wrong. I like it. But I prefer the green face. Reminds me of that sexy alien woman Captain Kirk slept with on *Star Trek*."

Kiki smiled. "Well, if it doesn't work out for me in New York, I'll always have a career on the Trekkie convention circuit to fall back on." She paused a beat. "Listen. I think you should be aware of something. There's been a breach in hotel security."

"I'll say," Fab said, his voice brimming with mock outrage. "Spontaneous acts of stripping are taking place in my lobby. I'd have the girl arrested, but all my guests are demanding an encore."

"I'm serious, Fab. Somebody tipped off the media that I was staying here. I think it might've been someone on your staff."

He shook his head. "No way."

Kiki started to protest.

"Not my staff. But I think I know who it was."

She waited for his answer.

"Zac Toledo. I got a call from a columnist just before I left for my investors meeting. Of course, I refused comment on everything. She got frustrated and let it slip that she already had a reliable source in Zac and that the story would run as is. The little punk pulls this shit all the time, apparently. He feeds columnists stories in exchange for mentions about himself."

Kiki knew the type. Society boys had to work much harder for the attention that girls like Paris Hilton got just for pulling dresses over their heads. "Does Serafina know?"

"At this point, I could give my sister proof that he's the Antichrist, and it wouldn't make a difference." His sigh was troubled.

"I know it must be difficult to sit on the sidelines, but it's just a phase. Most girls her age go through it. I did, too. I even lost a trust fund as a direct result of my stupidity over guys. But Serafina's stronger and smarter than I was at her age. She'll be fine.

Trust me. At the end of the day, your sister is Teflon-coated."

Fab managed a half grin. "Thanks. I needed to hear that." For a moment, he grew pensive, almost melancholy.

Kiki sat down. "What is it?"

"Nothing . . . it's . . . it's just hard for me to accept that my sister thinks that I'm like him . . . that I'm an overgrown Zac Toledo." He glanced up, and for the first time she saw him as . . . vulnerable. "I'll be the first to admit that I've got some commitment issues, but—"

"Commitment issues don't make you a Zac Toledo," Kiki assured him. "That just makes you a man. God, it makes you *human*. I've got commitment issues, too. For instance, I can't settle with a good facialist. And don't get me started on stylists and colorists." She leaned forward to whisper, "I'm a total hair *slut*."

Fab grinned. All the way this time. "I'll say this, Kiki. You do have a clever way of putting a sunny spin on things. That's why I think that book of yours is going to be a success."

Kiki paused a moment, allowing the comment ample time to evaporate. He talked about her book dream with such seriousness. It made her uncomfortable, because deep down, she knew that she would never finish it. And even if she one day managed to produce the discipline to get *something* down on paper, she'd never in a million years have the temerity to show it to anybody, especially a professional within the publishing industry. The thought alone terrified her.

"So put those thoughts out of your head," Kiki said, circling wide around the book talk and steering back toward Fab's sister. "Zac is certainly one of those creeps who breaks up with a girl by e-mail, if he even bothers to tell her that the relationship is over at all." She smiled at him shrewdly. "I'm sure all of *your* exes got a nice dinner and a lovely parting gift with their exit speech. At the very least."

Fab grinned and offered a modest, diffident shrug in a show of self-deprecating amusement, but, ultimately, the reaction revealed nothing at all. Which seemed to be a pattern with him. Revealing very little.

Kiki sat there as the Fab Tomba folklore tumbled down. The columnists had their spin. Kirby and Tiffany Lynn had theirs. Serafina got her licks in. Fab himself had a prickly nature when comparisons to Zac Toledo or any other womanizer from the same smarm pool came gurgling up. And all of it led back to the same dead-end cliché: a heartache waiting to happen. So why did she still believe that her experience with him would be totally different?

"What are you thinking about?" Fab asked. "I see a question trying to form, but you seem to be holding back."

"Oh, *I* seem to be holding back?" Kiki sniffed. "That's rich. You'll hardly tell me what your favorite color is."

"Green."

Kiki rolled her eyes skyward.

He leaned back in his chair and formed a pyramid with his fingertips. "Okay, ask me anything. Nothing's off limits. Shoot to kill."

It was her opening. She went for it. "Tell me what happened with Tiffany Lynn."

He smiled, saying nothing. But there was a wince. A slight one. "Nothing *happened*. She's a sweet girl. It just didn't work out. That's all."

"*It just didn't work out,*" Kiki repeated. "Let me give you a bit of advice. As it pertains to relationships, that's a word string you should probably delete from your vocabulary. It's almost as insulting as any apology that goes something like, *I'm sorry you feel that way.*"

Fab's smile deepened. "But those are two of my favorites."

"I have no doubt. Is that what the girl from *The Apprentice* heard, too? Didn't she come after Tiffany Lynn?"

There was an expression on Fab's face that was not far from irritation. "I'm not leaving women at the altar, Kiki. I date. I date *a lot*. What's wrong with that?"

"Nothing, I suppose," Kiki answered. "As long as

you're up-front about it and getting involved for the right reasons."

"Can you give me the Kiki Douglas version of a *right* reason to get involved?" He was getting angry, and his playboy baggage was filling up the small space of his office. Soon they would have to cut out of the room to make room for it.

"I can give you a *wrong* one," Kiki said. Enough dancing around the bush. Time to burn it. "It would be wrong to date the new dancer at Camisole because she's fresh from the West Coast and the club's number one girl. It would also be wrong to date a girl just because she's on television's hottest reality show."

"Or leading the headlines over the last few days," Fab finished. One beat. "The accusation being that I'm some kind of trophy dater who only gets off on novelty chicks." He waved his hand in a quick dismissal of the theory altogether. "Bullshit. I went out with Tiffany because for a quick minute Camisole was balm for my soul. I was stressed out and needed to loosen up after work. I walk in a club like that, and there's no asking, no begging, no charming. Just a one hundred percent guarantee that girls will get naked for me. It's a Barbie fantasy. And Tiffany Lynn's as gorgeous as they come. What man wouldn't want to go out with her? It was casual for me, but I saw her getting attached, so I cut it off before any more damage got done. I never wanted to hurt her. She's a sweetheart. As for *The Apprentice* girl, she has a name. *Amanda*. We met at a restaurant opening and went out twice. She canceled our third date and stopped returning my calls. Turns out she just wasn't that into me. Imagine that. And as for you, the fact that you've been leading the headlines in the *Post* is the *least* interesting thing about you. For once I've met a girl I can play serious verbal volley with. Sometimes it's frustrating, but it's never boring."

For long seconds, Kiki just sat there with nothing to say. And then she found the words. "Uh, I guess now is a bad time to ask for a room upgrade."

Fab grinned, leaning forward to access the information on his iMac. "The May-December suite just became available this morning. I'll set you up there." He spun around to retrieve something from a working table behind him. "I mentioned that I spoke to a few literary agents, right?"

Kiki nodded. Oh, God. The book again.

"Both expressed interest. They'd like to take a look at a proposal." Fab slid a packet across the desk. "Here's an explanation of the format and a model example to follow. Act now while your name is on people's lips. This is the kind of book that gets sold over lunch."

Kiki watched him, her chin balancing on the tips of her fingers, her elbows on the desk. "You actually think I can do this, don't you?"

"Absolutely. And I want to be on the book tour

when you go up against Bill O'Reilly." That should be an interesting match up.

Kiki held his eyes—honest eyes, and maybe, just maybe, even committed eyes . . .

From: kiki@misstexas95.com
To: numbersgeek@aol.com
    vshelton@kleinschmidtbelker
Subject: Just for Fun

Hi Girls!

Any word on the groomsmen yet? I know this sounds very seventh grade, but let's have a little fun and list our top three dream groomsmen and see if any of them match up. What a hoot!

KIKI'S GROOMSMEN WISH LIST
Brad Pitt (must have short hair and no facial hair)
Clive Owen (can show up with syphilis as long as he comes)
Michael Vartan (must go sleeveless to show his tattoo)

KIKI'S GROOMSMEN WISH LIST ALTERNATES (in the event that one or more from the main list can't fulfill their duties)
George Clooney (must agree to take me to his Italian villa after)
Jon Stewart (cute funny Jewish guys are always good in a pinch)
Jon Bon Jovi (has to sing "It's My Life" at reception)

Now it's your turn!
Air Kisses,
Kiki

Chapter Fifteen

The May-December suite was opulent, luxurious, and, at almost one thousand square feet, larger than Kiki's apartment.

A velvet curtain divided the romantic bedroom sanctuary (with an egg-shaped tub placed in front of an enormous Venetian mirror) from a separate living area complete with a dining table and a guest bathroom.

"I'm *never* leaving!" Kiki thundered as Tate followed behind, lugging her garbage bags filled with so many useless things that Suzi-Suzi had packed. "*Ever!* Do you hear me? I'm moving in."

Tate merely smiled as he struggled with her belongings, offering a respectful, "It will be our pleasure to have you."

Kiki cocked her head to one side. "By the way, how much is this room per night?"

The blank look on Tate's face matched his blank answer.

Oh, God, it must be an enormous amount. It was more than twice the size of her old hovel. But after seeing *this*, Kiki was practically insulted that Fab had ever put her in the Mistress Hideaway in the first place. It amounted to nothing more than a closet!

Okay, so the hotel had been booked solid. Still, *something* could've been done. A bit of rearranging, that sort of thing. It happened all the time in restaurants and clubs. For instance, if P. Diddy showed up at, say, Bungalow 8, with twelve bodyguards in tow, people would be plucked from tables to make room. Just ask Tori Spelling. Her night was cut short once. Anyway, why should that icky politician who liked to be dominated get a nicer room?

Kiki banished the categorical unfairness from her mind. Now that she had the proper accommodations, she could get some real work done. It was hard to accomplish anything without enough space or too much clutter junked around. A girl needed a clean environment.

She settled in at the desk and jotted down a quick checklist on Affair stationery:

KIKI'S THINGS TO DO
1) Write book proposal
2) Get agent info for Suzi-Suzi

3) Find Kirby a better job
4) Head-to-toe glamour treatment

Kiki reviewed the list and decided that the best thing to do would be to start with smaller tasks. That way the act of checking them off would serve as a motivator to get more done—as opposed to starting with some enormous project like a book proposal and then not being able to finish it.

Well, who knew the glamour treatment would take hours? Thank God for Suzi-Suzi's A–Z thinking in packing the complete beauty arsenal. Kiki was able to do a manicure, pedicure, body wrap treatment, eye mask, face mask, throat mask, deep hair conditioning treatment, light chemical peel, teeth bleaching, light waxing session (eyebrows, upper lip, bikini), and a cellulite-fighting cream blast. Exhausting!

But she did double up on tasks. Confused about the waxing directions, she called Bliss Spa for a bit of phone help and secured the name and number of that agent for Suzi-Suzi. Now, finally able to relax for a moment, she was soaking in a vitamin-enriched Sake bath and had time to make at least one phone call. She rang Suzi-Suzi.

"*You* are brilliant. I'll never doubt your packing judgment again," Kiki said without preamble.

"Oh, my God! You did the head-to-toe glamour

treatment," Suzi-Suzi said. "I can tell just by the sound of your voice. How amazing is that feeling?"

"More than amazing," Kiki agreed. "In a way, it's like great sex."

"I've never heard it described like that. But you're *so* right. And can I just tell you that it is also *exhausting*."

"I was just telling myself the same thing."

"People don't understand. I'd like to see some of these military guys go through a head-to-toe glamour treatment. Marines act like they can handle anything, but they'd fall down like ninepins."

"They'd be complete powder puffs," Kiki agreed. She sank down a bit to let the Sake bath lap over her shoulders and neck. "So how did the sex therapist thing go?"

"I won't know right away. It takes a few sessions. Otherwise, every girl would be clunking her guy over the head and dragging him in there."

"I'm so excited about this new agent for you. I think he's going to find you some wonderful projects," Kiki said.

"I was working on my resume earlier, and after today's caper, I think I'm going to add *Alias* to my list of shows that I've been on."

"I don't see why not," Kiki encouraged.

"Did you see me in the wig? I totally worked it. And then I jumped into the Taurus and dove down to the floor. By that measure, I'm not just an actress but a stunt woman, too."

"Put that down," Kiki said. "It shows you're very athletic, and sometimes casting notices come in requesting that."

"I want to add as many things as possible, so that I get tons of auditions."

"Knowing other languages is always good."

"I can't speak Spanish, but I love Latin male singers," Suzi-Suzi said.

"Hey, that's half the battle," Kiki said. "If you ask me, that makes you bilingual."

"And what about Japanese? Again, don't speak a word, but my nephew loves those Yu-Gi-Oh cards, and I'm constantly buying them for him."

"Okay, *fluent* in Japanese," Kiki decided.

"Really?"

"Totally," Kiki said. She signed off and slipped into a sexy pajama ensemble by Picalina. The little shorts were fuchsia and had the cutest little heart buttons splitting up the side, flashing skin from upper thigh to hip bone. The matching tank was snug and featured a rhinestone-studded hummingbird on the front.

Spritzing herself with Bobbi Brown's Beach, she inhaled the delicious Coppertone hints, a fragrance she loved but couldn't use as one. After all, it'd just be stupid to walk around wearing Coppertone all day.

Three knocks rapped the door.

Her first visitor in the new suite! She raced to answer. And this time she wasn't surprised to find Fab on the other side of the door.

For a second, his eyes did that crazy am-I-seeing-what-I-think-I'm-seeing thing. He swallowed hard. The bob of his Adam's apple was a main event.

Kiki left him standing there and walked, slowly, to the French four-poster bed with the sumptuous silk canopy and crawled into it like a lazy cat who just finished a big meal. Yawning and stretching, she made certain that the work of Dr. Mendez was being properly exhibited. "God, I'm *so* tired."

Without warning, Fab bum-rushed the show. He stormed inside, kicked the door shut behind him, and in a mangled voice growled, "You smell so damn good," as he climbed on top of her, kissing her like mad.

Kiki mocked his need, playfully pushing him away. "Fab, stop, I'm ready for bed, and you're getting me all messed up."

"I've never seen you like this," he murmured, hearing none of it, still nothing but hands.

"Like what?"

"Perfect. Beautiful. Like dessert. God, I just want to eat you up!"

Kiki laughed. "It's no big deal. This is my standard bedtime routine."

The expression was instant slave. The impression

was a thousand nights of bedtime with her could still be considered relationship infancy.

"I've never seen you look so gorgeous," Fab marveled. "Think about it. The first time we met you were running for your life from the paparazzi. Then I caught you with that Fango mud deal. Next time was the morning after your tequila raid. And earlier today, well, let's not even talk about that." He stroked her leg from knee to thigh. "But this is you." He lunged for her.

She twisted away from him. "Fab . . . wait. Don't you think we should talk about what happened this afternoon? Or rather, what seems to always happen to us whenever we're not having sex?" One beat. "Or trying to in the stairwell?" Kiki didn't wait for him to answer. "I don't know. Maybe we're two very passionate people. Or maybe we're just . . . not compatible."

It wasn't meant to be a question. But there seemed to be a now-or-never debate raging somewhere deep in Fab's eyes. A private war was being fought. He had her drift. The *compatibility* mystery was girl code for *commitment*. But here it was, hanging in the brief space between them, begging to be solved. His jaw stuck out. The mere idea of the conversation seemed to offend against his natural order of things in the way that a day without celebrity worship might hers. "I think we're compatible," Fab said.

"*Here*, yes," Kiki said, gesturing to the luxury that

was the bed. "I think that goes without saying. But what about when we're not . . . doing *that*. It's just one argument after another."

"You're infuriating," Fab said.

Kiki took in a breath, rising up in protest.

"But in a good way," he clarified. "It's refreshing. Honestly, I've never taken the time to fight with a woman before. Not like with you. I usually helicopter out when the conflict starts. Any conflict. So this is advanced female interaction for me."

"Until . . ."

"Until what?" Fab asked.

"Until you get bored with me?" Kiki threw down her greatest fear like a gauntlet.

"I just said you were refreshing."

"Yeah. Today. *Now*. What about tomorrow? The next day. The day after that."

He grinned. It was the grin of a man who wanted to end the argument and get things back in sexual gear.

But Kiki would have none of it. She felt desirable. She *was* desirable. His eyes were begging her to put the John Gray *Men Are from Mars* bit in deep freeze until he had his way with her. But Kiki just stared lasers, refusing to budge.

"What do you want from me, Kiki?"

"I want some honesty."

"I like to take things one day at a time. Is that honest enough for you?"

"It's better." Kiki drew back. The personal space invasion was no more. There were just a few feet between them on the massive bed. But in what she thought they could be for each other, the chasm talked doomsday.

He was itchy for sex. And now he was irritated. "What do you want, Kiki? My high school ring?" A coldness crept into his voice.

Kiki knew that she'd basically walked herself into that one. But it was something she felt very fortunate to come across. She could feel the red high up on her cheeks. Sometimes she thought that she led the ticker-tape parade when it came down to celebrating your own needs. For the most part, Kiki's world began with herself. And ended there, too. But she'd met her match in Fab Tomba.

He reached forward to her shoulder and touched her. "I didn't mean that." The too-late apology dripped from his lips, floating in the air around them like a bad script that was getting worse with each line reading.

Kiki flicked his hand away. "This is all just a little too *convenient* for you, Fab. I mean, come on, you don't even have to leave your job. You just take the elevator up a few flights and expect to star in a late-night Cinemax movie. The tabloid thing *will* blow over. I'll go back to my life. And somehow I just don't see you putting out the effort when that's what it will take. *Effort*. I think effort bores you. Maybe not in business. You built this hotel. You're building a nightclub. But building something with another person seems beyond you." She stood up, reached for a robe, and covered herself up, making a point to knot the tie. "I suppose there's a very good reason why you called this place *Affair* and not *Relationship*. Well, here's a new one for your dance card, Fab Tomba. *I'm* bored with *you*."

Kiki thrust her hands into the deep pockets of the robe and put forth her best been-there-done-that tough girl vibe, trying not to cry.

Without a word, Fab climbed off the bed and walked out of the May-December suite. He closed the door behind him quietly.

And then she did cry.

From: kbush@wma.com
To: kiki@misstexas95.com
Subject: CALL ME!

Kiki!

Where the hell are you? I've left messages at your apartment, and for some reason I don't have your cell. *All My Children* wants to bring back Jeannette. Apparently, after she got pushed off the cruise ship, she floated on a piece of driftwood and ended up on an island. They want to do a Castaway story arc with your character. Only in soaps. You're back, baby.

Keith

Chapter Sixteen

Kiki Douglas was a fire-breathing fashionista of ferocious feminine force. It looked that way. It felt that way.

The morning after the hurricane. Turns out, the damage wasn't as bad as she originally feared. So Fab Tomba was impotent when it came down to commitment. He wanted to show up whenever for easy sex and throw off pithy one-liners about his stupid class ring. Screw that. And screw him.

Why? Because the executive producer of *All My Children* wanted to marry her. Well, practically. At least he was talking to Keith Bush about an initial three-year relationship. These days, that was almost marriage.

Anyway, *there* was a worthy gentleman caller.

Kiki had a plan of attack. She needed to check out, move on, get beyond. The scandal. The mini-heartbreak. All of it. And since she knew that Fab's kryptonite when it came to her was the simple art of looking, smelling, and projecting a certain fabulousness that was Kiki's personal brand identity, there was only one thing to do.

Dressing to kill would be too easy. And why allow him a quick death? He deserved to be punished. So the strategy was this: Dress to make him cry.

God love Suzi-Suzi. Again, she knew how to pack for a girl. And there were enough so-sexy-the-cabbies-will-drive-up-on-the-sidewalk outfits in the garbage bags to make the selection process pure torture. Hmm. As nail-biters go, Meryl Streep had a far easier time of it when she had to decide which child to turn over to the Nazis in *Sophie's Choice*.

Kiki slipped on a paillette-dotted muslin blouse and silk crepe hot shorts by Marc Jacobs for Louis Vuitton. The neckline plunged dangerously. The breasts she charged on American Express spilled out ominously. Thank God for invisible tape. But one slip of it and Janet Jackson's famous wardrobe malfunction would be recommended viewing for children by comparison.

Kiki took one last glance and tottered out on Christian Louboutin platform sandals that were circus-act high. This was walking in the nosebleed section. But she found her balance, perfected the catwalk-worthy gait, and charged forward, never once losing the laser power of her focus. God, she looked good enough to slay dragons for. Sometimes it was okay for a girl to admit that about herself. This time was one of them. Put her next to Catherine Z right now and Mrs. Michael Douglas—even red carpet ready and diamond dazzling—would seem like a mess on the side of the road.

Running on the rich fuel of success as the best revenge, Kiki vamped toward the elevator, her Juicy Couture charm bracelet jingle-jangling all the way. Yes, *that* bracelet. The junk jewelry that had been the tipping point for her tabloid Waterloo was back on the wrist. It'd been the catalytic accessory for meeting Fab. Why not give it special billing as *and starring in the role of karma reversal* for the big goodbye scene that said she was leaving him?

Kiki had arrived at Affair quietly, sputtering like a broken-down car on its final cough to the Last Chance Auto Shop. But today she would exit loudly, revving like a twin-turbo Porsche. God, what a difference a few days could make.

The elevator went down. And so, as the saying goes, did Kiki's stomach. She stepped out into the lobby, took a deep breath, and made a beeline for Fab's office, the immaculate one where he worked his little hotel, worked his insecure plans for nightlife insurgence, and worked a speech yesterday that almost, just almost, made Kiki believe he might be capable of a relationship that didn't involve last names and job titles being exchanged as part of postcoital cuddling.

Kiki stood at the precipice of the doorway, the weight on her toes, a wonderful terrible feeling strong in her heart. She was mere nanoseconds from announcing herself, when, quite suddenly, she halted.

The hyper-real vision swamped her mind with such impact that it came close to shutting down her central nervous system.

Fab Tomba.

Tom Brock.

Kirsten Brock.

Together in his office. At this hotel. Kiki's skin heated up as her blood cooled down. It was fire and ice. With an inaudible gasp, she flattened herself against the door. And she prayed that she hadn't been seen.

The Juicy bracelet jangled.

Now she prayed that she hadn't been heard. God! This stupid jewelry! Always getting her into trouble. And yet she still wore it. This reminded her of that old *Brady Bunch* episode, the one where the boys competed against the girls in a house of cards challenge for the chance to pick out goodies at the trading stamps store.

Okay, there stands Marcia, about to louse it up for herself, Jan, and Cindy, all because her charm bracelet keeps dangling perilously close to knocking the whole thing down. Well, the question *now*, as the question should've been *then*, was . . . Why, Marcia, didn't you just take off the fucking bracelet?

Hmm. Kiki found the absurd linkage fascinating. Whoever would've thought that, at this particular moment of insanity, or any moment for that matter, she would find herself mulling a Marcia Brady incident. Basically, a true testament to the Brady's staying power in the cultural landscape.

One thousand one . . . one thousand two.

Kiki stopped counting. Obviously, Fab, Tom, and Kirsten hadn't seen her. Or heard her. Because they went on talking. And she went on listening.

"The May-December suite is our favorite," Kirsten was saying. "Tom and I stayed there the night I told him I was pregnant with Music."

"Third happiest day of my life," Tom said.

Kiki heard the smooch of a kiss.

"And what's number one and number two?" Kirsten prompted sweetly.

"My wedding day and the day Music was born," Tom answered dutifully.

"Isn't he adorable?" Kirsten asked. Now, most women who acted this way in public could make women who weren't in the throes of a happy relationship vomit things they might've eaten ten years ago. But somehow Kirsten Brock pulled it off, as she remarkably did with everything. In fact, it astonished Kiki that she didn't have the overwhelming urge to push Kirsten into a boiling vat of battery acid.

"There's nothing I would want more than to be

able to accommodate you," Fab said smoothly. "I feel honored that Affair has been a setting for some of your most precious memories."

"But . . ." Tom said, cutting to the chase with just a hint of edge.

"The suite is currently occupied," Fab said. One beat. "And I must be honest, although this is terribly awkward. Perversely amusing but still awkward."

"What?" Kirsten asked.

"I understand that it's been a rough couple of days for you in the tabloids, and I appreciate the fact that you thought of Affair as a place to go to get away from the pressure. But, as it happens, Kiki Douglas has sought refuge here as well."

"Are you serious?" Kirsten bellowed.

"This is one of those moments when Manhattan feels like a small town." Tom chuckled. "I've got to say, Fab, I didn't see that one coming."

"Yeah, well, that's only part of the irony," Fab said. He paused a beat. "She's staying in the May-December suite."

Kirsten was the first to laugh. A real laugh. From the belly.

It proved contagious, because Tom chimed in next.

Fab laughed, too, but not with quite the same abandon. "I'm sorry. But I'm glad you have a sense of humor about this. Especially since you came here for the express reason of getting away from it."

"It's not *your* fault," Kirsten said. "It's not Kiki's

fault, either. It's those awful tabloids. I can't stand them. And they've really raked that poor girl over the coals. How is she holding up?"

Fab cleared his throat. "Fine, I believe. Just fine. She's got a lot of . . . spunk."

Spunk. Please. If Kiki had a thesaurus within arm's reach, she would've lobbed it straight for Fab's head. Yellow lab puppies with a full meal in their fat little bellies had spunk. Precocious child actors with psycho stage mothers who annoyingly referred to themselves as "momagers" had spunk. Kiki Douglas did *not* have spunk. Thank you very much. She had *diva attitude*. So there.

"And you're absolutely right, Kirsten," Fab went on. "The tabs have really done a number on her. Kiki's got no designs on Tom, and she never said anything untoward about your child. If anything, she's a huge fan. Of both of you. This has been very stressful and upsetting for her."

"Oh, I'm sure of it!" Kirsten spat angrily. "This whole thing has been a ridiculous farce. They will come up with any rubbish to make it sound like our marriage is in trouble. It's completely insane. I would sue, but that just takes too much energy. And who wants to relive it for years with a bunch of expensive lawyers? I truly hate what the press has done to that sweet and beautiful girl. I'm just glad to hear that she's safe and sound. I've been calling her apartment for days, trying to reach out, but it just rings into the machine. We talked for a spell at Stella McCartney. I thought she was adorable."

Kiki was overwhelmed. No, "thunderstruck" was a better word to describe it. *Sweet and beautiful. Adorable.* This was huge. Okay, take a Sally Field moment. *Kirsten Brock liked her. She really, really liked her.* That just had to be done.

Suzi-Suzi and Danni were going to die. No, they were going to double die. Die first. Have a future life in some sort of weird Shirley MacLaine way. And then die again. Oh, God, it was just like being accepted by the most beautiful and popular girl in high school. Hmm. Kiki had *been* that girl in high school. Well, it was like what other girls must've felt like when Kiki accepted them back in high school. At any rate, it was a marvelous feeling.

"I'm happy to hear you say that," Fab said.

"Well, obviously, *you* find her adorable, too," Kirsten said shrewdly.

Fab was silent.

"There's a slight change in your eyes and face whenever you talk about her," Kirsten went on silkily. "I don't know what that is exactly, but I know it's something good. I saw the same thing on Tom's face shortly after we met."

"Permission to speak candidly?" Fab asked.

Tom and Kirsten clearly nodded yes, because Fab started talking.

"If I'm being completely honest, I have to say that I'm glad this scandal happened. I'm glad Kiki got raked over the coals. I'm glad your family got pulled through the mud. Because without all of that taking place, she might've never walked through the doors of Affair. And I might've never met the first woman I've ever really fallen for. I'm crazy about that girl. And Tom, those love songs that you sing all the time . . . they're finally beginning to make sense to me."

From: kiki@misstexas95.com
To: kbush@wma.com
Subject: Re: CALL ME!

Keith,

I'm sending you a tape from the Miss America Pageant 1995, featuring me doing a dramatic monologue from St. Elmo's Fire. Please show it to the network BEFORE you sign off on negotiations for my return to *All My Children*. ABC might want to build a prime-time special into the contract. If need be, I have enough dramatic monologues for a three-hour block! My favorite: The funeral scene from *Steel Magnolias*. Be a tough little bastard. If they don't show interest, tell them that this idea has to be better than those Nick & Jessica specials.

Air Kisses,
Kiki

Chapter Seventeen

Kiki tried to adjust to what she was hearing . . .

Fab's voice.

Fab's words.

To listen to him say these things seemed surreal. She'd given her all to get him to open up. Yet nothing. And now he was venting to Tom and Kirsten with on-the-sleeve emotions that only pros like Oprah were known for drawing out. Talk about the last to know.

"I think this could be serious," Kirsten said teasingly. "From what *I've* heard, a long date for you constitutes the cab ride from a nightclub back to your apartment. Clearly this is more than that."

"Yes," Fab said. "Clearly."

"You know what? We should go out together," Kirsten suggested. "All four of us."

"Yeah," Tom agreed. "A double date. That'd be fun." He laughed a little. "We're on the outs with another couple, so I guess you could say that we're in the interviewing stage for potential social hires."

"And I have to *apply*?" Fab asked in mock outrage. "I thought I'd just get an offer."

"This is a couples position," Tom said.

"Yes," Kirsten put in silkily. "And given your track record, you're a bit of an insurance risk."

Unable to contain her excitement, Kiki was practically jumping up and down. Okay, she was all the way jumping up and down. A double date with Tom and Kirsten Brock? Oh, God! That would be the ultimate social masterstroke in Manhattan.

Where would they go? Maybe Mas. It was a darling little restaurant in the West Village with a French countryside vibe. There was antique barn wood on the walls and a limestone bar. So charming. And the food was amazing.

What would she wear? Hmm. Something flirty and feminine. But classy. A look that would conjure up old Hollywood glamour. A memory downloaded. Her last visit to the flagship Prada store in SoHo. That chiffon dress that she cried over because she couldn't afford it. But now, with Keith negotiating a major offer from ABC, and her book as good as sold, she could definitely splurge. Okay, so she hadn't written page one of the proposal. But she could bang that out in no time. One sample chapter, a brief chapter by chapter outline, a marketing analysis. Please.

All that could be done before breakfast. Decision made. Definitely the six-thousand-dollar Prada dress.

The paroxysms of delight were still pulsing through her as she continued to jump for joy on the impossibly high Christian Louboutin heels. *Yikes!* All of a sudden, she noticed the jangling noise her bracelet was making. Kiki stopped in her tracks. But not before the heart charm fell off—again! It went bouncing, rolling, sliding . . . and then stopped . . . just inside the doorway of Fab's office.

Kiki crouched down on all fours. Holding her breath, she moved, inch by inch, hoping to just snatch it in a flash without being noticed. God, her shorts were really riding up high in this position. She glanced behind quickly, just to make sure someone wouldn't walk by and mistake her for Christina Aguilera. Then she turned back around, only to find a spotless pair of Gucci loafers in front of her face. Slowly, her gaze traveled all the way up.

Tom Brock was holding the heart charm. "Is it just me, or is this circumstance eerily familiar?" He offered a hand to help her up.

Kiki attempted to laugh it off. "Again, I *do* have better jewelry. You seem to always catch me when I'm feeling a costume vibe. It's the strangest thing."

Kirsten moved quickly toward Kiki to take possession of both of her hands. "I've tried to call you a *million* times. I'm so glad that you're okay. This whole mess has been awful."

"I know. For you, too, I'm sure." Kiki managed to get this out calmly, though deep down, she was hysterically praying that Kirsten had left messages on the machine so that they could be played back for Suzi-Suzi and Danni.

She peered over at Fab. Yes, he was the same. Deliciously gorgeous in a way that almost took her breath away each time she saw him. But there was something else, too, an effect mirrored in his eyes, an effect that she had on him.

"I have an idea!" Kirsten blurted. The confidence in her tone argued instantly that it was a damn good one. "We should call a press conference. The three of us." She looked at Tom and Kiki as she said this. "We'll dismiss all of these lies for the garbage that they are. Together. As a unified front."

Okay, no matter what Kirsten had suggested, Kiki would've eagerly gone along with it. *Let's give all of our couture fashions away and dress in Old Navy for a year. If you say so! Let's lock ourselves in a bunker and listen to Debbie Gibson CDs over and over again.* Right there with you! Really, it could've been anything. But the upside was, this was a truly fantastic idea.

Fab nodded to the beat of Kirsten's enthusiasm. "The image of the three of you standing in solidarity? That's a very powerful diffuser. I like it."

"We should do it as soon as possible," Kirsten said

eagerly. "I want an end to this nonsense once and for all." She looked at Fab. "What about your lobby?"

"It's yours," he said.

Tom merely shrugged, as if down for whatever.

Kirsten moved fast, commandeering Fab's desk phone first and asking permission to do so later. "Sarah Ann, it's Kirsten Brock . . . I'm fine . . . Listen, I'm at Affair with Tom, and Kiki Douglas is here, too. I want a press conference within the hour. Here in the lobby. We're going to take questions together and put a stop to all of this absurdity right now. . . . No, it's not a mistake. . . . Sarah Ann, this is *not* open for debate. Just get the media here, okay? I'll prepare my own statement. . . . This is me calling to ask for your help. If you're not willing to do it, then this is me calling to fire you." Kirsten checked her watch. "You've got five seconds to decide. . . . Good." And then she hung up and let out a frustrated groan, rolling her eyes. "She is such a bitch. After this is over, I *am* going to fire her."

Kiki smiled. If only she could be dancing in the room when Sarah Ann Duckworth got that news.

Kirsten turned to Tom. "We should go change. Kiki looks amazing, and I'm standing here in a Juicy warm-up with a baby formula stain on it." Now she addressed Fab. "So the May-December suite is out. What's the next best thing?"

"Wait," Kiki interjected. "I couldn't help but over-hear when you mentioned your fondness for that suite. I insist that you take it. I need to return to my apartment anyway."

Kirsten shook her head no. "Absolutely not. We can take another suite. In fact, I insist. Besides, you're already settled in, and after the press conference, we're all going out together. You can go back to your apartment tomorrow."

Kiki was quick to accept the new plan. It was, after all, Kirsten Brock's plan. Who was she to argue?

Fab concentrated on his iMac. "The Nine and a Half Weeks suite is available." He looked up. "It's like an adult playpen with lots of toys and mild fetish accessories." His expression turned doubtful. "Too hot for new parents?"

"Nothing's too hot for us," Tom joked. "Compared to us, Mickey and Kim were like clumsy band geeks on a first date in that movie."

"Tom!" Kirsten scolded, blushing an instant pink. Everybody laughed.

Tom and Kirsten ambled out to check into their S and M suite, leaving Kiki alone with Fab. She could feel the heat of his gaze burning up her body before turning to him.

"If you heard the bit about the Brocks, then I'm guessing you heard what I had to say, too." His eyes were still doing that intense survey thing.

Kiki had Fab hooked up like a light switch, and the sassy Vuitton number was flicking him up and down, playfully, cruelly, just because he was there, as if a bored child were operating the panel. She thought about responding coolly, to make him work harder, but in the end, she just gave in to her impulse. And that was to lose herself in his embrace. "Oh, Fab," she whispered, grinning against his chest.

His arms tightened around her. "I was miserable last night. I never went to sleep. No woman has ever made me lose sleep before." One beat. "That's not exactly true. But I've always been there. Rewrite. No woman has ever made me lose sleep when I *haven't* been with her. Except you."

Kiki leaned back and looked at him. "Now is *not* the time to bring up all of your ex-lovers. Relationship rule number one: Pretend you never had any."

Fab laughed and spun her around. And then he stopped, planting her firmly down before cupping her face in his hands and moving his lips millimeters from hers. "Haven't you heard? I'm a virgin."

Kiki felt his tongue brushing against her own, and she opened her mouth wide. They were kissing now. It wasn't the first. It wouldn't be the last.

Slowly, his lips retreated from hers. "Still bored with me?"

Kiki smiled the smile of a woman in love. "You know, I must admit . . . you're getting a bit more interesting."

* * *

The Manhattan press corps turned out in full force. Kirsten Brock, the media darling of the moment, had summoned them. No matter what she had to say, they considered the trip worth it just to get a new picture, some fresh B-roll footage, a quote about anything—the weather, what she ate for breakfast, her impressions of the new fall fashion lines, the last time Music pooped.

The photoreporters were flying by the seat of their Nikons. The broadcast news babes were tapping impatient pumps while their cameramen balanced heavy video equipment on tired shoulders. And the shock jocks were waiting, phallic microphones in hand, proving the old saying, "He has a face for radio," more relevant than ever.

Kiki could feel her heart pounding in her chest. Nervous sweat slicked her breasts. Out there were the vultures she'd been running from. And now she was standing in open field, inviting them to take another dive at her. She glanced at the woman to her left, uncertainty in her eyes.

Kirsten clasped Kiki's hand in a public gesture of friendship, female solidarity, and sisterly support, a move that triggered a blinding lightning storm of flashbulbs in overdrive.

Kiki prayed that the image would find its way to the front page, that no mistake would ruin the picture. Finally, a headline to be proud of.

Kirsten somberly stepped to the podium.

The Affair lobby was pin-drop quiet.

And then she began to speak in a voice serious, stoic, and more than a little angry. "Members of the press, thank you for accepting this invitation. The last few days have been very difficult for the Brock family *and* for Kiki Douglas. The gross speculations, offensive innuendos, and outright lies that have been brandished in newspapers, on television screens, on the Internet, and over the radio is a disgusting example of the Fourth Estate operating on its most vile and irresponsible impulses. There is nothing to explain or defend here today because *nothing* happened. My family has been put through undue stress and humiliation. For no reason. Kiki Douglas has endured the same. Again, for no reason. Other than the sick hunger certain media channels have for creating scandal when scandal is nowhere to be found." She cast scolding eyes over the crowd. "You know who you are."

Kiki observed a collective shame swamp down on almost every media representative in attendance.

Kirsten reached for Kiki's hand again, pulling her up to the podium, and raising their arms in a show of us-against-the-world unity. "This woman is not a home wrecker, ladies and gentlemen. She's my friend."

A belligerent tabloid scribbler elbowed his way to the front. "Kiki!" he screamed out. "If Tom Brock's not the man in your life, then who is it?"

Kiki aimed a secret look at Fab. "I appreciate your interest, but that's really none of your business. I will say this, though. He's *fab*ulous."

From: kiki@misstexas95.com
To: numbersgeek@aol.com
    vshelton@kleinschmidtbelker.com
Subject: A Fashion Tragedy of Epic Proportions
Avoided

Sydney and Vivien!

Okay, girls, even if you don't smoke, get ready
to light up a cigarette. Why? Because you just
might have an orgasm while reading this e-mail.
By now I'm sure you've heard about the little scandal involving me and Tom Brock. Ridiculous! Tabloids can lie better than married men at a
convention/conference in Vegas. Anyway, that is
so over. In fact, Kirsten Brock and I laugh about it
all the time. We're very good friends now. So
here's how it happened. I'm talking to Kirsten
about my brother's wedding and telling her how
worried I am about the bridesmaid dresses. I
mean, it's going to be impossible to find a dress
that we all look fabulous in. Think about it. Sydney, you're an accountant. Don't take this the
wrong way, but most dresses probably wear YOU.
That's just how it is with girls who wear too many
conservative suits. And Vivien, you know better
than anyone that your height presents a few fashion challenges. I'm sure prom night was murder

for you. Did your date have lifts built in to his rented shoes? I hope so. Anyway, Kirsten Brock (she's my friend now—did I mention that?) thinks this problem through. It takes her, like, a minute. And she's got a solution. Amazing. Meanwhile social security is still a mess after all these years. Send this girl to Washington!

Where was I? Oh, the best part! Kirsten's suggestion? VERA WANG! Yes! THE Vera Wang! Vera designed Kirsten's wedding dress. So she calls up Vera right there on the spot and says please, please, please design bridesmaid dresses for my friend and two other girls. And Vera said YES! Oh, my God! Can you believe it? Are you totally having a Meg Ryan diner scene moment from *When Harry Met Sally* right now?

Air Kisses,
Kiki

Chapter Eighteen

Kiki and Fab lived in Affair's May-December suite for a week following the press conference. It was heaven on earth. With maid service!

During the day, Fab would tend to the management of the hotel and work on details for the imminent opening of the nightclub, Foreign Affair. Meanwhile, Kiki worked slavishly on her book proposal, cranking it out page by page with the kind of iron-fisted discipline that Jackie Collins brought to her work.

Suzi-Suzi and Danni stopped by every day to read new pages. And Tiffany Lynn dropped in to proof the work line by line. A stripper who was a genius at grammar and spelling. What a brilliant paradox! Even Kirsten got into the mix, as she took Kiki shopping to find the perfect outfit for the first lunch with her new agent, Marc Weisberg, a friend of Fab's. He was a mere baby at twenty-four but knew his way around the publishing world like Doogie Howser had known the ins and outs of an operating room. Everything had happened so fast. Exactly the sort of whiz-bang turn of events that could make a girl stand in front of the refrigerator and sample everything in sight while she left the door open. Luckily, the minibar was small. Because it could've been a serious situation.

Marc had sold the book in a flash. He sent it out to his top three editor picks. They all wanted to pounce, so it ended up going to auction. So exciting! Of course, waiting for *The Call* had been pure torture. Especially with Suzi-Suzi beeping in every three minutes to ask, "Has he called yet? Has he called yet?" Ugh! Annoying. But so sweet. You *had* to love her.

Finally, Marc had phoned her with the low six-figure offer. Amazing! Of course, now she had to actually write the damn thing. With the signing money, though, she planned to begin building her promotional tour wardrobe in earnest. Basically, that was more important than composing the book itself. Because the right image was invaluable to an author.

Marc's incredible news had arrived right on top of Keith buzzing by to announce the official closing of the ABC deal. A three-year contract to return to *All My Children* as Jeannette *and* a one-year talent-holding deal with the network for a prime-time drama, sitcom, or reality-based program.

Still, it was the simple things that filled her chockablock full of happiness. Like right now. Here she was sitting in a hot bath with Fab. The egg-shaped tub was easily built for two, and their ritual all week had been to indulge in a long soak with a bottle of red wine while they shared details about their days. Kiki did most of the talking, though. Fab mainly just listened, interjecting only occasionally.

"Did I tell you that Chad is back under hypnosis with the sex therapist?" Kiki asked.

Fab shook his head, massaging her right foot under the soapy water. He was practically a reflexologist. Phenomenal hands.

"Oh, Suzi-Suzi is a wreck," she charged on in speed-talk. "I told you what his problem is, right? He cries when he comes, hates a hand on his penis. Well, turns out it's all trauma from a repressed memory of getting caught masturbating in the high school library. The first hypnosis worked. Sort of. There's *no* problem with a hand on his willy anymore. As long as it's his own. Now he's addicted to Internet porn. The man will sit there and do this even if Suzi-Suzi's in the room. He's only got dial-up access at home, and, apparently, that's way too slow for online smut. So he spends all his free time on Suzi-Suzi's computer. She said he got come on her keyboard and that it was totally disgusting."

"Here's an idea for your friend," Fab cut in. "End the relationship."

Kiki sighed. "It's not that simple. Suzi-Suzi's the

kind of girl who sticks with things until they're right. Like modeling. Anyone else would've quit a long time ago. But she stuck with it, and now with her new television agent, she's got a callback for a national commercial. She's not thrilled that it's for a vaginal itching cream, but the pay would be great. Anyway, she actually believes that Chad is the one for her. Oh, and Chad knows that you own a hotel. He wants to stop by and talk to you about putting Tempur-Pedic mattresses in all the rooms. There's a whole spiel he'll take you through on the advanced construction, and you'll have to endure some bad mattress jokes, too. Chad's never been to Spice Market, so I told him you'd let him take you out for lunch. I know it's crazy with the nightclub getting ready to open, but the restaurant's just around the corner. I figured you could squeeze the appointment in. Spicy food gives him gas, though, so steer him clear of the really hot dishes. Next Thursday works great for him."

Fab nodded helplessly, love and amusement beaming from his eyes.

"Great," Kiki chirped. "Suzi-Suzi will be so excited. Chad's been depressed because he hasn't opened a new account in months. All the sexual problems have been a huge distraction for him."

"I didn't agree to buy anything," Fab warned, starting the magic rubbing on her left foot now. "I'm just having lunch with the guy."

Kylie Adams

"Oh, you've *got*, to. Suzi-Suzi let slip that it was a done deal, and Chad's already told his boss that he landed a hotel account. You can't change your mind now."

"*Change* my mind?" Fab asked. "This is the first I've heard of it."

Kiki shrugged. "Whatever . . . oh, keep it right there . . . God, that feels amazing." Suddenly, she lurched forward, kissing him full on the mouth with the desperation of a love addict, then leaned back against the basin.

He smiled. "What was that for?"

"For helping out my friends. It's very sweet."

Fab gave her a quizzical look. He seemed hung up on something. "You said *friends*." The impression lingered that the plural usage was troubling.

But Kiki returned an upbeat nod. "Suzi-Suzi, Danni, and Tiffany Lynn."

"I'm almost afraid to ask, but exactly what have I done for Tiffany Lynn?"

Kiki splashed him playfully. "Oh, stop!"

"I'm serious," Fab said. "I have no idea what you're talking about."

"Kirby's going to manage the bar at Foreign Affair." Kiki announced this as if it were common knowledge on the AP wire.

Now Fab splashed back. "Absolutely not."

"I didn't tell you? Oh, my God! This week has been so insane, what with the book proposal, shopping with Kirsten for my lunch with Marc, the whole ABC thing, trying to schedule fittings with Vera Wang for the bridesmaid dresses. It completely slipped my mind. Anyway, you *have* to say yes. He's already given notice at Camisole. Besides, he'll be fantastic. And he's got really big arms. So not only can he keep the drinks coming, but he's strong enough to throw someone out if they get too rowdy."

There was the slightest hint of a smile curling onto Fab's lips. Tacit agreement. But agreement nonetheless.

"You're going to end up thanking *me*," Kiki said with self-satisfied confidence. "Kirby will be a true asset. And Tiffany Lynn is on the moon about it. I mean, at first she was a little bummed because it meant they wouldn't see each other as much. But now they're going to be working together again, so it's really—"

"Wait a minute." Fab laughed the laugh of the weary. "I've hired Tiffany Lynn, too?"

Kiki hit her forehead with the palm of her hand. "God! I am *such* a ditz!" She took in a deep breath. "Tiffany Lynn is going to dance in a cage at Foreign Affair."

Fab shook his head in disbelief. "There *is* no such cage at Foreign Affair."

"Oh." Kiki bit down on her lower lip. "Well, there has to be now. Where else is she going to dance? You don't want her dancing on the bar. She might knock someone's drink over. Or what if a guy gets too fresh with her? Then you've got Kirby kicking a customer's ass in the middle of peak bar time. Not a good situation. Better make arrangements for a cage. That way she's safe from jerky guys. And Kirby stays calm and concentrates on the job you hired him to do."

"I believe *you* hired him for the job, but I suppose that's a moot point at this stage."

"Oh, and by the way, in case Danni asks, you considered *several* top choreographers for her job. Including Paula Abdul and Debbie Allen."

With that, Fab sank down into the water and pretended to drown himself, staying under for at least sixty seconds.

"Fab!" Kiki cried. She tried pulling him out, slipped, and ended up on top of him.

"Okay, I give," he whispered. "What have I hired Danni to do?"

"Well, *somebody* has to choreograph Tiffany Lynn's routines. Besides, Danni's doctor boyfriend—he's the one who looks just like George Clooney—said that she couldn't keep up with the same dancing schedule. It's *killing* her knees. Plus, she's a Christian, so your nightclub is a better fit with her values. I told her that you'd put up a sign in the employee lounge, too. She wants to start a Bible study group right away."

Fab lay still beneath her, except for one essential

part of him: his sudden erection. It pushed shamelessly against her slick stomach. "You . . . are the most impossible woman I've ever met . . . *in my life.*"

"*Impossible?*" Kiki repeated softly, angling her pelvis above his, slyly preparing for the entry. "You know what? I don't think I like the sound of that."

"How about the sound of this then . . . I love you." Fab's voice broke with exquisite helplessness. He thrust upward, taking her by surprise, instantly deep inside her.

Kiki rose up on the force. She found his eyes and stroked his cheek, telegraphing the same sentiment, a slight mist building in her eyes as the emotional realization became so beautifully clear.

Norman Mailer had said it once about sex. But Kiki Douglas was feeling it right now about Fab Tomba. Loving him would be like lava from a volcano. Once it erupted, you could never stop the flow.

From: kiki@misstexas95.com
To: breckin@withthisring.com
Subject: The Impossible Bride

Breckin!

I know this may be a terrible thing to say about my soon-to-be sister-in-law, but I think Julia just might be the most impossible bride I've ever heard of in my lifetime. I don't know how my poor brother is going to live with her. The girl can't decide on anything! We've been killing ourselves on whim after whim of hers, and frankly, I've had enough. I say stop the madness. Let's just take a few steps back and see where the wind takes her. Okay, now that you're free, start working on my wedding. It's a bit soon (I haven't been asked yet), but I know this guy is THE ONE. Oh, my God. His name is Fab. Could there ever be a more perfect name for a man? I mean, every girl wants her future husband to be fab. And mine will be fab and Fab! Anyway, I want the wedding to be out of this world. Do you remember Celine Dion's ceremony? She got carried in like an Egyptian goddess! I want something equally mind-boggling. I'm thinking waterfalls and synchronized swimmers wearing veils. Play with that, and I'll post back other ideas as they come to me.

Air Kisses,
Kiki

Epilogue

Excerpt

First Runner-Up . . . But Still a Winner
by Kiki Douglas

"Bette Midler Knew of Which She sang . . .
and Other Truths"

True story. This happened in Fredericksburg, Texas, where I grew up. It's a very inspirational tale. Sort of like Jessica Lynch, only it's got nothing to do with war or the Middle East. But it did take place during high school, which, it can be argued, is very close to the Middle East in terms of unrest, potential dangers, fear at every turn, etc. At least socially.

I didn't make cheerleader. I know, it seems impossible. I'm completely the cheerleader type. But I didn't make the cut. The coach and I were worlds apart on what a cheerleader should be. She maintained that the opportunity was an athletic endeavor with lots of jumping, flipping, flying through the air, that sort of thing. Well, I just wanted to look cute in the uniform, flounce around, yell out, "Go team!" and flirt with Barry Shamblin (quarterback, matinee-idol dreamy). Anyway, I was denied the dream—of cheerleading, that is (totally made out with Barry!). Depression hit. So bad that I stopped watching *21 Jump Street*. Yes, I sank that low! Thank God for Breckin Andrews. My lifesaver of a friend and the school's only gay person. At least openly. Nobody had the nerve to say so, but the health teacher, Mrs. Heath, did *not* share a house with her "cousin." Everybody knew that the lady truck driver was her lover!

Luckily, Breckin had all the episodes of *21 Jump Street* on tape and forced me to watch them. The healing benefits of Johnny Depp kicked in, and suddenly, I could see the light at the end of the tunnel. God, what would I have done without Breckin? I was so close to taking a dark turn back then. It was practically *Girl, Interrupted*. You know, the movie with Winona Ryder and Angelina Jolie in the mental ward.

Friends are important. You *must* have them. Example: Ted Kaczynski. Things would've been so different if he'd had a few friends. First, those endless manifestos! Likely, a first reader (you just *know* a friend would've been asked to take a look) might've said, "Ted, this doesn't make any sense. Writing's not your bag. Pick up the guitar, dude!" Think about it. With a friend or two, he could've been a John Mayer instead of the Unabomber.

Making and keeping friends is not easy, though. Especially for girls. The whole *Sex and the City* vibe is practically a fantasy. Do *you* have a Charlotte, Miranda, and Samantha in your life? Most girls don't. First of all, there's the whole issue of time. I mean, with work and everything, there just aren't endless hours available to sit at a coffee shop and deconstruct every millisecond of life like they do on that show!

My advice is to be open. Sometimes the girl at the office who annoys you could be your best friend in disguise. That's how it happened with me and Suzi-Suzi. I'd just moved to New York and gotten a job as a waitress in a very chic restaurant. Suzi-Suzi worked there, too. Anyway, she found out that I had one of those little calorie counter books at home, so she used to call my apartment after our shift to tell me everything that she'd eaten that day. So here I am sitting there and adding up her calories. *Every night*. Ugh! But now we know each other *so* well. When Jude Law proposed to Sienna Miller, she called right away to find out how I was holding up. Now *that's* a true friend.

I think an intimate little circle of friends is essential to navigating through life. My advice: Buy a generous plan for your cell phone and keep in touch about *everything*. You never know when someone will have a kernel of wisdom that could stop you from setting a destructive event into motion. What I'm about to tell you is a true story, and it's a frightening, cautionary tale that illustrates this point.

So, I've been in a million weddings and have a closet bursting with hideous bridesmaid dresses that I'll *never* wear again. Well, one day I just up and decided to give them away to women at a transitional shelter. I figure, it's a perfectly good dress, and these women are trying to get their lives back together.

Enter Danni, another best friend of mine. She'd seen the ghastly frocks and thought—in addition to being awful—that they were just too dressy. Well, everybody knows that *over*dressing for a job interview is almost as bad as *under*dressing for one. I mean, it's a very fine line.

So I didn't donate the dresses. At the end of the day, it would've been a disservice to those women trying to reclaim their lives. Thank God for Danni! She stopped me just in the nick of time. I ended up taking in shoes instead. And what happened? Greta totally worked her secondhand Manolos in that temp service interview. Now she's an executive secretary for the CEO of a major corporation. All because of Danni!

It's like that Bette Midler song—" 'Cause you got to have friends/Da, da, da, da, da, da, da, da, da/ Friends . . ."

From: kiki@misstexas95.com
To: crownjule@aol.com
Subject: Dramatic Reading

Julia!

I've got the most brilliant idea for your wedding. Yes! Another one. First step: Ditch the singer. Why? Because it's so yesterday. Do we really need to hear some second-rate vocalist croon "The Reason" by Hoobastank? That's a rhetorical question, by the way. The voice inside your head should be screaming, "No!" So my wedding gift to you and Roman will be a dramatic monologue at the ceremony. This was my talent showcase for the Miss America Pageant, so you know I'll be well rehearsed. All pageant girls have a steely self-discipline for such things. Anyway, I'm thinking about doing something from Jerry Maguire. You know, the Tom Cruise and Renee Zellweger movie with the famous "You had me at hello" line. Trust me. There will be a river of tears!

Air Kisses,
Kiki

ABOUT THE AUTHOR

Kylie Adams is the author of *Ex-Girlfriends*, *Fly Me to the Moon*, *Baby, Baby*, and the *USA Today* best sellers *The Only Thing Better than Chocolate* (with Janet Daily and Sandra Steffen) and *Santa Baby* (with Lisa Jackson, Elaine Coffman, and Lisa Plumley).

Two new projects will be published later this fall—*Ex-Boyfriends* and *The Night Before Christmas* (a holiday anthology featuring the novella *A Good Girl's Guide to a Very Bad Christmas*). Also set for release is the mass-market paperback edition of *Ex-Girlfriends*.

Kylie lives with her shih tzu and bichon frise in Brandon, Mississippi, where she is currently at work on her next novel and involved in a twelve-step program for *Us Weekly* addicts.

To contact Kylie, visit her online at www.readkylie.com. Or write: Kylie Adams, c/o New American Library, 375 Hudson Street, New York, NY 10014.

If you fell in love with Sydney in *First Date* and laughed out loud at Kiki's misadventures in *First Kiss*, there's one more bridesmaid you'll have to meet before the big wedding in . . .

First Dance

BOOK THREE IN

THE BRIDESMAID CHRONICLES

Vivien Shelton is Manhattan's top female divorce attorney . . . and Julia Spinelli's best friend and future bridesmaid. Except Vivien has seen the ugly side of love—and alights at the wedding in Texas with the perfect present: an ironclad prenup. But the groom's good ole boy lawyer is itching for a fight—especially with Vivien, a woman he has tangled with in the past. . . .

Read ahead for a sneak peek of Vivien's story.

Vivien Shelton kissed the five doggie noses arrayed at varying heights in front of her and backed out of her Manhattan apartment. She clutched a tape roller and her computer bag in one hand, and a tall espresso-strength coffee in the other. Ellis whined mournfully, and Brooklyn gave a sharp, disapproving bark.

She looked regretfully at her gaggle of greyhounds. "I know, guys. But I can't stay and play. Klein, Schmidt and Belker pays me for my legal expertise, not my Frisbee skills. Tabitha will keep you company, okay?" She glanced at the tiny blond walker, still incredulous that the dogs didn't pull her right off her feet.

"Queenie has a two p.m. vet appointment, remember. Just have them send me the bill—forty-three greyhounds later, they know I'm good for it."

"Will do." Tabitha crunched down on a Granny Smith apple and waved goodbye. "What about the couple who's interested in Brooklyn? What should I tell them?"

Excerpt from FIRST DANCE

"I'm not comfortable with him going to them. There's something 'off' about those people. Tell them he's already been placed."

"Okay. Have a good one, Viv."

"You too!" She dropped another quick kiss on little Mannie's speckled pink nose—he was practically an albino—and he licked her cheek, probably taking off half of her makeup. Mannie was the latest in her long line of rescued greyhounds, and he hadn't left her side all day on Sunday. She felt guilty leaving him, but he was in good hands. Cranky old Schmidt would have a stroke if she brought Mannie anywhere near the office.

Viv glanced at her watch and galloped toward the elevator, madly tape-rolling the little white hairs off of her left trouser-clad thigh. She did her lower left leg while waiting for the car to arrive, and her right leg on the way down from the seventeenth floor to the first. A slurp of coffee, then the right front of her jacket. Another slurp, and the left front.

Mr. Duarte from the eleventh floor watched eagerly as the roller skimmed over her breasts, and she sent him a quelling look. This only made him look hopeful that she might punish him. Duarte gave her the creeps.

Once they got to the ground floor, Viv waited for him to scram. Then she sidled over to Timmy, the doorman, raised a come-hither brow, and dove down the service hallway. Timmy appeared within seconds, she presented her backside, and he tape-rollered her from nape to ankles.

"Oooooh, Timmy. Was that good for you, darling?" She winked at him once he was done. "Because, as always, it was *sensational* for me."

"You're lucky I'm here to service you, Miss Viv." Timmy winked back.

"That I am," Viv agreed. "That I am. Thank you!" She popped the tape roller into her bulging computer bag and rushed out the door just as the firm's car and driver appeared.

Viv had once thought that the chauffered car was a nice perk of working at Klein, Schmidt and Belker: a luxury. She now considered Maurice and the Lincoln Continental to be her jailer and paddy wagon, respectively. Maurice made sure she was working hard to generate the big bucks for Schmidt and Belker by seven forty-five a.m. each weekday morning, and by nine forty-five a.m. on too-regular Saturdays. (Klein was technically out of the picture, after he'd dropped dead at a urinal in the men's room three years ago. He'd left behind a spectacular courtroom win ratio and an exposed trouser-snake that bent even farther right than his politics.)

"Good morning, Maurice," Viv said crisply as she stepped into the Lincoln. "And how are you today?" The usual nauseating smell of wintergreen gum and tropical fruit carpet freshener assailed her nostrils.

The wizened little man looked at his watch and frowned. "Better, now that you're in. Four times around the block today, Miss Shelton!"

"Four, really? How frustrating. Were you early?" Viv was never late. Not by as much as thirty seconds. And tardiness in others was one of her biggest pet peeves.

"Early, schmurly," grumbled Maurice, lurching forward and left in the heavy traffic and cutting off an irate and vocal cabdriver. Then he floored it for all of eight feet before dodging right again, barely missing a bike messenger, and slamming on the brakes.

Viv took it all in stride. She had a strong suspicion that Schmidt and Belker awarded Maurice an annual bonus for delivering her hundred-and-thirty pounds of flesh before eight o'clock each day. She and the other five attorneys on his run were his responsibility.

She had at least fifteen minutes to kill before the car got from her Upper East Side building to the law offices in midtown, so she checked e-mail on her Palm Pilot.

Please, she prayed, let there not be any more wedding horrors awaiting her. Since the troubling news that her best friend, Julia Spinelli, was getting married to some redneck she'd only known a month, Viv had tried to digest the fact that she'd have to be a . . . She shuddered, unable to wrap her mind around the concept.

A *bridesmaid*. Vivien didn't want to be anybody's maid, not even for a day. The whole concept was foreign; it implied servitude and worse, it spanned all the possibilities of polyester.

She'd already had to leave a deposition one day to find a full-length, strapless foundation garment in her bra size. Julia had then commanded that she purchase a pair of satin Manolo evening mules and a flaring *petticoat*. Viv had never in her life worn something as fussy as a petticoat, and she dreaded seeing the hideous taffeta creation that went over it. Oh, God! Please let her not have to wear anything with a bow on the butt . . .

Under any other circumstances, she'd laugh her ass off at the idea of one of Manhattan's top divorce attorneys moonlighting as a bridesmaid in a wedding. But all the humor went out of it immediately when *she* was the top divorce attorney in question. Viv had represented some high-profile clients, and she only hoped the papers didn't get hold of this. She could see the headlines now: RAPTOR IN ROSE-BUDS! WILL SHELTON SERVE GROOM PAPERS AT RECEPTION?

Viv shook off what she knew were selfish thoughts under the circumstances. She should be a lot more concerned about Julia than she was about herself. She'd already questioned her delicately on the phone about this guy Roman. She'd also told Julia that coincidentally she knew his sister, Kiki Douglas. Unfortunately Viv had represented her ex-husband in their Manhattan divorce three years ago.

"Listen, hon," she'd said to Julia. "If Roman is anything like Kiki, you want to be careful."

"Roman is nothing like Kiki!" Julia had exclaimed, even though to Viv's knowledge she'd never met her.

Viv had closed her eyes to ward off a migraine—impossible—and sent an urgent e-mail to Sydney Spinelli, Julia's older sister.

Today there was a reply, and Vivien scanned it quickly.

Subject: Re: Your little sister has gone crazy!

Date: XXXXXX

From: numbersgeek

To: vshelton

Tell me about it! Yes, I've met him, and there's something fishy with the guy. What kind of Texan speaks Italian, wears designer clothes, and has a vineyard??? And Viv, here's the really awful part: the ring he gave her is FAKE!!!!!!!!!!!!!! I think he's marrying her for the $$$. But I can't talk sense into her.

Syd

Excerpt from FIRST DANCE

"Fake?!" Viv said it aloud, with enough force that Maurice squinted at her in the rearview mirror. *"What?* She has *got* to be kidding!"

Viv typed a quick reply. She'd call Sydney as soon as she got to the office.

Subject: FAKE ring???

Date: XXXXXX

From: vshelton@kleinschmidtbelker

To: numbersgeek

What do you mean, the ring he gave her is fake?! HOW COULD HE??? I'm speechless. xoxoxo, Viv

Sydney was obviously online at the same time, because before Viv had finished reading one of the work e-mails her reply popped into the mailbox.

Excerpt from FIRST DANCE

Subject: Re: FAKE ring???

Date: XXXXXXX

From: numbersgeek

To: vshelton@kleinschmidtbelker

Viv, supposedly it's not his fault. The grandmother sold it way back when and he didn't know. (Do you believe this? Not sure, myself.) But it doesn't matter! Our Julia has got it bad: she's STILL WEARING the ring, and says she doesn't care that it's fake. Why? Because HE gave it to her. I give up . . . I'm going home. Can you at least get her to sign a prenup? I'm serious!!!!!!!

Syd

Viv stared in disbelief at the text. Julia was still wearing a fake ring! She logged off and shut her laptop with a snap. This was insane. This Roman guy must be damn good in bed to have her so deluded. He sounded like one hundred percent bad news, and if he was related to Kiki Douglas, whose face had been *all* over the tabloids lately, then he was a prize schmuck.

Julia needed a prenup, all right. The question was how to convince her of that. People in love and planning a wedding did not want to think about the ugly death of that love and the dissolution of the wedding. You couldn't really blame them.

Excerpt from FIRST DANCE

Viv shuddered at the idea of grabbing Julia and telling her that the fabric, cut and design of her gown didn't matter, because she'd be burning it in a back-yard bonfire in less than a year.

"Julia, honey," she saw herself saying, "don't worry that the doves they delivered for the event are both male. You'll be roasting them on the barbecue with veggie kabobs by Christmas." Or . . .

"Sweetie, don't bother freezing the top of that cake—unless you want something heavy and icicle-encrusted with which to brain your husband after he absconds with your trust fund." Or . . .

"Lacy white bridal lingerie imported from France? Don't spend the money—unless you've got some red or purple dye on hand. You can transform them for your divorce trousseau."

Viv winced. Julia, the poor thing, wouldn't want to listen to any of this. But Vivien had seen the rough side of marriage. She dealt with it every day: the ugly accusations, the dirty little secrets, the infidelity, the asset hiding, the custody squabbles—even the occasional kidnapping of the miserable couple's children by one spouse.

Viv had seen some strange things. She'd attended a Divorce Dirge for a client of hers and downed a dirty martini as a doll of the ex-husband was burned in effigy.

A caterer client had baked a large, penis-shaped

chocolate cake for a luncheon, serving a stunned Viv a good chunk of the balls on a china plate. The client had then thanked her in front of everyone for her great work.

And during one case the cheating SOB of a husband had propositioned Viv right in front of her client, his wife!

But Viv's mistrust of marriage went far deeper than her job. Not only were her own parents divorced, but their parents before them. She simply did not believe in marital bliss.

As the Lincoln pulled up in front of Klein, Schmidt and Belker's building, Viv pulled her things together. She got out with an unenthusiastic thanks to Maurice, who gunned the engine and pulled away before she even had the door closed. Then she schlepped inside.

The first face she saw that morning belonged to grumpy old Schmidt, whose yarmulke hung precariously from a bobby pin attached to one of three final strands of combed-over hair. Now, in Schmidt's favor, he'd been married to the same woman for forty-eight years.

But Viv had a suspicion that Mrs. Schmidt hung around more out of inertia and fear of the man's divorce-law expertise than out of any burning passion for him. And she'd long ago decided that Schmidt stayed with *her* due to a fondness for her

chocolate babka cake and light touch with potato lat-
kes. He was also far too fond of his money to part
with any of it in a divorce.

Schmidt grunted at her and she nodded back as
she passed him on her way to her office, navigating
the sea of dark mahogany tables, tasteful green plants
and leather seating.

Belker, the younger partner, had covered the walls
of the firm with his dour, very minor, old-master
Flemish paintings, which Viv referred to collectively
as the sourpusses. Belky, unlike Schmidt, had been
divorced twice and had given each wife a considerable amount of money for his freedom. But since the
firm dumped more on him by the truckload, he
didn't seem to mind overly much.

Unfortunately Belky had a thing for Viv's assistant
Andie, a former client whom she'd hired in an un-
wise moment of sympathy. She'd negotiated a fabulous settlement for Andie, the bulk of which was her
husband's 2.3-million-dollar house. Unfortunately
he'd stopped making the insurance payments on it
and burned it down with himself inside it.

Andie was terribly sweet and had a way with Viv's
usually upset female clients, whom she plied with
tea and sympathy and great gossip.

Belker was sitting on the corner of her desk with
his scrawny knees apart when Viv appeared, his
chest puffed out like a rooster's. "I had the judge in
the palm of my hand," he said, eyeing Andie's

plump assets in their tight black sweater. "Had her *purring*."

"Good morning," Viv interrupted him, hardly able to refrain from rolling her eyes.

" 'Morning!" Andie sang.

Belker nodded coolly and removed his vile, skinny buns from their perch. "Ah, Vivien," he said. "I have something to discuss with you."

Ugh. She didn't want to discuss anything with Belky other than a promotion and a raise—or taking some of the six weeks of vacation owed to her by the firm.

"Certainly, Howard," Viv told him, accepting the stack of phone messages Andie handed her.

Belky followed her into her office, picking at the dead skin on his left hand—caused by his psoriasis.

She averted her gaze and crossed her arms in front of her, waiting for him to begin, as tiny little flakes of his flesh spiraled toward her carpet. The same carpet she walked on in stocking feet when she worked late.

"You may not be aware, Vivien, that I've just taken on the divorce case of one Samuel Buckheimer."

"Congratulations," she said, infusing her voice with just the right amount of cordiality.

"Yes, well. Sam owns a couple of large operations both here in New York and in Florida. Greyhound tracks. And he happened to come across your name as a large donor to—"

Viv felt her face freezing. "Oh, he did, did he?"

"Yes. He was very pointed in his questioning. Frankly, it was embarrassing."

"Howard. While I feel for your being put in such a position, I must respectfully say that my personal donations or activities outside the firm are a private matter."

"I'd just like you to think about it, Vivien. Okay?"

"He's also being represented by *you*, not me."

"He's concerned about any of his money adding to . . . er, your bottom line. Since you two are philosophically opposed," said Belky smoothly.

Viv gritted her teeth. "Yes, that we certainly are. I don't think that the torture, starvation and neglect of animals for profit is acceptable. Do you?"

Her boss ignored the question. "Great work on the Alderson case, by the way," he said to soften her up.

"Thank you."

"See you at the meeting later."

"Yes."

Viv glared at his hunched little back as he left her office, trailing more tiny bits of his decayed flesh. This wasn't the first run-in they'd had over work she did outside of Klein, Schmidt and Belker. As far as he was concerned, pro bono activities were a waste of time, unless they were accompanied by the firm's name in huge letters and reported in the media.

She'd learned that it was useless to lobby Klein,

Schmidt for charitable contributions, unless they involved a fat tax write-off and good spin.

Vivien sighed and began to return phone calls, eyeing the towering stack of briefs and files on her credenza. Just a little light reading to pass the time . . . She glanced at her watch. She had less than twenty minutes before her first appointment.

She'd resolved a couple of issues with one client and left a message returning another one's call when Andie beeped through. "Miss Sydney Spinelli is on line four."

"Okay, thanks." Viv punched the button. "Syd? I was just going to call you."

"Vivien! How are you? How's your mother?"

"I'm fine. She's fine. You?"

"I'm . . . great, actually." And Syd—*Syd!*—actually giggled. "I'm still here in Fredericksburg. I've, uh, met someone."

"Well, I hope you're not going to marry the guy after a week," Viv said dryly.

"Not yet," Syd chirped.

Syd never chirped. She, like Viv, had studied the entire time that Viv, Julia and Sydney had spent at boarding school in Massachusetts. Well, she'd played field hockey, too. She'd never gotten into trouble, that was for sure. And she'd never been upbeat and bubbly, like her sister. But today, Sydney's voice could almost be mistaken for Julia's.

"Syd, what is going on down there in Texas? Julia's wearing this fake rock, and she believes this BS story about the grandmother hocking it without anyone's knowledge?"

"Yup. And I can't talk any sense into her. I've been accused of jealousy and meddling. And now that I've met Alex, I especially can't say anything to her, because she throws my own romance into my face. Viv, you're Julia's best friend. You're the Ball-Busting Bitch of Manhattan. The *New York Post* said so."

Viv glanced at the framed copy of the article that she'd proudly hung on her wall. Her lips twitched at the unflattering photo, which made her look like Dracula's trailer-trash mistress on a bender.

"You have to come down here and reason with her," said Sydney. "At least get her to sign one of those ironclad prenups of yours. This Roman guy says he's head over heels for Julia, but he's expanding the family vineyard and looking for cash to do it—I heard him say it myself. He thinks we're like a blue-collar version of the Hilton sisters: the Marv's Motor Inn heiresses."

"Syd, if she didn't respond well to *you* talking with her, she won't listen to me, either. I'm not even family."

"She'll listen to you because there's no sibling rivalry involved. And you're so frighteningly businesslike. You just tell her you want to protect her legally.

Excerpt from FIRST DANCE

You say, 'Here, Julesy, sign on this dotted line and I'll take care of the rest.' "

Andie buzzed through. "Mrs. Bonana is here for your eight thirty."

"Okay, thanks," Viv told her. "Can you put her in one of the small conference rooms?"

"They're all full."

"Oh. All right. Send her in." Viv went back to Sydney. "Look, hon, I'm glad you think I'm frightening, but I doubt that even I can scare Julia into doing something she doesn't want to do. That dent in her chin means, as you very well know, that she's stubborn. And she's also a bona fide romantic. Plus, as usual, I'm up to the eyeballs in work right now, and I'll be lucky if I can get away to be there for the wedding."

Andie brought a dubiously sun-streaked brunette to her office door. Viv nodded and held up a finger.

"Please, Viv. You've got to do something."

"Syd, it sounds as if you might need a prenup soon yourself, doll."

"Oh, no. Alex is completely trustworthy."

Viv groaned. "See what I mean? And you don't think your sister will have the same reaction?"

"No, really, this is different."

How many times had Viv heard that before? "I've got to go—I have an appointment."

"Please say you'll think about coming down and

talking to her. I can't do anything else. It's all up to you."

"I'll think about it," Viv promised, more to get off the phone than anything else.

"Okay. Thanks."

She hung up the phone and smiled reassuringly at Mrs. Bonana, who looked a little manic and frayed around the edges. "Hi. I'm Vivien Shelton. What can I do for you?"